THE VISCOUNT'S PEARL

MELISSA ADDEY

For Ben, Claire and Otis and their new life by the sea.

Have you read the Moroccan Empire series? Pick up the first in the series FREE from my website **www.MelissaAddey.com** and join my Readers' Club, so you will be notified about new releases.

A gifted healer. An impossible vow. An empire's destiny.

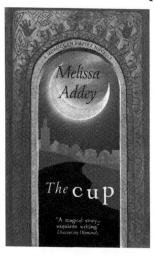

11th century North Africa. Hela has powers too strong for a child – both to feel the pain of those around her and to heal them. But when she is given a mysterious cup by a slave woman, its powers over-take her life, forcing her into a vow she cannot hope to keep.

Trapped by her vow, Hela loses one chance after another to love and be loved. Meanwhile, in her household, a child is born. Zaynab will one day become Morocco's queen and Hela's actions are already shaping her destiny.

Can a great healer ever heal her own wounds? Will Hela turn her back on her vow or follow it through to the bitter end? And will her choices forever warp the character of Morocco's greatest queen, and so shape the destiny of a future empire?

Northdown House, Margate

England, late August 1813

CHAPTER 1
The Spinster

FRANCES LAY ON THE COLD FLOOR. SHE WAS AWARE OF water trickling nearby, the leaves rustling in the late August breeze as she gazed at the pattern above her. It had taken hours of painstaking work, standing on a tall ladder while her mother had wrung her hands, forcing two of the footmen to stand holding it hour after hour while Frances reached upwards till her arms ached. But now it was complete, and she could happily lie here in the rotunda forever. Modelled on a Greek temple, the delicate open building boasted twelve columns and a floor of white marble, topped with a domed copper roof which had started out shining and was slowly acquiring the desired green patina. A pretty addition to the grounds of Woodside Abbey, situated next to a waterfall sculpted from the natural stream which criss-crossed the estate. Frances' father, Viscount Lilley, was keen that nature should be shaped to his will, and so the grounds were under the strict supervision of an army of gardeners as well as his watchful eye. Frances' odd interest in shells had been grudgingly given a home here, more than four thousand of them set into a spiralling pattern within the domed roof.

Round and round and round…

The spiralling pattern was the only way to block out the word also going round and round in Frances' mind.

Spinster.

The word most dreaded by all the *ton*. A curse, the worst insult one could throw at a young woman. It was whispered by those of mean spirit if a young woman was presented at court but then too many seasons passed without receiving a suitable marriage proposal. Or indeed any marriage proposal, in Frances' case. And how many seasons were too many? This would be her fourth season. Too many. Now that summer was drawing to a close, the household was already planning for London, her mother talking endlessly of new modistes and fashionable milliners, as though their combined efforts would somehow change Frances sufficiently to accomplish the marriage proposal which three previous seasons had failed to achieve.

Spinster.

To Frances, lying on the cold marble floor, the word was appealing. No parties, balls, picnics, rides along Rotten Row. No modistes and milliners. No tickling ribbons and scratchy lace and ballrooms either too hot or too cold. The exhaustion of coming home with aching feet and ravenously hungry after eating almost nothing so as to seem ladylike. Above all, no small talk on tedious subjects like the weather, minor ailments or the latest gossip. Spinster. Frances stared up at the spiralling cream shells. She could have a house, somewhere by the sea, and a handful of servants who would care for her. She could walk on the beach every day and have somewhere to keep her finds without people interfering with them. She could spend whole days without being required to speak. She could curl up in a rocking chair with books by the fire and have a hot chocolate or tea brought to her without asking, at a set hour. In the summers, the breeze would fill the house and the sound of the sea would reach her wherever she was, its soothing rhythm keeping her calm.

"Miss Lilley?" The anxious voice of one of the footmen, Nicholas.

With a sigh, Frances sat up. Nicholas was standing just outside the rotunda, dark green and gold uniform immaculate, looking worried.

"Yes, Nicholas?" She knew why he was here.

"Her ladyship would like you back at the house, Miss Lilley. The visitors have arrived."

Frances suppressed a groan. Already the spiralling shells above her were losing their power to soothe. "Coming."

She trailed Nicholas back to the imposing grey stone house, surrounded by immaculately tended lawns and intricately cut box hedges before the gardens swept into the wider grounds where the stream and waterfall, rotunda and other decorative follies were situated. As Frances entered the hallway, her lady's maid Deborah appeared from the shadows where she had clearly been lurking to catch her.

"Her ladyship said I was to make you... that is, dress you for the visitors, Miss. Come quickly, they're already in the drawing room."

Make you presentable, was the phrase she had bitten back, thought Frances, following the maid up the stairs. Her mother knew her too well. If it had been down to Frances, she would have entered the drawing room as she was, in dirty boots and a dusty dress from lying on her back in the rotunda.

In the bedroom, Deborah set about Frances in a flurry, tugging off her boots and replacing them with dainty cream kid slippers, muttering over the buttons as she lifted away the plain blue cotton dress and replaced it with a floaty muslin in a shade of pink which Frances detested, adding a delicate fichu for a modest neckline which made Frances want to scratch.

"I don't have time to do ringlets," Deborah said. "I'll use the combs."

Frances' shoulders sagged. Much as she disliked the process of creating ringlets at the front of her face, she despised the false hairpieces attached with tiny combs even more. The thought of someone else's hair attached to her scalp was even worse than the endless fussing and curling required to make her hair look fashionable.

Deborah hastily added a pearl necklace and Frances made her way downstairs, taking a deep breath before entering the drawing room where, as she had expected, she was met with a waft of strong perfumes, emanating from her mother as well as from the visitors. Frances found perfume too strong at the best of times, and scents mingling from multiple sources made her nauseous.

"Ah there you are, Frances," her mother said, her lips smiling while her eyes glittered a warning. "Have you been walking? She is *so* fond of nature and fresh air," she added to the guests. "Such a country girl."

Lady Ridlington and her daughter Miss Ridlington nodded approval. Lady Ridlington's son was on the market for a wife, and very much a country man himself, preferring hunting and fishing on his estate to balls and life in London. Frances gave a curtsey and seated herself at her mother's side, opposite the two women, as instructed by her mother in a briefing before the visit, "So that they can look at you," her mother had said. Frances hated being stared at.

"Such a shame my son could not come with us," began Lady Ridlington. "It is the end of the shooting season, so I could not drag him away from his guns. But he will find time to pay a call very soon, I hope. What are your interests, my dear?"

"The natural world," said Frances. She had been trained to say this by her mother, as apparently "shells" sounded too blunt and obsessive.

Lady Ridlington beamed. "How delightful. Do you draw?"

Lady Lilley gave Frances a dig in the ribs. Frances obediently got up and fetched her drawing portfolio, which she handed over to Lady Ridlington.

Lady Ridlington opened it. "Oh, how pretty," she said. "Shells. From a visit to the seaside? Brighton, perhaps?"

"Margate," said Frances quietly.

Lady Ridlington nodded. Brighton was more fashionable of course, but Margate was not without its charms.

"Frances has a godfather who keeps a house in Margate for his health," said Lady Lilley. "Lord Barrington. He is very fond of Frances and often invites her there. He is an invalid, so although his estate Ashland Manor is in Surrey he prefers to spend time in Margate, he says the sea air and the bathing relieve his symptoms. He likes to have youthful company about him as he is unmarried and without children, so he dotes on Frances as well as his other younger relations."

Lady Ridlington gave a nod, and Frances knew she would be correctly locating Viscount Barrington in her mental list of peers as a wealthy and respectable, if reclusive, member of the *ton*. A wealthy unmarried uncle was always useful for a young lady, especially if he were an invalid, one never knew if there might be an addition to Frances' dowry in due course. Frances Lilley's marriage portion was already twenty thousand pounds, which, if properly invested in the five percents would bring in one thousand pounds a year, a generous sum to add to Lady Ridlington's son's already comfortable income. Yes, no doubt Lady Ridlington thought Miss Lilley was promising, especially as she was unlikely to want to relinquish the control that she currently enjoyed as the widowed mother of an unmarried son with a handsome estate. A quiet obliging daughter in law would be just the thing. She gave an encouraging smile.

"Did you draw these while visiting your godfather, Miss Lilley?"

"Yes," she replied, as instructed.

Frances had actually drawn them at home at the behest of her mother, who had doggedly insisted that Frances must have at least one accomplishment to show off on such occasions. A drawing master had been secured and Frances had, after much coercion, at last consented to learn to draw shells. Her mother and the drawing master had both suggested adding flowers and other elements of the natural world, but she had refused and in the end they had given in.

"Tell me a little about shells," Lady Ridlington suggested. "They are so pretty."

Frances stared at her. "Many people foolishly dismiss shells as only pretty objects, without fully understanding their scientific interest," she began, heedless of Lady Ridlington's expression at being called a fool and of her mother's sudden sharp nudge in the ribs. She continued, leaning forwards, sifting through the pages of the portfolio to find what she was looking for. "Even those marine bivalves and gastropods which we most commonly find on our English shores, and indeed use for culinary purposes, have their own interest. This, for example, *Mytilus edulis*, the common mussel, thrives on our coastlines, showing resilience even in brackish waters, attaching itself to rocks with its delicate yet strong byssal threads. The nacreous interior gives a pearlescent effect as the light catches it."

Lady Ridlington opened her mouth to reply but Frances continued to speak, pulling out another drawing.

"Here is a cockle, or *Cerastoderma edule*, which has a globular shape with between twenty-two and twenty-eight concentric ridges on the outside, while the interior has shallow grooves running from the notched margin, but fading before the pallial line. They bury themselves in the sand at great speed to escape predators such as gulls and of course humans."

Miss Ridlington's mouth was now open while Lady Ridlington's face had grown stiff, but Frances was fully engrossed in her descriptions, not even glancing up to see if her audience was paying attention.

"Observe this: *Buccinum undatum*, the common whelk. Seven to eight spiraling whorls with the last one making up the majority of the overall size, the light and dark colouring irregular. *Buccinum undatum* may be confused with the so-called 'red' whelk, *Neptunea antiqua,* by those who do not note the finer ribbing of *Neptunea antiqua*. And while the common whelk is edible, the red whelk is not, therefore such subtle differences are important." Frances drew breath, turning to another drawing. "The oyster, or –"

"Frances, dearest," interrupted Lady Lilley desperately, "would you ring the bell for more tea?"

Frances looked up and surveyed the table. "We haven't finished this tea yet," she pointed out.

Lady Ridlington held out a hand. "Please do not trouble yourself, Lady Lilley," she said. "Mary and I should be leaving."

"But you've only just arrived! I was going to ask Frances to show you the gardens..." tried Lady Lilley, but Lady Ridlington was already standing.

"Such a long drive... unlikely we can visit again soon... perhaps we will see one another in London..."

Snatches of conversation drifted back to Frances as the visitors, escorted by the disappointed Lady Lilley, made their way out of Woodside Abbey and into their waiting carriage. The crunch of the wheels faded away as Lady Lilley returned to the drawing room, where she sat down and took a long drink of tea.

"I'm sorry," Frances muttered when it became clear her mother was not going to speak.

Lady Lilley sighed and slumped back in her armchair, entirely losing her usual immaculate posture. "I had such high hopes for Lady Ridlington taking a fancy to you for her son. We could have avoided your fourth season if... well, never mind." She gave a forced smile. "I have heard that there is a wonderful new modiste who is a marvel when it comes to..."

Frances let her mind drift away from the thought of another exhausting season. Her fourth. Too many. There would be new dresses and bonnets and shoes, new fans and gloves and stockings, for her father was generous enough and anxious to marry her off.

"And the latest fashions might suit you, bosoms are not being worn so high now, so even though you are not so well-endowed they will look becoming and perhaps something can be done with your hair..."

"Mama."

Lady Lilley paused in her recital of everything that might be attempted in making Frances more marriageable. "Yes?"

"Could you not speak to Papa about my plan?"

"Your plan?"

"If he were to settle the marriage portion on me now, I could live very comfortably alone. Somewhere by the sea…"

"Frances!" Lady Lilley sat bolt upright again.

She fell silent, staring down at her portfolio.

"Frances, I do not want to hear this sort of talk again, it is ridiculous."

"I am going to be a spinster," said Frances. "So I might as well start now and be happy, rather than dragging it out for season after season, until you and Papa realise I am right."

"Frances Diana Charlotte Lilley! You are *not* going to be a spinster. If it comes to it, your father and I will choose a suitable husband for you and arrange a marriage that will see you respectably wed. There is to be no more talk of spinsters!" And with that, Lady Lilley swept from the room, her cheeks pink with annoyance, while Frances escaped to the familiar comfort of the rocking chair in the library next door and rocked the hours away until dinner, staring out at the neatly clipped lawns and wondering how she might persuade her parents to let her live as she wished and not subject her to yet another miserable season.

Her hours of thought bore fruit, however, and after dinner, in the drawing room, she made her move, sidling over to a writing desk in a corner of the room.

"May I write to Uncle Barrington?"

"If you wish, dear," said her mother distractedly from

behind a copy of *La Belle Assemblée,* which boasted a new fashion plate she was considering. "I am not sure about yellow gloves with a rose-pink dress…Is it too bold? I favour cream gloves, myself…"

Frances ignored the wholly uninteresting and uninspired fashion advice and sat down at the desk to compose a letter to her godfather, which she then sealed and gave to one of the footmen to post before her mother could ask to see the contents.

> *Dear Uncle Barrington,*
>
> *Please will you write to Mama and invite me to Northdown House for as long as ever you can? She talks of nothing but London and my fourth season and I can't bear it. Please send for me.*
>
> *Your respectful goddaughter,*
> *Frances*

A week went by. But as Frances had hoped, Viscount Barrington could be relied upon.

> *My dear Lady Lilley,*
>
> *Will you do an old man the great pleasure of sending my beloved Frances to stay with me in Margate for the duration of September and October? I am here for my health as you know, but the days are lonely and conversation with a young spirit would do me good. I hope you will do me this kindness.*
>
> *I remain your faithful servant,*
> *Barrington*

"Your godfather wishes you to visit him," said Lady Lilley.

"Does he?" said Frances, trying to maintain a tone of surprise. "In Surrey?" she added disingenuously.

"No, in Margate."

Frances waited, holding herself back from looking too eager.

"I suppose," began Lady Lilley, "we could send you there once we reach London. The main season is not until March anyway and if you were with him for what is left of September and October, there will still be time to take you to a modiste in November and engage in some parties and balls before Christmas."

"Whatever you think best, Mama," said Frances in her best meek voice.

"But you are to make yourself *agreeable*," fretted Lady Lilley. "He is in want of conversation, he says, and you…" she paused.

"Oh, we do talk together," said Frances quickly. "We are both so fond of shells and the natural world, we walk on the beach every day and his gardens at Northdown are very fine. We spend a great deal of time conversing."

Her mother looked as though she found this hard to believe, but reluctantly agreed and put the plan to Lord Lilley, who generally went along with whatever Lady Lilley decided was suitable when it came to Frances.

"You must take Deborah, of course," Lady Lilley decreed and although being obliged to have a companion with her everywhere she went usually annoyed Frances, in this case, once at Northdown, her maid would mostly leave her be, for she was fond of one of the footmen there and would take every opportunity to disappear below stairs or to some other room and see him. Besides, Deborah was something of a snob when it came to anywhere that was not London and would therefore, if coaxed, allow her to wear her plainest clothes, without fussing so much over ringlets or ribbons. The thought of being back in Margate, of walking on the beach every day and collecting her beloved shells, made Frances tingle with happiness.

Over the next week, she was on her very best behaviour, agreeing with everything her mother said and even managing to make polite conversation at the table. Deborah, likewise, became tractable, turning a blind eye when Frances removed jewellery and all but the plainest bonnets from the boxes and trunks she had packed.

The journey from Berkshire to London in the Lilleys' carriage was always slow and tedious, but at least this time, when they arrived in Berkeley Square, Frances would only be spending one night there and would then depart for Margate with Deborah, who had travelled behind in the second carriage with the luggage. She could therefore ignore her noisy older brother, who was greatly looking forward to a season in town, and would avoid seeing her two older sisters, who would no doubt be visiting regularly, along with their boring husbands. Frances was fond of her nieces and nephews but her sisters' constant references to Frances' unmarried state were hard to bear for long.

The following day, with Deborah at her side, Frances travelled by post-chaise to Margate. The journey took another dreary day, but at last Frances saw the welcoming gates of Northdown Park and shortly thereafter the familiar sight of Northdown House. It was a fine house, both inside and out, but not grand in the way that Lord Barrington's main estate Ashland Manor in Surrey was, nor overly imposing like Woodside Abbey. Instead it maintained a comfortable feel, a lived-in warmth of which Frances was very fond. This was how a home ought to be. When she had her own home, after however many more seasons she had to endure before her parents accepted her spinsterhood, she would make the grounds like those at Northdown House. Its flowering meadow-like gardens were filled with fruit trees and a hothouse full of roses, orchids and grapes, in stark contrast to Woodside Abbey's clipped lawns and geometric hedges, which did not allow for any rest for the eye, drawn endlessly to its repeating patterns in shades of green and to trying to solve its maze-like layouts.

The carriage pulled up outside and Frances and Deborah stepped down. Jeremy Barrington, or Viscount Barrington to give him his correct title, made his appearance in the hallway, manoeuvring his bath chair, with its two back wheels and one at the front, with practised ease. As his legs had slowly lost their strength, Northdown House had been altered over the years to accommodate the viscount's chair, so that his bedroom was now located on the ground floor, in what had been a little-used morning room, leaving the upper storey of the house largely unused. Approaching his seventieth year, with greying hair and a lined face, he wore his customary kindly expression as he greeted his goddaughter.

"I have something to show you," he said, dispensing with any further niceties, a habit of which Frances heartily approved. "Come."

She followed him as he rolled along the corridor. A footman sprang to attention to open the side door leading to the gardens, which had been fitted with a wooden ramp which allowed him to roll out, unlike the grand stairs at the front door. Unlike most gardens, which favoured gravel paths for keeping one's feet clean even in wintertime, Lord Barrington had commissioned a wooden walkway, built from the side door all the way around the gardens, including a deviation into the hothouse, allowing him to make his way around without assistance until he had to re-enter the house. A footman was always positioned there to help him back up the ramp.

The meadow was full of autumn's long grasses, through which were threaded the delicate blue of harebells and forget-me-nots, the pinks of cranesbill and red clover, as well as the vibrant yellow of hawkbit, while the walls of the nearby vegetable garden were draped over with ivy and old man's beard.

"I wish I lived here," said Frances.

Lord Barrington paused on the walkway. "Your mama still determined for you to marry?"

"Yes. And I don't care to! All the young men I meet during the season are dreadful. They're either boors or they fawn over me until they realise I don't wish to make small talk and then they run away. Can none of them be companiable without twittering on?"

Lord Barrington chuckled. "Not looking forward to your fourth season?"

Frances rolled her eyes. "Must everyone keep count?"

"I am afraid they do."

Frances sighed.

"There."

Frances looked where he was pointing and brightened at once. "A swing!"

From an ancient oak had been hung a large wooden swing, already tantalisingly moving in the warm breeze. Frances hurried towards it, carefully took her seat and then pushed off with her feet, the swing lifting her up towards the green leaves and blue sky before returning her back towards the grass beneath her feet.

"Happy?" asked Lord Barrington, watching her.

"It is wonderful," she said, without opening her eyes, a contented smile on her face. The smooth rhythm, the steady to and fro, was much like the rocking chairs she so enjoyed. The air rushing past her face, bringing delicate scents of the flowers around her and the faint tang of salt air from the nearby sea, was a delight to her sensitive nose, so unlike the overly-heady perfumes of the *ton*'s ladies. Here at Northdown House she could be herself and not be endlessly disappointing to anyone, for Lord Barrington always seemed happy with her. If only these two months would last forever.

CHAPTER 2
The Rake

THE GENTLE AUTUMN SUN HAD MADE FOR A PLEASANT morning's sport on Lord Ludlow's estate and the four young men and their loaders would soon be finishing for the day, but the beaters had just regrouped to start the last drive to flush out the remaining partridges, so there was a brief pause in the shooting, which had lead to conversation.

"Lady *Montsbourne*? You rogue!"

Laurence gave a lazy smile and handed his gun to his loader for reloading. "I escorted her to the opera. It is a perfectly respectable entertainment."

"The opera is. What she allowed you to do to her in the carriage afterwards, is another matter entirely!"

"Who said I did anything in the carriage?"

"Anyone who knows you, Mowatt."

"I escorted her home to her husband, like a gentleman."

"You're a rogue and a rake, Mowatt, admit it."

Laurence gave a laugh. "I admit nothing."

"And *that* is why the married ladies are so fond of him,"

pointed out Lord Ludlow, taking aim and firing. "He admits nothing, only smiles and bows. The perfect gentleman."

"The married ladies either want him in their bed or want him for their daughters," rejoined Lord Beauchamp. "He may be Mr Mowatt now, but it can't be long until he's a viscount, and a future Lord Barrington sounds quite fine on the marriage mart, don't you agree?"

"Uncle Barrington is not dead yet," admonished Laurence.

"He's an old man and an invalid," said Lord Ludlow. "Whereas you are a young man and rich enough already even if you aren't titled. The viscountcy, whenever it comes along, will just be that extra flourish the mamas are after for their daughters. I wonder you haven't been snapped up already."

"Having too much fun with the married ladies," said Lord Beauchamp. "Why would he want a simpering miss who has to be taught everything when he can have a lady who knows what she wants and isn't shy about it, eh?"

"Enough of your nonsense," said Laurence. "Might have to marry this season anyway, my father keeps mentioning it."

"Ah! On the marriage mart at last!" exclaimed Lord Ludlow. "I shall be sure to let the gossip-mongers know, they'll have your name around town in a moment. You'll have a queue of mamas standing outside Albany with their daughters in tow ready to make you fall in love."

Laurence waved them away. "No need for any of that romantic nonsense. All I need is a sensible woman who knows how to run a household and is fond of children."

"Romantic nonsense? Are you dead set against a love match then?"

"I don't see the value of them," said Laurence as they began walking back across the fields towards Lord Ludlow's shooting lodge. "Falling in love with someone doesn't mean they're suited to you, it just means you think they're a pretty face."

Lord Beauchamp grimaced. "I don't think you've ever been in love, Mowatt," he said. "You wouldn't dismiss it so easily if you had."

Laurence shrugged. "Maybe not," he said. "But why wait about for love? The woman I marry will have to run the households of two large estates and keep our family line going more abundantly than my parents. One son doesn't really secure the family line, now, does it? Look at my uncle. Never married, no children. When he dies everything will go to me, his sister's only son. And it's only because he's titled that his name will keep going. There's a lot to be said for a practical approach to marriage."

"And a lot to be said for married ladies who are disappointed with their practical husbands and enjoy sporting with a young rake, eh?" said Lord Ludlow. "Come on, I'm famished."

A week later, the hunting season completed and the first days of September now upon him, Laurence returned to London and his set in Albany. The imposing building contained sixty-nine apartments for young, rich, well-connected gentlemen who did not choose to reside with their families, preferring the conveniences of being close to the clubs and shops of St James. They were also, should they be required to attend Parliament, not far away from that hallowed building. It was rumoured that Lord Byron himself was about to take an Albany lease, no doubt making the address even more desirable to the young men who wished to be seen as stylish rakes about town. Women and children were absolutely forbidden from residing, and no lady of quality, married or unmarried, would have risked visiting, in case rumours should spread about her.

Making his way down Rope Walk, up the stairs to his set and opening the door, Laurence looked about in satisfaction at the ample hallway. At the front of the building were a comfortably large dining room and drawing room for entertaining, while the three rooms behind were made up of his bedroom, a study and a small kitchen-pantry where his manservant Roberts could rustle up simple repasts, from cakes and coffee in the morning to carved ham, a tasty pickle and fresh bread at midday. Laurence was rarely at home in the evenings, but when he was Roberts would arrange for anything from an amply filled pie to a more elaborate repast should Laurence have friends to dine. A soup, oysters, roast pheasant with boiled potatoes and fried artichokes sent up by the nearest cookhouse, followed by a damson tart and a plate of sweet oranges and macaroons from the pastrymakers, all accompanied by fine wines and an enjoyable port, was all that was needed. Roberts was a good fellow, who kept the wine and coal cellars well stocked and arranged for cleaning and laundry to be done. His sleeping quarters were in the attics, where all the servants for the sets had rooms provided as part of the lease. He could be relied on for discretion when the occasional outraged husband appeared demanding to know Laurence's whereabouts. Roberts' look of injured innocence on behalf of his master had spared Laurence at least one threatened duel.

The set was comfortable and well appointed, although Laurence did occasionally smile to himself when he drove through Grosvenor Square and saw the house that would one day be his. Lord Barrington's wealth was considerable and he was known for his appreciation of fine things, from houses to the statues and art collected within them. There was not only the Grosvenor Square townhouse but the main estate, Ashland Manor, in Surrey, not to mention Northdown House in Margate, which itself would not have disgraced any peer as their home.

"Welcome home, Sir," said Roberts. "I hope the shooting party was pleasant."

Usually Roberts travelled with him, but on this brief trip Laurence had simply made use of Ludlow's extensive staff to valet him.

"Hello Roberts," replied Laurence. "We had excellent sport at Ludlow's, but it's always pleasant to be back in town."

"Will you be dining in, Sir?"

"Yes, I shall need some decent sleep after the journey here. You can bring a drink and the post to my study and then I'll dine early."

"Very good, Sir."

The tray with his post on was piled high. He selected the first letter from the top of the pile and opened it, casting an eye over the contents, then dropping it onto another tray, a reminder to himself to answer in the affirmative to an invitation to the Halesworth ball. As he slowly opened one missive after another, so his social commitments piled up. Despite the Little Season having barely started, with many families still arriving in London from their country estates, Laurence found he was already in demand. There were the first balls of the season, new plays and operas opening, a few dinners and, making the best of the still-clement weather, picnics and walks in Vauxhall's Pleasure Gardens all being offered up for his delectation. Most of the invitations came from respectable sources; the mamas of the *ton* preparing their strategies for the battlefield ahead.

These were obvious because of the additional notes added to the invitation cards, oh-so-subtly mentioning that their dear Caroline... Anne... Beatrice... Lydia was coming out this season and therefore they were delighted to invite him to a ball or dinner in her honour. The mamas whose daughters had not been so fortunate as to snare a proposal in their very first season were more circumspect, only mentioning that they would be pleased to see him at whatever social occasion they were hosting. A few were familiar to him from last season or even (horror) the one before. He could recall their daughters and what it was about them that had been off-putting: too noisy, an irritating laugh, too tall, lacking any real accomplishments yet determined to show them off anyway... the list went on. Their mamas would have regrouped, found new milliners and singing or dancing instructors, ready for the fray of a new season. Good luck to them.

The invitations that drew his interest were different. These consisted of a calling card, often scented with a memorable perfume, and a brief note to the effect that Lady so-and-so was very much looking forward to visiting the theatre or opera, or perhaps a new art gallery or concert and that she would 'value his company'. One from Lady Kingsman brought a smile to his lips, while another from Lady Selkirk occasioned a raised eyebrow.

Married women were Laurence's pastime, for they had many advantages over escorting the young women on the marriage mart. To begin with, they were respectable. Married to boring men who paid them little attention, often having already produced an heir and a few spares, they were now free to conduct themselves as they wished, so long as they were able to maintain a veneer of propriety. They were often more interesting, for they had lived longer and experienced some of the ways of the world, and therefore were better conversationalists and generally better social company than the wide-eyed simpering girls thrust in his face every season. Aged seventeen or eighteen, these girls were still excited by the very idea of a ball, no matter how poorly hosted, and had barely any conversation to offer other than to nod earnestly at anything he might say, no matter how ridiculous, and to mention whenever possible their supposed accomplishments. A kiss on the hand left them blushing and certain of an imminent proposal. Whereas the married ladies, ah, they were a very different matter. They had experienced enough boredom in the bedroom with their husbands to be open to anything and everything that Laurence might care to suggest trying between or even out of the sheets, were more ladylike and cleaner than the so-called ladies of even the finest brothels London could offer and, above all, were extremely discreet. An affair with such a lady could last for anything from one delightful night to several pleasurable months, then be terminated with very little fuss or resentment, both parties wishing the other well. Indeed, quite a few of Laurence's latest amusements had apparently been 'advised' by their friends that Laurence was well worth their time and attention.

But Laurence would soon need a wife to run his households and raise their children who would be the sons and daughters of a viscount and viscountess. He had a possible candidate in mind, perhaps he should have a word with her this season, just to sound her out and see if she might be agreeable to the notion. Lady Honora Fortescue was an heiress in her own right and a practical, cheerful sort of young woman, one who would fully understand what was expected of her. He did not personally find her particularly attractive, but she was handsome enough and after all, he was not looking for love, but for a wife. Love was one of those irrational emotions that foolish young girls and the lower orders aspired to, the stuff of plays and songs as well as the tediously sentimental poetry which young women were forever quoting with hopeful glances in his direction. No, what was wanted was affection and respect, which would enhance any appropriate marriage, and he felt both of these for Lady Honora. He respected her practical nature and excellent breeding and had warmed to her ever since she had once stopped a hack driver who was passing and pointed out to him that his horse was limping, probably from a stone lodged in its foot. The man, who clearly had little care for his horse, had shrugged and said he would see to it when he had finished work, whereupon Lady Honora had produced a hoof pick from her reticule, lifted up the horse's foot and seen to the matter herself before she would allow him to drive any further. The combination of a kind heart, a commanding air and a practical solution had greatly endeared her to Laurence, and she had, ever since, been at the top of his list of possible future brides. From passing comments she had made at various events he was fairly certain that she was not one of these girls who pined for a love match, rather she was sensible enough to weigh up her options carefully and then choose someone suitable. And he, Laurence, was eminently suitable. He was not yet titled, but he would be one day and therefore Lady Honora, daughter of a marquis, would not be marrying down too much to make the match unlikely, and would anyway enjoy the same level of wealth she had been raised with, for the wealth of the Mowatts, once combined with the Barrington estate, would be considerable. Yes, he should speak to her this season, he resolved. He could tell Uncle Barrington about it beforehand, he would probably be pleased to hear that his heir was thinking of settling down. Perhaps, he mused, they might even get married next spring, there was no reason why not and then a child or two could be born before the old man died, giving him some pleasure in his later years and the knowledge that his name and legacy would live on. Laurence had already planned to change his name to Barrington when the time came, to honour his benefactor. And speak of the devil, here was a letter in his uncle's distinctive writing, all flourishes and loops.

My dear Laurence,

The last warm weeks of the year find me in my beloved Margate, enjoying the sea air and bathing, both of which have always cheered my spirits and improved my ailing health. My days pass well enough here, but my evenings find me sadly at a loss for good conversation and companionship, for the Assembly Rooms and the society here have never been much to my liking, in part owing to my infirmity. Will you do me the kindness of joining me at Northdown House for a few weeks? It has been too long since your dear mama's passing, and I still miss her greatly. It would bring me pleasure to see her again reflected in your visage, for you were always extraordinarily like her to look upon. And as Northdown House will one day be yours, I should like my loyal staff here to look upon you as much the master of the house as I am and grow to know your ways such that they might serve you well when I am gone, which cannot be long now. London will be keeping you busy, I know, but as the great

*philosopher Socrates warned us, we must beware the
barrenness of a busy life.*

*Believe me, your affectionate Uncle,
Barrington*

It was just like Uncle Barrington, thought Laurence with
a wry smile, to pull upon the heartstrings, both in reminding
him of the closeness he and his mother had shared, as well as
the fact that he was Uncle Barrington's heir and therefore duty
bound to behave to him as a son might to his father. He had
written plenty of letters to Laurence since his mother's passing,
always with the reminder that he was welcome to visit him at
any time, but he had never requested his presence so forcefully
and so Laurence had neglected the old man, even though he
was fond of him. It was just that...

Laurence took a gulp of his drink. His mother had died
over three years ago now, but the thought of her absence still
brought a leaden feeling to his stomach. In the past there had
been many merry visits with her to visit Uncle Barrington but
now, without her, he dreaded a visit which would only remind
him again of her absence. During her lifetime he had eschewed
the lure of London, preferring time on his family's estate,
enjoying the warm embrace of his family and their small but
intimate social circle, all of whom he had known since he was
a boy. Oh, he had gone to London, of course, and enjoyed the
balls and dinners and the young ladies, but he had also been
happy hunting with his father, escorting his younger sisters
about the countryside to their various social engagements and
his mother on regular visits to Uncle Barrington, her favourite
brother, either in Surrey or Margate. But since his mother had
gone, he had found their family home too quiet and empty

without her vital presence, and had eventually taken out a lease on his set in Albany, spending more and more time with his friends, at his club or out and about. The married women had given him an education in the bedchamber and then become both a safe outlet for any desires and an always agreeable way to pass the time without much required of him in return.

Still, he must steel himself to visit, even though it would remind him of his loss. He owed the old fellow a visit, indeed he had neglected his duty to him somewhat. A visit to Margate for a couple of weeks would put that right and cheer the old man's spirits. It was the least he could do. He would spend an evening with Lady Kingsman, an old favourite, and then make his way to Margate by carriage. He had never been fond of the option of a sea voyage there from London, for although the captains promised every comfort and smooth waters, his experience had been that plenty of people grew nauseous on board and both the sound and the smell of the afflicted passengers made the journey unpleasant. No, he would travel post and bear the tedious eight hours or so, after all, based on previous experience he might need some sleep after a night with Lady Kingsman. At least once in Margate his uncle kept both a carriage as well as a fine riding horse named Hippomenes whom Laurence enjoyed riding. Roberts would accompany him, and the dutiful visit would pass soon enough.

"Roberts!"

"Sir?"

"Tomorrow I will make a few calls and take Lady Kingsman to the theatre in the evening. The next day we travel to Margate to visit Lord Barrington. We will probably be gone for a couple of weeks. Pack accordingly and make all necessary arrangements."

"Very good, Sir. Dinner will be served in a few moments."

Laurence made his way to the dining room, where Roberts soon had a decent meal on the table. First a mutton broth, followed by a game pie served with peas and cardoons, and finally some peach tartlets, a modest but tasty repast since he was dining alone. He ate well, then wrote two quick notes. One to Lady Kingsman, a woman whose company he had much enjoyed that spring before going away for the hunting season. He would be glad to renew their acquaintance and promised to escort her tomorrow night to the theatre. The second note informed Uncle Barrington that he would be with him late on the second day and not to wait up for him, for the old man kept early hours. Having made these arrangements, he took himself off to bed and slept soundly.

The next morning, after a leisurely breakfast and having answered a few other items of correspondence, he visited his tailors, Schweitzer and Davidson of 12 Cork Street, where he bespoke himself some new clothing to be collected on his return, then shoes and boots at Wood, as well as a new hat at Lock & Co. None of them would be needed in Margate, which was hardly a place of high fashion, but all of them would be required for the rest of the season. Laurence prided himself on being well turned out for all social occasions and while Roberts could be relied upon to keep him well stocked in shirts, stocks and stockings, a gentleman should see to commissioning his outer clothing himself, for fit was everything and there were always small modifications, season by season, which showed attention to detail and marked one out as a man of fashion. A new item known as a frock coat was being worn by some men who were considered forward in their fashion choices and although it was very new, Laurence had one ordered, in case the style should catch on. It would not do to be seen as behind the times and if it did become the fashion, no doubt all the tailors would be busy creating them for their customers. Better to be ahead of the crowd. There were also so-called Cossack trousers, voluminous items with ribbons at the ankle, but Laurence frowned when shown them and decided against such a departure from Brummell's accepted leadership.

A meal at his club, Boodle's, led to a brief rest at home before the enjoyment of a bath and then the matter of dressing for the theatre.

He arrived promptly at Lady Kingsman's house and was there to take her hand and help her into the carriage as she emerged, appreciating both the quality of her perfume and her sequin-studded green silk dress, made up in the very latest style. He admired a woman who took care of herself and made the most of the finer things in life, as he did himself.

"You've been gone too long," she murmured when the carriage started. "I didn't know what to do with myself all summer."

He changed sides of the carriage, taking the seat beside her, their bodies pressed close together. "What *did* you do to… I mean, *with* yourself all summer?"

She leant against him. "You wicked man."

"The summer was very warm," he said in a low voice. "I cannot imagine that all those layers of clothing were wanted. Surely you must have removed some of them so that you could be more comfortable?"

"I might have done."

"May I be so bold as to inquire which layers you felt were not needed?"

"I could not possibly say."

"May I be permitted to guess?"

Her lips parted. "You may."

He looked her over. "To begin with, a silk dress is far too hot for the summer. So I think that would need to be removed."

She inclined her head.

"Which leaves... a petticoat? Surely unnecessary without a dress."

"Entirely," she whispered.

"In that case, let me think. I believe that under this..." His hand slid over her silk-clad breasts and she shivered at his touch, her breathing growing faster "... there must be a corset or stays of some kind, to take care of these beauties."

"There is."

"Well, that is far too restrictive for a hot summer's day and besides, as I recollect, they required very little help in remaining... uplifted. I think we could entirely dispose of that item."

"You leave me clad in very little, Sir," she murmured, her hand on his knee.

"A shift, I believe? And stockings?"

"So little? I am covered in shame."

He leant towards her, whispered into her ear. "If you are covered in shame, madam, I see no need for the shift. I will remove it at once."

"And my stockings?" she breathed.

"Those I will leave. But only if they are held up with these." From his pocket he pulled out a small box. "A gift."

She opened it and pulled out two silk ribbon garters, each one delicately embroidered with flowers and letters. She held them out, looking at the words on one and then the other. "*Laisse-moi te tenir les cuisses… jusqu'à ce que nous nous revoyions.*"

He traced the words with one finger. "Let me hold your thighs… until we meet again."

She sighed with delight and slid her hand down the inside of his thigh. "Laurence…"

The carriage halted. In a moment the ribbons had vanished into her reticule just in time for the door to be opened by a footman, who found them seated on opposite sides, not even their knees touching. Laurence sprang lightly out of the carriage and held out his hand for Lady Kingsman, who alighted with careful dignity and was escorted by him first into the theatre and thence to her private box – and the small room behind it to which they repaired for a large part of the evening's entertainment.

CHAPTER 3
The Birth of Venus

Waking in Margate each day was a source of happiness for Frances. She rose early, dressed simply, breakfasted on toast and hot chocolate with Uncle Barrington and then the carriage would arrive for them, so that they reached the town and shoreline well before most visitors, allowing her to pace the beach in glorious solitude. Uncle Barrington kept watch over her from the promenade and occasionally she would bring him a particularly fine specimen, which he would admire. About midday they would be served a meal in the sunshine and then continue shell seeking until late in the afternoon. It was a wonderful life and she was somewhat put out at the news that they were to be joined by a visitor.

"My heir, Laurence Mowatt. He travels tomorrow."

Frances nodded, uninterested except for one particular. "Will he be staying long?"

"A week, perhaps two."

She had been hoping for only a few days, but never mind. No doubt a young man would spend his time socialising with local society or riding, bathing and so on. She only hoped he would not commandeer too much of Uncle Barrington's time.

The journey from London to Margate was as tedious as Laurence had feared, but he spent much of it asleep after the late evening he had enjoyed with Lady Kingsman. Arriving late at Northdown House, he was informed, as expected, that Lord Barrington had already retired. The servants, however, were welcoming to their future master, serving him a hearty meal accompanied by a good wine, then taking him to the warm and comfortable Cherry Bedroom, where Roberts had already unpacked and made everything homely. Dressed in a warmed nightgown, lying in a well-aired and exceedingly comfortable feather bed, Laurence blew out the candle by his bedside and slept.

In the morning, freshly washed and dressed, he made his way to the drawing room for breakfast but was surprised to be informed by the butler that Lord Barrington had risen early, breakfasted and was "on the beach with Miss Lilley."

"Miss Lilley?"

"His goddaughter, Sir, she is visiting at present. His lordship desired that you join them at the beach when you had breakfasted. Your horse will be saddled and waiting for you when you are ready."

Laurence ate a couple of slices of a rich plum cake, drank his coffee and then made his way out via the gardens and to the stables, where a groom was waiting with Hippomenes, a fine grey. Laurence re-acquainted himself with the horse, offering him a freshly-picked apple from the orchard before getting easily into the saddle. He prided himself on being able to ride most horses well, but he did have a soft spot for Hippomenes, the first fully grown horse he had ridden as a boy. The horse had been only a couple of years old at the time, but standing at a fully grown sixteen hands, he had seemed very impressive to the young Laurence, who was only just graduating from his favourite pony. Uncle Barrington had always kept a riding horse for guests, despite no longer being able to ride himself, and so Hippomenes had an easy enough life, ridden mostly for exercise by the grooms to keep him even tempered and in good form. It had been the best part of four years since Laurence had visited Northdown, but the horse still whinnied with recognition, fresh and eager for the day's outing.

The ride to the sea from Northdown House was a short and fairly direct route, mostly downhill and Laurence took it at a brisk trot, enjoying the bright autumn morning and the fresh air. Once in the centre of Margate, close to the promenade overlooking the sandy beach, he dismounted and paid a young boy to watch over Hippomenes for him while he sought out Lord Barrington.

His uncle was easy enough to spot on the already busy beachfront, for while there were bath chairs here and there, Uncle Barrington went about with two strong footmen, who had been chosen for their burly arms. Andrew and Benjamin had been with his household for years, taking Lord Barrington wherever he wished to go, whether it be gently pushing him along the promenade in his chair like the other invalids or on more intrepid adventures, when they would carry him onto beaches both popular and deserted, even down difficult-to-manage cliff paths. Laurence quickly reached his uncle and presented himself before him with a small bow.

"Uncle Barrington."

"Laurence, my boy! You are most welcome to Margate. I am sorry I was not at home to greet you when you rose, but I thought you would be weary after the journey from London and wish to rise late. Frances was keen to get to the beach early, while the strandline was still fresh. We are but servants to the tide."

Laurence made a bow. "I am very pleased to see you, Sir. You are looking well."

"I rarely look well, but you are kind to say so. Frances! Come and join us!"

A young woman some way off turned and made her way towards them. She was not particularly noticeable, Laurence thought, being of average height and dressed in plain blue cotton with little decoration. An equally severe blue bonnet with a white ribbon contained most of her hair, though a few dark brown tendrils had escaped in the breeze. Her feet were shod in worn leather boots and she carried a small straw basket lined in green linen, in which were a handful of shells, none of them remarkable. Her skin was browner than it should be for a lady; clearly she had spent too much time in the sun without a parasol. She could easily have been mistaken for a lady's maid or the daughter of a merchant, so plainly was she dressed.

Uncle Barrington, however, was beaming at the sight of her. "Laurence, may I introduce my goddaughter Miss Frances Lilley, daughter of Viscount Lilley. She has been a regular visitor here over the years and is staying with me for a few weeks. Frances, this is my nephew and heir Mr Laurence Mowatt, son of Mr Mowatt and my dear late departed sister Cecilia.

He used to come to me often when he was a boy along with his mother, for she was fond of the sea. We have not seen one another nearly enough since her passing, so I wrote and asked him to join me here for a visit."

Laurence bowed. The young woman, eyes fixed on the ground at their feet, gave a curtsey in return, but did not say anything, nor so much as smile. So much for Uncle Barrington being lonely, thought Laurence, he already had one "young spirit" as he liked to call them, for company, and hardly needed Laurence to attend him at Northdown. Still, if Miss Lilley were staying she would be company for his uncle. He might be able to leave sooner than he had thought.

"Are you enjoying Margate, Miss Lilley?"

She did not raise her gaze to him. "Yes."

Laurence waited for some other comment, some pleasantry about the sea air or doting on her godfather, but nothing was forthcoming.

He blinked and tried again. "Do you come for your health, or the pleasure of Uncle Barrington's company?"

Simpering flattery of Uncle Barrington was what he was expecting, but Miss Lilley only shrugged – shrugged! – and said, "I come for the shells."

Laurence frowned, but Uncle Barrington let out a laugh. "Her bluntness does me good," he said. "I grow weary of the *ton* and all its falsities disguised as niceties. You will no doubt meet some of the local society while you are here, Laurence, and then you will see why I prefer Frances' company to theirs."

Laurence tried to smile in return at the jest, but to his consternation Miss Lilley had already turned away from both of them and had begun walking away along the beach, following an invisible line of her own, head down, turning slightly from side to side. She occasionally stooped to pick up a shell and add it to her basket, then continued. She did not look back at the two men, did not in any way suggest that they might wish to follow her or indeed that she had anything to do with them.

Disconcerted, Laurence turned back to his uncle, who was watching Miss Lilley with a fond smile.

"She does me good, Laurence."

Laurence murmured something that he hoped sounded agreeable, though he could not for the life of him understand what his uncle saw in the girl, who was not only plain (and plainly dressed) but entirely deficient in manners. Her terse replies, her seeming inability to meet his gaze when conversing, her abrupt departure, none of them were what he expected from the daughter and goddaughter of viscounts.

He cleared his throat. "Shall we follow along the promenade?"

"Yes, let us do so. We can talk while Frances gathers her shells. Andrew and Benjamin, you may wait here. We will wave if we have need of you."

Laurence took hold of the chair and pushed it slowly along, so that they kept pace with Miss Lilley on the beach below them. After a few moments Laurence could not help asking more about her, for he found her presence odd.

"Does Miss Lilley visit you often, Sir?"

"A few times a year, mostly when I can spirit her away from her mama, an excellent woman but altogether too preoccupied with marrying the girl off, for which there is still plenty of time, though she will go *on* about it being her fourth season." He sighed, looking out to where Frances continued along the shoreline. "I am sorry this is the first time the two of you have met, I suppose when you were both very young you were not much in company and when you grew older… well, Frances is not overly fond of meeting new people and you usually visited with your mother, so I would not have invited many other guests, so that I might better savour her company and yours."

Laurence had stopped listening partway through this explanation, having caught hold of a fact which had caused his eyebrows to raise. "This is to be Miss Lilley's *fourth* season?"

Lord Barrington chuckled. "You sound just like her mother and the rest of the *ton*, Laurence. Who cares how many seasons a girl has? If it takes longer to find one's soul mate, so be it."

Laurence was glad he was walking behind his uncle's chair, for he was aware that his expression would have been in direct conflict with Lord Barrington's unusual views. Her fourth season? A spinster, then. And hardly surprising, given how she looked and behaved. Her parents must be sorely disappointed. He thought of his two sisters, attractive, cheerful women who had adored balls and pretty dresses as young girls and who had both successfully married in their first seasons. Both were now with child. Miss Lilley would no doubt stumble through this fourth season and then her parents, if they had any sense, would encourage her to forgo excessive social outings. She could take to wearing a cap and continue looking for shells, would no doubt be treated with baffled politeness by the inhabitants of Margate for her all too obvious but harmless eccentricities, protected as she was by wealth, her local connections with Lord Barrington and her titled family. It was possible that she was not entirely right in the head, certainly based on their brief exchange so far and his uncle's excessive explanations for her behaviour. He felt a little pity for her and resolved to treat her with kindness. She could not help how she was born, after all.

At the end of the promenade the two men paused for a

while, looking out to sea, where ships passed on the far horizon and bathers and fishermen came and went close by.

It was annoying, thought Frances as she walked along the sands, that her godfather had seen fit to invite along his heir. The one thing Frances was keen to do was escape the notice of young men, and here was one where she had hoped to find none, and worse, a young man certain that he must pay her attention out of politeness to Lord Barrington, so that he would inevitably ask too many questions in an effort to make conversation. When they were alone, she and Lord Barrington often spent more than half a day at a time barely speaking, only enjoying the amiable company of the other. She would bring him a particularly fine shell and he would turn it over in his hands and nod at her description of it, then hand it back and she would be off again. They spoke more at meals, but again there was no sense of obligation to ward off silence. If they wished to speak, they would speak, if not, not. Her mother, had she been with them, would have chattered away incessantly, and no doubt this young man would spoil the silence she had been enjoying. At least she was to stay longer than he was. Frances hoped to stay at least a month and perhaps two if she could keep her mother at bay long enough.

But for now the sand slipped gently under her feet and the sun shone, the gulls cried above and the salt air from the sea was a pleasure to breathe. She found a large mussel shell with a tiny hole bored through it by the sea and beside it a tiny shell which was a plain white and brown from the outside, but inside revealed a delicate rosy pink. *Limecola balthica* came in a surprising array of shades of pink or white or brown, always different the one from another. And something out of place – a pale brown and white whorled shell, not a seashell at all, but *Helix aspersa,* the common or garden snail. Those who did not know their shells often did not notice the difference, and they were pretty enough but Frances never collected them, they were part of the land, not the sea. From time to time the legs and skirts of passers-by interrupted her view, but she did not raise her head to acknowledge their greetings. They were merely an obstacle to her search and she found them irritating. No doubt they thought her odd, rude or even deaf, but she did not care. If she must succumb to the coming season and all its horrors then she was determined to enjoy herself for now, to revel in her collecting and the freedom of life under her godfather's wing.

The slow stroll along the promenade to the lighthouse and back again, as Miss Lilley prowled the seashore, head always down for the next hour and a half, was pleasant enough. Laurence listened to his uncle speak of Northdown House and Park and its upkeep with interest, for not only was his uncle knowledgeable, but of course one day it would all be his, and he must know how best to manage it or whether it would be better to dispose of it altogether.

"…And I think I will expand the orchard, it has always been a favourite part of the grounds for me, and the trees seem to do remarkably well there, no doubt the gentler seaside weather helps them along, we rarely have hard frosts. The mulberry and cherry in particular are bountiful each year, Mrs Norris can barely keep up with preserving them. I think perhaps espaliered pears along the southern wall would be a welcome addition. Are you fond of pears, Laurence? I recall you were always fond of cherries, you used to eat them in such quantities as made your dear mother fear you would be sick, but you never were. Always climbing the tree and sitting there contentedly, eating cherries by the handful." He chuckled and Laurence smiled, remembering the happy days when he would visit Northdown with his mother, indulged at every turn by both her and his uncle, the freedoms he had been allowed away from his nursemaid and later his tutor.

"...And speaking of eating, after such an early start I think we should have nuncheon, let us rejoin Andrew and Benjamin, they have care of the provisions."

The footmen, accustomed to the viscount's ways, had with them in the carriage not only a large hamper of food but also, strapped to the back, a set of cunningly wrought table and chairs, all of which folded up entirely flat, to facilitate their transport. In a matter of moments, a fully-laid dining table had appeared at the base of the lighthouse at the base of the lighthouse and two chairs to go with it for Lord Barrington's guests, while he himself remained in his wheeled chair. A large roast chicken, individual pigeon pies, an intricately laid out salad platter of salmagundy, bread rolls and butter, cheese and plain biscuits, a lemon syllabub and fresh white grapes as well as little rout cakes, were placed upon the white tablecloth and both lemonade and ale were offered as they began their repast.

"I have never seen such folding furniture." Laurence popped a grape into his mouth.

"They are naval campaign pieces," said Miss Lilley, engaged in buttering a roll. "They are designed to take up as little space on board a vessel as possible, as well as to be stored safely in case of a storm and, of course, to be easily transported to one's destination once land is made."

Laurence stared at her. He had thought that perhaps she was simple-minded, but now, hearing her speak with authority, he was forced to reconsider that opinion. "I was not aware of such items before," he said. "How do you come to know of them, Miss Lilley?"

She did not look up, merely held out her plate so that Lord Barrington could help her to the roast chicken, which he had just finished carving. "My younger brother is in the navy. He took me aboard his ship once, that I might see where he would be spending his time. They have very many excellent inventions on board, to take account of the sea's movements. Hammocks to sleep in, for example, may seem a crude form of bed, but actually they are both comfortable and practical. I tried one myself and found it most agreeable, I suggested to my mother that I might have one in my bedchamber but she disliked the idea."

She nodded to Andrew, who filled her glass with lemonade, from which she took a small sip. "A hammock is not just for sleeping in. Should a sailor die at sea it is used as his shroud. They dress him in his land clothes, sew him into the hammock with a cannonball at his feet to weigh him down and put the final stitch through his nose – a superstition designed to keep him in his shroud and prevent his spirit from following the ship – although of course it also serves as a final check that the man really is dead."

Laurence stared at her. Not only was her topic of conversation unexpected, it was downright inappropriate for a young lady to know of, let alone talk of, such things. The lives and deaths of sailors? Shocking details of their preparation for burial at sea? He was speechless. He glanced at his uncle, but Lord Barrington appeared to be entirely attentive to his meal, although a small smile lurked at the corner of his mouth.

In the ensuing silence, Frances looked up at Laurence, meeting his gaze directly for the first time. "I have shocked you," she said. "I apologise. My mother is always telling me that gentlemen do not like to hear a lady discourse on anything considered unfeminine." She gave a resigned sigh. "Would you prefer me to speak of art or music? I have been subjected to enough tuition of each that I can hold a tolerably staid conversation regarding them."

Now that he was close to her and she was finally looking directly at him, Laurence could see that her eyes were her one redeeming feature. They were a deep grey in colour, very large and fringed with long black lashes. There was, he had to admit, something refreshing in not having a girl simper at him or flutter her lashes excessively. Miss Lilley was speaking to him more in the way his sisters had done as children, directly and honestly, with no artifice or intentions to snare him. He had forgotten what such conversations had been like, when these days every woman he met had her eye on him for matrimony or something else.

Relieved at her offer to change the topic, he tried to steer the conversation back to safer ground. "Are you fond of art, Miss Lilley?"

She nodded and straightened her shoulders, as though accepting a challenge. "Gainsborough's portraits are very fine. The landscapes in which his subjects are placed show an understanding of nature which can only come from dedicated attention to the details of the natural world, which he was known to study and indeed sometimes created small models of, the better to recreate it in his works. Were you aware that some of the supper boxes in Vauxhall Pleasure Gardens were painted by him when he was still an unknown? They are quite charming."

Unexpectedly, Laurence wanted to laugh. She sounded like a particularly poor actress at the theatre, repeating her lines without any emotion or interest. "Did your mother teach you that monologue?" he asked.

"Yes," she said, without any indication of embarrassment at being found out. "Was it more to your liking?"

He could not help it, he chuckled. "Not really," he confessed. "I thought it would be but now I think I would prefer you to speak of the navy and their odd practices rather than a topic in which you have clearly been schooled, yet have no real interest in."

She gave a short nod. "I would prefer that also," she said. "Have you ever slept in a hammock, Mr Mowatt?"

He shook his head.

"Frances enjoys rocking motions," Lord Barrington said. "She is fond of both swings and rocking chairs, I have had both installed for her at Northdown. I was not surprised when she confessed to liking the motions of hammocks. She would make an excellent wife to an admiral, for she could travel with him."

Laurence raised his eyebrows in surprise. "I thought sailors objected to having a woman aboard."

Frances nodded. "They think it brings bad luck," she said, lifting up her cup of syllabub and taking a spoonful.

"A shame," said Lord Barrington. "Think how many shells you could collect if you were to travel the world, Frances."

She shook her head. "I do not need shells to be from far off climes," she said. "I am content with the many specimens available to me here."

"Do you have a wide collection?" asked Laurence politely.

"She has thousands of them," said Lord Barrington.

"What do you do with them all?" asked Laurence.

She put down her spoon, the syllabub unfinished, and turned her frank gaze on him again, the grey of her eyes almost slate blue in the afternoon light. "I decorate with them."

Laurence nodded. He had seen such items as she was referring to. "Turning them into flower petals and suchlike," he said. Some ladies painted shells in pretty colours, and then stuck them together so that they took on the appearance of baskets of flowers or added them to the frames of looking glasses.

"No," she said and there was a sharpness to her tone.

He raised his eyebrows. "No?"

"They look ridiculous when painted. Their natural patterns and the subtle variations between specimens are beautiful as they are. People who paint them do not understand anything about them. They might as well be painting pebbles or little scraps of paper. It would be better if they stuck to quilling."

He tried again, surprised by her vehemence. "How do you decorate with them then?"

"I lay them out in patterns which make the most of their existing colours and similarities or contrasts. It accentuates what is naturally present without lending them artifice they do not possess."

"Do you collect shells daily while in Margate?" Laurence inquired, ostensibly addressing Miss Lilley but hoping for his uncle to declare that they would not be doing any such thing.

But his uncle seemed entirely happy with the idea, nodding vigorously. "We do indeed. We will return here tomorrow, and perhaps on one of the days after we can visit Botany Bay as well, we can work our way along the coastline. We spend most days on the beach when Frances is here."

Laurence quietly resigned himself to the idea of spending most of his time here on the beach, but at least he would be able to talk with his uncle while the odd Miss Lilley collected her shells, and the weather was fine. So be it.

A pale sunset of pink and gold saw them return to Northdown House after several more hours of Miss Lilley gathering shells and Lord Barrington alternating between speaking with Laurence and occasionally dozing off, during which moments Laurence watched the sea slowly creeping up the beach as the tide came in, no doubt depositing more shells for Miss Lilley's collection, whose cheeks looked pink from the sun, despite her bonnet.

"Miss Lilley, you are catching the sun again," fretted Deborah that evening, ineffectually dabbing a cold cream on Frances' cheeks. "Your mother will scold me when she sees you with brown skin like a farmer's daughter."

Frances retied her stocking ribbons, which had grown loose. "You were not on the beach, how could you have stopped me?"

"Then she'll say I should have walked beside you with a parasol."

"I would not have liked that, I wanted to be alone. It is bad enough that Mr Mowatt joined us." She poked her toes into her evening slippers and Deborah knelt to tie them.

"He's a very handsome gentleman," said Deborah, bringing out a blue silk evening dress. "He might be a first-rate match for you. Imagine your mother's face if you came away to Margate and got a husband here instead of in London!"

"I have no interest in Mr Mowatt. I wish he would go away," protested Frances from within the blue silk as it was drawn over her head.

Deborah sighed. "The sooner you get married, the sooner your mother will stop twitting you about not being married," she said. "And you don't need to see your husband all the time. Lord and Lady Lilley don't spend more than an hour a day together."

It was not clear from her tone whether she approved of this or not, but at any rate she was correct. Lord and Lady Lilley dined together each day and sporadically crossed paths in the drawing room, but other than that they lived their own lives, with the occasional visit to Lady Lilley's bedchamber when Lord Lilley chose to make use of his conjugal rights.

"Now your hair," said Deborah as she finished dressing Frances in the blue silk.

Frances sank onto a chair and waited for Deborah to fuss about with hot tongs to ensure neat ringlets, her mind elsewhere. She wanted more oyster shells but they were in short supply in Margate. In Whitstable, there would be mounds of them everywhere, for many people went to Whitstable expressly to eat them. Perhaps she could ask for the carriage to drive there one day. It might give her some respite from Mr Mowatt.

"Done," said Deborah with pride, for Frances had sat unusually still and for once her hair was a credit to the maid.

Reluctantly, Frances made her way down to the dining room.

Dinner was served, during which Lord Barrington mostly spoke about philosophical texts he had been reading while both

Laurence and Frances nodded along and turned their attention to the food. Mrs Norris, Lord Barrington's cook, was a woman who knew how to please guests, providing a meal which made the most of both their seaside location and Northdown's fine orchard, with cod in oyster sauce, roast lobsters and fried whitebait all making an appearance, as well as plum puffs, apple pie with a rich custard and some dainty jellies made with her own bottled elderflower wine. As the meal came to an end, Frances abruptly stood up, forcing Laurence to do the same.

"I suppose I should retire so that you can drink port and talk about whatever it is you men talk about when there are not ladies present. I shall be in the library, in my rocking chair."

Laurence watched her as she left the room. Andrew the footman placed port and cigars on the table. Laurence filled the two glasses and shook his head at the cigars, while Lord Barrington lit one and leant back in his chair. "What delightful company I am to enjoy. First Frances, now you, joining me here. How are you getting on with my goddaughter?"

Laurence sipped his port. "She is... a little odd in her manner, Sir."

Lord Barrington chuckled. "She is indeed. She speaks her mind as she sees it and she does not suffer fools. She follows her heart's wishes, and I admire her for it. She claims she does not want a husband, that she would rather be a spinster all her days, but I think the man who sees her true beauty will be a lucky fellow."

"I think a husband might wish to change some of her ways, Sir."

"Ah, I hope not. I love her as she is and hope a man who feels the same will claim her as his bride one day. We do not change those we truly love, Laurence, we see their strange ways and their little faults and we love them all the more."

"Even if they do not meet the expectations of those around us, Sir?"

Lord Barrington gazed into the fire for so long that Laurence thought he might not be going to answer at all. At last he sighed, looked up and gave him a small smile. "When we love someone, we forgive the pain they may cause us, for we cannot stop loving them once we have been bound together."

It seemed an odd speech from a man who had never been married, Laurence thought, but perhaps Lord Barrington had had his heart broken in his youth, possibly on the Grand Tour he always spoke of with such fondness, some French or Italian beauty he had never forgotten. His uncle was a romantic, that much Laurence had always known. His mother had been wont to tease her brother, lovingly calling him a romantic fool. The visit would be dull compared to life in London, but Uncle Barrington was a kindly fellow and Laurence was prepared to make an effort for him. Once done, he would return to London, and it would be some time before he would feel obligated to return. And as for Miss Lilley and her odd ways, well that was none of his business. He would be civil but no doubt she would spend her days on the beach while he discoursed with his uncle on matters unlikely to be of interest to a lady. They need not spend much time together, only meals, and that would not be too taxing.

But the next morning it was raining, a grey steady rain that looked unlikely to stop and Lord Barrington shook his head over breakfast.

"I know you would go to the beach even in the rain, Frances, but your mama would never forgive me if I allowed you to catch a chill. Come, we shall walk in the gallery instead, one of my favourite parts of the house. Do you remember it from when you were a boy, Laurence?"

Laurence dimly recalled a room full of light and colour, of statues and echoing walls when he ran or laughed, his mother telling him to be quiet and respectful but Uncle Barrington only smiling indulgently and saying that a joyful child should never be disciplined, that there was not enough joy in the world as it was. "I recall parts of it, Sir."

Lord Barrington waved at the door and a footman opened it. "It is where I keep all my treasures from my travels."

"From the Grand Tour, Sir?"

"Indeed. It was the happiest time of my life. Venice, Florence, Rome, Naples, then on to Athens and Istanbul before we came home. My father was astonished at how much art travelled home with me, sculptures, paintings, even masks and chandeliers. Most of them I keep here at Northdown as a real-life memory palace."

Frances paused in the doorway of the gallery, looking about the vast space. Even with a grey sky outside, the room was full of light from the large windows along one wall, while the other walls were adorned with paintings. Sculptures and statues sat on plinths where the light might best illuminate them. "What is a memory palace, Uncle Barrington?"

"It comes to us from the Greek poet Simonides of Ceos. In order to memorise something, you place it within an imaginary space in your mind. So you might imagine a house with many rooms and in each room of that house you place an object that reminds you of something you wish to remember. Usually it is all imaginary, but here in my gallery I could take you on a journey which recalls the Grand Tour I undertook with Lord Hyatt in our youth."

He pointed to a painting close to the door, showing a landscape of snowy mountains. "We crossed the Alps and were snowed in for a week by an unseasonable snowstorm, staying in a wretched little inn we had intended to avoid altogether, but we had little choice."

He moved along past a sculpture of a young man asleep, a rose held in his hand, then gestured to a cabinet of Venetian masks, bright with colour and gilding, faces both beautiful and horrible in their aspects. "Venice was our first real glimpse of the beauty available to us on the Grand Tour. Hyatt and I attended the Carnival, we stayed there longer than we had planned, enjoying all the city could offer." He looked upwards, to where a magnificent chandelier hung. "Venice lit up my heart and my life, I was never so happy before or since."

"You travelled with Lord Hyatt?" asked Laurence. He remembered the name being mentioned in connection with Lord Barrington, but had not known the two men had travelled together.

"Indeed. He was not in possession of the title yet of course, neither was I of mine, we were young men, free of any ties or responsibilities. We travelled for over a year before we returned to London where we lived in adjoining apartments close to St James' – something like your Albany is today for young gentlemen who wish to spend their time in the city. We were there for another two years before his father died early and he came into his title." A small sigh left him. "After that of course he had many responsibilities – the management of the estate, securing an heir. He married and had children, after which we saw each other less frequently."

"Where was his estate?"

"In Kent, close to Margate. He would visit me here at Northdown, which I built when I came into my title. It allowed us to see one another as often as possible, when he had time."

"Is he still living?"

Lord Barrington shook his head. "He was lost to us ten years ago, before his time, like his father before him. His children must be your age by now, grown up and out in the world."

"Do you still see Lady Hyatt?"

A shadow passed over Barrington's face. "Lady Hyatt and I were not always the best of friends. She wanted her husband at home, naturally enough, not off visiting his old companion."

He sighed again, then pointed beyond the cabinet of masks to a large painting of a naked woman with long golden hair, standing on a giant shell, surrounded by the sea. "That is from when we moved from Venice on to Florence and I first saw Botticelli's Venus. Legends tell us that the goddess of love, known as Aphrodite in Greek, was born from the waves, *aphros* meaning foam, and that she came ashore on the island of Cyprus. Because of her origins, she was also considered the goddess of the sea. Here Botticelli shows her arriving on a giant scallop shell, blown ashore by the winds. It is only a copy of course, made by a local artist, it does not have the true delicacy of the original, but I could not resist bringing her home to better recall my time in Florence."

Frances was peering out into the gardens, where the rain was slowing to a drizzle. "Your mulberry tree still has some fruits on it," she said, surprised.

Lord Barrington wheeled himself over to the window beside her. "That tree is a wonder. It positively pours down fruits every year, Mrs Norris can barely keep up with it. But you are right, those ones are very late." He smiled. "The orchard is my delight. I have planted many trees in my years here. Lord Hyatt was always the one for sweet pastries and fruit drinks, so many of the trees were there to satisfy his desires. Quinces, apples, cherries… it was our Eden."

He was silent. "I am weary," he confessed. "I have grown lazy in my old age and now often allow myself the indulgence of a nap in the late mornings. Will you both excuse me? The servants are at your command should you require anything and I will trust that you are not in need of a chaperone."

"Of course, Sir," said Laurence, surprised at his uncle's tiredness. He was weaker than when he had last visited, some four years ago. "May I assist you?"

"No, no, I can manage, dear boy."

When Lord Barrington had gone, Laurence turned back to Miss Lilley, somewhat dreading the duty of staying by her side and making polite conversation. But to his surprise she was already tugging on the stiff handle of the door which led outside.

"Let us go into the gardens," she said, the door opening, a chilly breeze entering the room.

"It is still raining," objected Laurence.

"The walkway will keep our feet clean," she said. "And the swing is set under a vast oak, the canopy will keep us dry." She looked round at him. "You need not accompany me if you do not wish to," she added. "I will be quite all right by myself."

It was an easy escape, he could nod and make his way to the library to read in front of a warm fire, but Laurence felt that Frances had been left to his care in his uncle's absence and that it would be ungentlemanly of him to leave her to get wet and cold outside. "Allow me to fetch an umbrella to at least take you to the swing," he managed although by the time he had gone to the hallway and back, now armed with a large umbrella, she was already out of the door and he had to hurry to catch up to her, carefully holding the now open umbrella over her as they made their way along the walk.

She was right, the wooden planks kept their feet away from any mud and they soon reached the swing, where Frances took her seat, and began to swing herself back and forth, her eyes closed and her lips curved into a peaceful smile. Laurence stood under the umbrella and watched her for a few moments, but it seemed as though he were witnessing too intimate a moment, almost as though they were together in a bedchamber, a thought which startled him, considering how unlike she was to the women he had bedded over the years. Flustered, he turned away and looked out over the orchard, which boasted a fine array of pears, apples and quinces. The view reminded him of his uncle's words, which had confused him at the time.

"What do you think Lord Barrington meant by this being an Eden for himself and Lord Hyatt?" he asked, turning back to Miss Lilley.

She did not open her eyes. "That they were lovers and this was their paradise," she said, as though this were an obvious interpretation.

"I beg your pardon?" said Laurence, truly shocked. She could not possibly have said what he thought she had said, nor be referring to the Italian Vice, jokingly referred to amongst his racier friends when in their cups.

She opened her large grey eyes and fixed them on him, still swinging to and fro. "Lord Barrington and Lord Hyatt were lovers in their youth. They went on the Grand Tour together and lived close to each other in London. That is why they spent so much time here away from their families and why Lord Barrington never married. It is why Lord Hyatt used to visit him here alone after his marriage. It is why Lord Barrington speaks of him with such sadness and spends much of his time here, even though his proper estate is in Surrey. Northdown House is the place where they were happy together. Surely you knew that?"

Laurence stared at her in silence. How could this young woman know such a thing and not be shocked by it? She seemed entirely unperturbed about such a scandalous matter, her feet still kicking the ground in a gentle rhythm which kept her swing moving evenly back and forth.

"You're very quiet," she observed at last. "Have I said something to shock you?" She narrowed her eyes at him. "I suppose I must have done. Is it that you did not know of their liaison, or that you consider it scandalous? Or both?" She made a face. "Or is it that you think *I* should not know about it?"

Laurence cleared his throat. "I am surprised," he began, sounding pompous even to his own ears, "that a young lady should..." he trailed off.

She nodded. "Oh, it is me, then, not that you did not know or consider it scandalous yourself?"

"I did not know."

"And it bothers you?"

"Does it not bother you?"

She gave a small shrug, still swinging smoothly back and forth. "It does not concern me with whom Lord Barrington was or is in love," she said. "It would concern me if I were his wife, I suppose, which is probably why Lady Hyatt did not care for my godfather. And why Lord Barrington never married. But otherwise... what has it to do with me?"

"To associate with..."

She regarded him calmly. "Lord Barrington is the kindest man I know," she said. "He has always been good to me, he has never chastised me for being odd or different, for failing to meet the *ton*'s expectations of me, which everyone else in my life most certainly has. He has always tried to help me. I am here now because I wrote to him and asked him to invite me, for I could not bear the thought of my fourth season and all the whispers that will accompany me wherever I go."

Laurence was still disconcerted by what she had said, even though he was beginning to glimpse the truth of it. Lord Barrington had never married, which was odd enough, but on top of that he had always spoken fondly of Lord Hyatt and indeed of the importance of loving and being loved. There were several portraits of Lord Hyatt about Northdown, both alone and with Lord Barrington on the Grand Tour from their youthful days. The truth had been there for all to see, it was not very well hidden, yet it had taken this slip of a girl, this odd creature, to point it out as though it were common knowledge, and not only common knowledge but also entirely acceptable, which it most certainly was not by polite society. He was unsure of how to proceed. Yet Uncle Barrington had also always been kindness itself and Laurence's mother had loved him dearly. Now that Miss Lilley had brought the matter up, he recalled a time, some ten years past, when he had accompanied his mother to Northdown House for an unexpected, extended stay. He remembered entering a room where his mother was embracing Uncle Barrington who was sobbing on her shoulder, his confusion and bewilderment, her gentle smile and gesture to close the door, to leave them alone. Had that stay, then, been occasioned by the death of Lord Hyatt, had his mother come to comfort her brother in his grief at losing his beloved? His muddled thoughts were interrupted by the footman, Andrew, appearing in the doorway to summon them for the midday meal. Miss Lilley rose promptly from her seat and went indoors without a backward glance, leaving Laurence to join them at the table, still trying to decide how he felt about this new information.

They were joined by Lord Barrington, who was in fine spirits. "Now that I am rested, we will eat and then we can play cards in the drawing room or Frances can play the harp for us, though she will have to spend some time tuning it. The sea air is no friend to the harp, I am afraid, they are very sensitive instruments."

Laurence nodded politely.

"I have also received word that there is to be a ball next week at the Assembly Rooms, and one of my neighbours, a Mrs Pagington, has forcefully insisted that I attend – I told her I am not well enough to do so and have instead suggested you go in my stead. She is an amiable woman," he added indulgently. "A pillar of local society here and means well. She was delighted at the idea of making your acquaintance, since you will be a man of some importance in these parts in the future, when Northdown is yours."

Laurence, having just taken a mouthful of sliced beef, was not able to answer, so he only nodded again.

"Excellent. I am indebted to you for this kindness. Frances and I will stay at home, as she does not care for such events and, unlike her mother, I am of the opinion that her preferences should be honoured. Frances is more comfortable amongst select friends than at vast gatherings, are you not, my dear?"

Frances looked up from buttering her roll. "Yes," she said. "Mrs Pagington is too loud and never stops speaking. She gives me a headache."

Lord Barrington chuckled. "They are not a comfortable match at all," he said. "Frances can barely say a word in her company. I see her growing pale with the strain within an hour of being there. We will be content here alone, while you stand in our stead, Laurence, since you are a man who can conduct himself well at balls."

CHAPTER 4
Intentions Regarding Marriage

A WEEK WENT BY IN WHICH THEIR DAYS FOLLOWED the same patterns – on dry days Frances collected shells while Lord Barrington and Mr Mowatt conversed. On wet days the gallery and library became their haunts, while Mrs Norris continued providing her excellent meals. But Mrs Pagington's invitation loomed ever closer and on the appointed evening Laurence dutifully prepared himself to meet Margate's society.

To a young man accustomed to the finer haunts of London, the Assembly Rooms of Margate in Cecil Square proved every bit as dull as he had feared. The ballroom itself was of a decent size, amply provided with large looking glasses and well-lit with five glittering chandeliers, but the card room was full of elderly locals who all knew one another and clearly held long-standing grudges over their ongoing games of Commerce, constantly referring to previous gambling success or failures such as to make any newcomer nearly bored to tears. The billiard room contained only those men who were reluctant to dance, and Laurence felt himself obliged to be sociable since he was representing his uncle. The dancing had not yet begun and the musicians, rather than playing something to make those already in attendance feel welcome, were still tuning up, a far from pleasant sound. The tea room was well provided however and Mrs Pagington, delighted at the sight of Laurence, would barely leave his side, introducing him to everyone in the room.

"The future master of Northdown House, you know, when our dear Lord Barrington is no longer with us,"

This information swiftly had the effect of all the local mamas lining up their daughters in what amounted to a parade of faces before him, each one hoping to be chosen for the first dance and thereafter to be shown favour throughout the evening.

"My daughter Miss Reid…"

"Miss Thrup, Miss Susanna Thrup and Miss Patience Thrup…"

"Lady Emilia…"

Mrs Pagington also saw it as her business to keep up a positive babble of instructions regarding etiquette to Laurence, as though she were the Master of Ceremonies and he had never attended such an event before.

"This will be one of our final assemblies, Mr Mowatt, for our social season runs quite contrary to London, since we are quiet in the winter and busy in the summer, nothing like the city! Now, the dancing will begin at *eight*, gentlemen are to change partners every two dances – so as not to show too much favour to one pretty face and have it remarked on, you know! The cotillion will be danced *after* tea, and we end *promptly* at eleven, even if we are *mid dance*! It is quite late enough for a social gathering, do you not agree?"

Laurence, who rarely got home before three in the morning when attending a ball in London, nodded politely.

"And of course, every lady of precedence shall be entitled to her proper place at the top of the set, but once a dance has begun, any lady joining *shall* be obliged to take her place at the bottom of the set..."

Eager to escape the monologue, Laurence threw himself into the dancing, offering himself as a partner to most of the young women in the room. The locals blushed and giggled at the attention from the man who would one day become a viscount with an estate both here and in Surrey. The ladies visiting from London affected superior airs, implying that a titled gentleman would naturally prefer a more sophisticated bride. All of them were anxious to point out that they were not in Margate for their own health, far from it, they were only being thoughtful daughters, sisters and nieces to family members who suffered from one malady or another which would benefit from the sea air and the salt water. More than one mama mentioned their intention to call on "dear Lord Barrington" soon, indeed the very next day, perhaps, if he were at home.

Laurence, understanding full well that they had no interest in Lord Barrington until such time as he died and left his title and estate to an eligible bachelor, thought that he must devise some means of being out of Northdown House on most of the following days. He smiled and danced, danced and smiled, made polite conversation with as many local dignitaries as possible and was infinitely relieved when the clock struck eleven and, as promised, the music stopped mid-dance and he could escape back to Northdown House. It was odd to be so eager to escape a social occasion, but the society at a resort such as Margate was too limited for his tastes. He had no intention of marrying a local girl and it would not do, in such a small community, to form intimate acquaintances with married ladies, it would be far too noticeable in a place where everyone knew everyone else and had nothing to fill their days with but gossip.

He envied Lord Barrington and Miss Lilley for having avoided the entire evening and wondered whether his natural inclination to attend far more social occasions than was strictly required was in fact as diverting a path as it seemed. There were certainly evenings, like this one, where he would have preferred to stay at home. His parents had eschewed most such social obligations, preferring to keep their social circle more intimate, comprising their family and close friends, going to London only infrequently and, although good-spirited while there, always returned to the countryside with pleasure, saying that they had had enough of the city and its delights until the next year.

"Society is best in small doses," his father was fond of saying.

Laurence, as a child, had never understood this statement, since London's society was to him a place full of extraordinary delights and excitements, which he had certainly made the most of in the years since his mother had died, after he moved to Albany and took up life as a stylish young man about town. But tonight he understood his father's view.

The next morning Frances was curled up on a sofa, hot chocolate clasped between her hands. She had come to breakfast early and eaten Mrs Norris's buttery seedcake, half-hoping to hear Mr Mowatt's description of the night before so that she could congratulate herself on having avoided the event entirely. But when the two men joined her Laurence ate heartily without much description of his outing at all, while Lord Barrington had dry toast and a cup of broth and seemed quieter than usual.

"I feel a chill coming over me," he said. "Frances is eager to go down to Margate, would you accompany her, Laurence? I will follow in an hour or so, when I have warmed my old bones longer."

"Of course, Sir."

Frances was disappointed, but she supposed that an outing to find shells was better than staying at home, so when Mr Mowatt asked if she were ready to depart she only nodded and rang for Deborah to fetch her pelisse and bonnet, both in dark brown velvet and silk with fur trims. Deborah was additionally pressed into service as a chaperone and followed them into the carriage with a sulky countenance, since she disliked the chilly breeze that came in off the sea.

They walked along the soft sands, feet occasionally slipping in the sifting grains.

"You should walk where the sand is damp," said Frances after a while, becoming annoyed by Deborah's huffs of irritation as sand got into her shoes and Laurence's taking odd zig-zag steps to try and avoid the worst of the slippage. Could they not see the darker sand, how much more compact it was? She wished she could have come alone, for being trailed by two unwilling attendants was an encumbrance she would gladly have done without.

"When do you return to London?" asked Laurence.

"My mama has written to me, telling me I should hurry back to London as there is a most eligible young man lately arrived in town," she said. "I have told her I cannot possibly leave Lord Barrington when he has invited me personally. But in truth I have no interest in chasing after some young man when every young miss in London will be doing the same. The poor man must feel like a fox chased by the hounds. I shall stay here as long as possible. I am in no hurry for my fourth season."

"I am sure there is still time for finding a suitable husband," he said politely.

Frances suppressed a smile. No doubt he found her entirely unsuited to marriage. Excellent. The more men who thought so, the more likely her parents would give up and allow her the freedom she craved.

"I wonder you are not yet married yourself," she said after a while, turning a white *Cochlodesma praetenue* or spoon clam over in her hands and then discarding it, since it was cracked. "Are you more of Lord Barrington's bent?"

"No!" he said, looking shocked at the very suggestion.

She shrugged. "Do you prefer not to marry, then?"

"Of course I will marry," he said. "My father is keen that I should be wed. He would like to be surrounded by grandchildren. I intend to secure a wife this coming season."

She was intrigued. "You have already fallen in love then?"

"One does not need to be in love to marry," he said stiffly. He seemed put out by her interest, as though he did not wish to discuss any intimate particulars of his life with her. "Of course, affection is to be hoped for in a marriage, but so long as there is respect between the parties, that is all that is needed. As I am sure you will one day find yourself," he added, with a lecturing tone.

"I do not wish to marry," she said, eyes still searching the sand.

"Perhaps not now," he said, stooping to pick up a small pink-tinged shell and passing it to her. "But no doubt one day you will wish to marry and have children."

"No," she said. "I do not ever wish to marry."

"You do not want children?" he asked, surprised. Surely all women wanted children.

"I would not object to children," she said. She added a delicately pink *Tellina tenuis* to her basket, the two halves still together, so that it looked like a tiny butterfly instead of a shell. "But I would not wish to be obliged to carry out the other duties of a wife; to host or attend social gatherings, to be forced to spend a great deal of time in company. It would be both tiring and tiresome to me."

He had known she was odd, but this was beyond what he had thought. "What would you propose to do with your life, then?" he asked, with an indulgent chuckle. "Collect shells, all alone?"

She turned to him at once, her face suddenly lit up. "Yes," she said. "I wish to have a small house by the sea, with an income of my own and time to be alone. I would collect shells and walk by the sea and enjoy all that the natural world has to offer, its beauty and its mysteries. I would keep to myself and have a well-managed life, with things done as I wished them done. I would be happy, I think. But my parents do not agree with me, so I will have to wait until they have given up on my ever marrying." She turned away again and continued along the beach, head down in her usual stance.

Laurence stood still watching her, drawn to a halt by her extraordinary statement. What could she mean by it? She did not wish to marry at all? She would forgo the desire to have children in order to live a strange solitary life by the sea, collecting shells for the rest of her days and speaking to no-one? He shook his head. Well, her parents were right to persevere in finding her a husband, it was absurd to let a young woman who knew nothing about the world make such a reckless choice. He looked behind him, back to where Uncle Barrington had arrived and was now following their progress from the promenade, his chair rolling along at a slow but steady pace. There were some steps nearby, where the beach led back to the promenade and now Laurence took them two at a time, reaching the pavement as his uncle drew abreast.

"May I walk with you, Sir? Miss Lilley is happy enough alone." Happy alone, not just now but forever, was that truly her intention? There was something about the thought he found disconcerting.

Uncle Barrington gave a warm smile as he watched Frances continue down the beach, seemingly unaware and uncaring of whether Laurence were behind her or not. "Most certainly, my boy."

Laurence walked for a few moments in silence, before his thoughts could no longer be contained. "Miss Lilley said she does not wish to marry," he blurted out. "Ever."

"Had you made her an offer?" inquired his uncle.

"No!"

"What made her say such a thing then?"

"I – I had made mention of wishing to find a wife this coming season."

"Are you in love?"

"No, Sir. But it is my duty to marry soon and I intend to find a suitable wife."

"Duty… suitable… would you not wish to find someone you truly love?"

Laurence thought of Lord Hyatt and how he had found a wife, despite his youthful connection with Lord Barrington. Had he felt anything for Lady Hyatt or had the marriage been one of convenience, his heart lying elsewhere? The thought seemed sad, but then Lord Hyatt had done his duty to his family and sired heirs, which Lord Barrington had not. Laurence was still unsure of whether his uncle's path was acceptable. "Love is not required for a marriage, Uncle."

"Is it not?"

"No, Sir. I would hope for affection, of course, and mutual respect."

Lord Barrington sighed. "And do you have such a woman in mind? One who is suitable, who will afford you mutual respect and possibly affection?"

"Perhaps."

"May I inquire as to her name?"

"Lady Honora Fortescue."

The viscount thought. "Daughter of the Marquis of Halesworth?"

"Yes, Sir."

A small smile twitched at the corner of Lord Barrington's mouth. "An excellent woman," he pronounced. "Practical. Well bred. Good-natured but not weak-willed with it."

"Yes, Sir. We have known each other a long time."

Lord Barrington stopped his chair and Laurence stopped with him. "Will you do your uncle a favour?"

"If it lies within my power, Sir, of course."

"Do not marry this season. Next year, perhaps."

"Why?"

"Only a whim of mine, to keep you young and free of duty, as you said, a little longer. Will you do that? Oh, by all means court whomever you like this coming season, but without obligation, without any understandings being entered into. Will you do that for me?"

"If you wish it, Sir. Although I do not understand why you would be reluctant for me to marry."

"I am not reluctant for you to marry, far from it. But I would like you to marry for love, Laurence, and therefore I beg your indulgence; one more year for your heart to bloom. If it does not, then you have my blessing to marry whomsoever you choose, with or without love."

Laurence shrugged. "As you wish, Sir, though I do not think I will change my mind on this subject."

"Then it will not matter if you wait only one more year." Lord Barrington gave his nephew a warm smile. "Now, perhaps you would be so kind as to push my chair for me. My arms grow tired and Miss Lilley, as you can see, is rapidly outstripping us, for all that she is walking on the sand, and we have a firm path beneath our feet. Let us make haste and follow her."

"Yes, Sir."

As he pushed the chair along the promenade, Laurence turned over Miss Lilley's determination to remain a spinster in his mind. It was very odd, certainly, but there was something about the certainty of her vision that appealed. She had depicted the life she wanted with great clarity and seemed determined to achieve it. He half wished he had such certainty about his future – his images of married life were half-formed, with no true shape to the woman who might be his wife, only the knowledge that he should of course have a bride, one who would take her place one day as Viscountess Barrington. But that was all he could imagine for now: that she would be fit to take such a position. Nothing more. Miss Lilley was an odd fish, but at least she knew her own mind.

"Today I will go to the baths," announced Lord Barrington at breakfast the next day. "There is a place on the seafront where they have heated baths with seawater, it is most convenient and brings the benefits of the salt water to those of us no longer able to enter the sea itself." He smiled. "Shall you both join me?"

"Yes, but I will go into the sea," said Frances.

"A brave woman indeed," said Lord Barrington. "Laurence?"

Laurence could hardly settle for the warm baths provided for invalids if Miss Lilley was going to brave the cold of the sea. "The sea, of course," he agreed.

"Excellent," declared Lord Barrington. "Then we shall return home cured of all our ills this afternoon."

The carriage deposited Lord Barrington at the warm baths close to the promenade, then took Laurence to the gentlemen's part of the beach, before driving away to the next section of the beach, reserved for ladies, although the two were quite close.

The summer sun had lost its powers, showing only its pale autumn face. The sky was mostly grey, there was a chill in the air and the sea was downright cold, there was no two ways about it. Still, Laurence climbed the steps into the bathing machine standing waiting for him and undressed while it rocked along the beach to its destination.

"Ready for you, Sir!" called the attendant.

"Ready!" Laurence replied and the door was opened, revealing the steps down into the sea, the grey water sloshing against them, a few cold drops catching his bare legs. He braced himself for the impact, but still gasped as he dived in and the cold struck him. Spluttering, panting, he swam vigorously to and fro for some minutes, the activity bringing him enough warmth to bear the water at least a while longer. Now better able to withstand the cold, he struck out for a longer swim, heading away from the shore, inspired by the exhilaration which the sea had always brought him, the sensation of being very small and insignificant whilst also being at one with a vast untameable element. When he had swum some way out he turned, treading water, and looked back towards the beach, where he could see the tiny figures of the attendants and their bathing machines. He had come out further than he had thought, the bottom was quite untouchable, despite most of Margate's shoreline being shallow. He would head back.

But something caught his eye to the left and a sudden shock took hold of him. A corpse! Then a secondary shock as he realised that no, it was a woman, floating on her back, eyes fully open to the grey sky above. Miss Lilley, clad only in her bathing dress, a heavy navy-blue costume which had drifted up her legs, now gathered at her knees. He had veered to one side as he swam out and now was too close to the female bathing section. He averted his eyes and made to swim away, but something made him want to look at her again. She had swum out as far as he had, which made her a strong swimmer. She was not gasping and spluttering or shivering, merely lying on her back gazing at the sky, as though on a comfortable bed, unworried by the cold, unconcerned by what must be the heavy weight of her thick blue dress, pulling her downwards. She looked peaceful, content. Laurence trod water a few moments longer, unable to take his eyes off her, then struck out for the shore, his mind entirely on Miss Lilley. He looked back from time to time, fearful lest she suddenly cry for help when he was already too close to the shore, but she did not move from her position, staring up at the sky.

The sky. Grey it might seem to the casual onlooker, but it was not such a flat colour. There were clouds layered upon clouds, with some patches darker, others lighter. Occasionally the sun would send hesitant, searching rays through the clouds, before they were lost again.

The gulls. They swooped overhead, calling out with their harsh voices, sometimes flying together, at other times entirely alone, wheeling on invisible eddies of air.

The sea. Cold seeping through to her bones yet oddly not unpleasant, its harsh salt smell all about her, in her nose as well as her mouth, but below her a gentle rise and fall, akin to her rocking chair, to the swing she was so fond of, the motion bringing her a deep calm.

She would have stayed for far longer, but she supposed, reluctantly, that she should head back to the shore. More than once, she had experienced concerned bathers dragging her back, all but submerging her in the process when she had been in no danger of drowning, or attendants calling for her in ever more panicked tones, despite her being entirely peaceful and happy. She turned onto her front and began the swim back to shore. The dress she was forced to wear for modesty's sake was heavy, pulling her downwards, but Frances was a strong swimmer; the narrow but deep stream on the family's estate had taught her well over the years.

She headed towards her bathing machine, which in her

opinion there was entirely no reason for, why could she not stroll down the beach and walk into the water naked, as the men did? But social conventions were social conventions, so she obeyed them, knowing what a fuss people liked to make otherwise. It was not worth the energy it would take to withstand their protestations. Frances had long since learnt to keep her oddities to herself unless they were truly worth battling for, when she would turn intransigently stubborn. Back at the bathing machine, she gripped the handrail to pull herself up the stairs, her dress three times its former weight, pulling her back towards the sea. Turning her head as she climbed, she saw, not thirty yards away, Mr Mowatt, standing naked halfway up the stairs of his bathing machine, looking her way, an anxious expression on his face. Had he seen her out on the waves, fretted about her? If he had, he had shown remarkable restraint in trusting that she was happy, in not pulling her from the sea, and for that, she was grateful. She nodded to him and he looked away, as though uncomfortable at seeing her in her soaking wet bathing dress, not that there was much of her that could be seen in it. Long sleeves, a long hem, heavy fabric. It was absurd to go swimming in it. At home, she had been wont to swim in only her shift, and sometimes not even in that, to the consternation of the gardeners and the horror of her mother, who had eventually insisted, with dire threats, that Frances must only ever swim in a proper bathing dress.

Peeling off the wet dress with the assistance of her attendant, then carefully rinsed in fresh water, Frances emerged from her bathing machine tolerably well-dressed again, though her hair was still very damp, her ringlets nowhere to be seen.

"Did you enjoy your swim?" Mr Mowatt asked her, meeting her at the carriage, where they waited for Lord Barrington to join them.

"Yes. Thank you for not rescuing me," she said.

His face flushed with embarrassment. "I did not – that is to say, I saw you but thought you seemed…"

"Content," she said. "I was perfectly content, Mr Mowatt, and in no need of being rescued. I am grateful you saw that. Not many men would have done."

Laurence had never had a lady thank him for leaving her alone before, but it was clear that she did not speak in jest and her words made him feel oddly proud that he had seen her strange behaviour and interpreted it correctly. "You are welcome," he replied, feeling that an answer was called for. "You are a strong swimmer," he added, meaning to repay the compliment.

She shrugged. "I am not afraid of the deep water. Indeed, further out it is usually less rough, the waves break on the shoreline while out at sea they are often gentler. One feels held by the sea, in no danger of drowning if you do not fight it. If you fight its nature, it is dangerous, but if you understand it and allow it to be itself you will be safe in its embrace."

"You sound like Uncle Barrington, a true philosopher," he said.

"He makes a study of human nature. He understands those around him far better than they understand him."

He wondered if she meant it as a rebuke for his shock over Lord Barrington's past love life, but she gave a small smile which indicated some degree of friendliness, which he returned.

"I shall be leaving in a day or two," he said.

"So soon?"

"The Little Season is beginning and I have invitations which it would be rude of me to refuse."

She looked away. "I have refused plenty, my mama says I am a hopeless case of rudeness."

He could not help a small chuckle. "I do not think you care what the *ton* thinks of you, Miss Lilley. If you did, you would not be here, gathering shells, you would be fretting at your modiste to make you yet another ballgown."

She looked at him with a serious countenance, before her lips twisted into a wry smile. "Why, Mr Mowatt, I believe you are beginning to know something of my character. First you do not rescue me from my sea bathing and now you know my secret: that I am only waiting for the *ton* to declare me a spinster once and for all, so that I may lead the life I wish to."

He nodded, still surprised at her insistence on not marrying, but pleased that there seemed to be an amicable understanding developing between them. "If I know something of your character and you of mine, perhaps we are becoming friends, Miss Lilley."

She tilted her head. "Do you have many female friends, Mr Mowatt?"

He thought of the married women with whom he spent his London nights, but they were not what he would call friends. He did not converse with them on any topic other than those which led to compliments and caresses. "No," he admitted at last. "I believe you are my only female friend, Miss Lilley."

Lord Barrington arrived and was swiftly made comfortable in the carriage by Andrew and Benjamin, ready for them all to go home.

On Laurence's last day his uncle gave him a generous sum of money in addition to his usual allowance and followed him to the door, where the carriage stood waiting. "Now remember what you promised, my boy. No rash promises of marriage, not this year at any rate. Wait a while longer and have faith in providence. 'There are more things in Heaven and Earth, Horatio, than are dreamt of in your philosophy.' It may seem responsible, to marry for practical reasons, but I promise you that love, when it comes, is worth the wait."

This advice, hopelessly romantic as it was, was well meant, and Laurence held out his hand to Lord Barrington, only to be pulled down for an enveloping fatherly embrace. "Go now, my boy, and enjoy yourself."

"Yes, Sir. I hope your health will not suffer this winter."

"That, I can always hope for. Goodbye."

Behind him, Miss Lilley appeared in the doorway. She did not say anything, only watched him.

"Goodbye, Sir. Miss Lilley." Laurence gave her a small bow and she returned it with a silent curtsey.

CHAPTER 5
The Halesworth Ball

HER PEACEFUL TIME WITH LORD BARRINGTON HAVING expired, Frances had reluctantly returned to London as promised and was once again enduring the boredom and strain of social expectations. The current day promising nothing but grey drizzle until the social calls of the early afternoon, Frances had taken up residence in the drawing room, curled into the rocking chair, accompanied by volume two of Donovan's *Natural History of British Shells.* Her peaceful morning was interrupted when the door opened and a footman appeared.

"Lady Lilley requests that you join her in the morning room, Miss."

Reluctantly Frances followed him to the morning room, where her mother usually spent time managing the household. She was dismayed to find a larger than usual selection of magazines laid about, opened up at the fashion plates, and her mother looking unusually bright and cheerful.

"You will recall the tragedy that befell the Buckinghams?"

Frances did not recall anything about the Buckinghams,

but whatever the tragedy was, her mother looked altogether too happy to be recounting it.

"No," she replied, hoping by her tone to indicate her lack of interest.

"You cannot have forgotten! The Duke of Buckingham died of apoplexy and directly afterwards his son, the new duke, died in a hunting accident. It was all anyone could talk about."

Frances gave a grimacing nod, as much to indicate that yes, she was now aware of what the tragedy was and still had no interest in it.

"So *now*," continued her mother, oblivious to any hints, "the younger brother, Edward, is Duke of Buckingham and is to be married."

Frances nodded again but her mother was looking at her as though this time, a nod was not sufficient. "To whom?" she asked, hoping the answer would be brief.

"I meant he is *looking* for a wife," said her mother. "The Duchess his mother has made it clear to her acquaintances that His Grace intends to find a wife this very season. They are already in town; the Duchess, the Duke and a cousin, a Miss... Miss Seton, I think. Of course, the Duchess cannot be seen to be too lavish in her clothing, since she is so recently in mourning, but her modiste told me, in the strictest confidence, that she has ordered more than a dozen dresses already, and for Miss Seton, twice that number and with a promise of more to come. They are only accepting the occasional invitation during the Little Season, they say because of the mourning and so on but we all know really it is to draw more attention to themselves. Every hostess in London is desperate to have them accept an invitation."

Frances yawned.

"Frances!"

"Yes?"

"You are not paying attention."

"I am paying attention," said Frances. "Every hostess in London is desperate to have them accept an invitation."

"Repeating my words back to me like a parrot is not the same as listening, Frances," said her mother sulkily. "You must see that this is news of great import to us."

"Why?"

"Because he is looking for a wife. And he is a young man, who has not previously been much in town and will not know that you are…. that this is not your first season."

"Someone will tell him, no doubt."

"Whether they tell him or not, for him you are new, he has not met you before."

"How old is he?"

"Twenty-two, I think, so the same as you."

"Where has he been?"

"What?"

"Where has he been all this time? The young men of the *ton* generally spend years in London before they seek out a wife. Where has he been?"

"Stop repeating that, you still sound like a parrot!"

"It's an obvious question."

"I don't know. Studying, travelling, I believe there was an uncle in Ireland he visited…" said her mother vaguely. "The Duchess said he was fond of astronomy."

Frances didn't respond.

"Astronomy is part of the natural world," tried her mother desperately.

Frances raised her eyebrows.

"We will visit the modiste this afternoon. The Halesworth ball is in two weeks and the Duke will be there."

Frances felt the threat and braced herself for all that was to follow. As she had feared, the following days involved milliners and modistes, leaving her on the day of the ball concealed beneath layers of fine green muslin and silk, her hair in the tightest of tight ringlets and under strict instructions to "*try* and be appropriate." She had not answered this plea, but her mother had found it necessary to add, "The Duke of Buckingham will not want to marry an odd girl, Frances, so try to behave *normally*."

The Halesworth ball, held by Lord and Lady Halesworth, was both large and well attended, being one of the first major balls of the Little Season, the first chance to see and be seen, to assess this year's marriage mart and judge its worth. Boldly decorated with autumnal shades of flowers and berries, brilliantly lit with hundreds of beeswax candles which perfumed the air with a sweet honey scent, it was generally acknowledged by all attendees that Lady Halesworth had certainly done a fine job as hostess. Champagne flowed freely and there were pretty paper fans with tiny silver pencils provided for all the young ladies who would be dancing, listing the dances that would be played with an adjacent space for their partners' names.

Frances shook her head at the champagne, which only ever made her feel dizzy, took her fan and silver pencil, then retreated as fast as possible behind two large palms in a corner of the room.

"Frances."

She turned and her shoulders dropped in relief. "Elizabeth."

Elizabeth Belmont, daughter to Lord and Lady Godwin, was a delicately built young woman, with dark hair and such a quiet voice that everyone called her "the mouse" behind her back. Frances had known her since they were children and had always relished her company, Elizabeth being one of the few people she knew who neither wore strong perfume nor minded sitting in companionable silence while reading or drawing, one of Elizabeth's favourite pastimes. Excellent at capturing a sitter's features in a few simple strokes of charcoal, she would happily sit and sketch Frances while Frances read to herself or occasionally out loud. She was a couple of years younger than Frances and had only recently come out.

"Are you on the marriage mart this year?" Frances asked.

Elizabeth nodded. "My parents are determined I should marry the Duke of Buckingham. He is new to town, young, rich, handsome... and a duke. They can barely contain their excitement.

Frances nodded. "Mine too."

Elizabeth gave a laugh. "And all the other mamas of the *ton*, no doubt. Poor man, he will not know a moment's peace until he is engaged." She scanned the floor, then stiffened. "Here he comes now."

A tall young man, elegantly dressed in the finest tailoring but with unfashionably long fair hair which brushed his shoulders, stood before them. "May I have the next dance, Miss Belmont?"

Frances watched as Elizabeth held out her fan and the new Duke of Buckingham wrote his name, before turning vivid blue eyes on her and bowing again. "Miss... Lilley? May I also claim a dance from you?"

Frances dropped him a curtsey and held out her fan. He wrote his name and she noticed his hand shook as he did so, wondered whether he, too, would rather not be here, before he bowed and stepped away from them. She glanced at Elizabeth to see what she thought.

"Shy," said Elizabeth.

Frances nodded. Shy might be promising, she supposed, he might at least not be one of those loud men who stomped about with boots and gave their opinions when they were not wanted. But he had made a beeline for Elizabeth, already briefed by his mama as to whom he should pay attention, hesitating over her name. Elizabeth, freshly out after a ball held two weeks previously, would be considered the better catch, even though they were both daughters of viscounts.

"How was your first ball?" Frances asked.

Elizabeth wrinkled her nose. "Stiff. Mama was so very disappointed that the Queen was not holding a Drawing Room to present me that she made me wear court dress anyway. Can you imagine? Plumes and all. It was ridiculous, no-one else dressed that way. Only Lady Celia Follett seemed to enjoy herself, but then she's already promised to the Earl of Comerford, so she doesn't have to worry about finding a husband. She can enjoy a season of balls and parties and then be married. I think I envy her." She pointed with her closed fan to a young woman dancing, whose face was alight with merriment at something her partner had just said. "She is always in fine spirits, I am sure she will make the Earl a happy wife."

"Is he here?"

"Not yet. He will return for the opening of Parliament in November."

Frances watched the dancers as they formed and reformed the patterns of the quadrille. If she could only watch dancing, it might be enjoyable, for there was something pleasing about the way the dancers moved between one another, repeating the same figures. But to dance among them was to keep perfect count of the moves and to interminably smile and nod, to sometimes talk to one's partner, which many young ladies did with great charm and vivacity, but which Frances found exhausting, her bright smile soon turning to a grimace or an expression of burden. Despite not wanting to marry, she somewhat envied the Earl of Comerford and Lady Celia. A marriage already settled on while they were still in their nurseries, no wooing required or expected. They could go about their lives and wait for the day when they were to complete the ceremony. There would be none of this false flattery, this simpering to catch the eye of some foolish young man and hope to chain him down as quickly as possible.

She sighed as she saw the first of her partners heading towards her. There was nowhere to hide, it would have to be borne.

The ball passed as they always did, a chore to be got through, one drudgery of a dance after another. The Duke of Buckingham was all but silent, although he performed their dance admirably, with neat steps and a gracefulness which Frances herself did not have. Frances imagined that if the Duke were to show any interest in her, their marriage would be all but silent, a thought that very nearly made him seem interesting, but it was clear his mind was elsewhere and that she had not caught his attention. Lord Radcliffe also made it abundantly clear he was disinterested in her, looking around the room for better options, while Lord Frampton made a gallant effort at pleasant conversation but fell silent after a while when her responses did not provide much to build on. Frances would happily have left early, but she could see her mother watching her, an anxious expression on her face, which only served to remind her that she was failing yet again.

"Miss Lilley! I did not expect to see you here."

The familiarity of the voice brought a half smile to her lips. She turned to see Mr Mowatt before her and held out her hand without thinking, which he readily took and bowed over, placing a small kiss on her glove. She pulled her hand back, fearing she was being too forward, but his expression seemed pleased.

"I was obliged to attend," she managed.

He gave a rueful smile. "Always so blunt," he said, but there was something warm in the way he said it that did not sound like the chastisements of her mother. "Will you dance?"

"I would rather not."

This time he laughed out loud. "Then may I escort you for an ice, at least? Lord Barrington would be disappointed in us if we did not at least share some refreshment, in view of our connection through him."

She took his proffered arm and nodded to Elizabeth, who was speaking with Lady Honora Fortescue.

"And now that you have been obliged to attend, are you beginning to enjoy yourself?"

"No," she said. "I look forward to leaving as soon as possible."

"Surely you have a list of eligible young men with whom your mother has insisted you dance?"

"I have already danced with the Duke of Buckingham. No-one cares about anyone else."

He nodded. "That is true. I have met him, he is a pleasant enough fellow, quiet but thoughtful. I like him. He will make someone an excellent husband."

"I doubt it will be me. He can have anyone he chooses."

Perhaps he felt obliged to give her some small compliment. "Anyone who marries you will have a wife who will always be honest with them," he began, then hesitated, before adding, "Besides, you are interesting to talk with."

She gazed at him, assessing his words for some hidden slight but did not find one, he seemed to believe what he was saying. "I am not sure those are the qualities men seek in a wife," she said at last.

"What qualities would you say they sought, then?"

She gave a rueful smile. "Prettiness, polite conversation, breeding and money." She paused. "I have the last two, but not the first."

"You are pretty," he said, and he sounded surprised, as though the opinion had only just come to him. "But your conversation perhaps is not quite what young men are used to," he admitted.

She nodded, pleased that he had not attempted to deny that she was at least right about her lack of polite conversation. "Have you seen Lord Barrington since we were last there?" she asked.

"No, though he wrote to me to say he feels more tired these days. I will try to visit him before Christmas."

"In Margate?"

"Yes, he leaves Margate just before Christmas, as you know, to be at the main estate during the festive period. He takes most of the staff with him, since they are used to his ways and needs. A few stay behind to keep the house in good order against his return. Will you be visiting?"

Frances shook her head. "I doubt I will be allowed to escape all of this."

"I will give him your compliments, then."

"Thank you."

He would have stayed longer, but Lady Celia Follett was turning her head to look for him, he had promised her the next dance. "I must go."

She nodded and gave him a brief curtsey. "Goodbye, Mr Mowatt."

"Miss Lilley."

He left her and walked across the ballroom to Lady Celia. Lady Celia would have been one of the season's brightest stars and most desirable brides, were it not for the fact that her right hand was oddly deformed. She had been born with a full-size thumb and little finger, but the three fingers in-between were only tiny stubs, like baby toes, incapable of much movement and of no use in daily life. Fortunately, two points stood her in good favour in avoiding spinsterhood. Firstly, she was the daughter of a duke, with a large dowry to accompany her unfortunate disfigurement, which might perhaps cancel out the risk that her children might be born with a similar fault. Secondly, she was already promised in marriage, for her family had, at her very birth, already arranged a betrothal with the Earl of Comerford's second son, who had at the time been all of ten years old. The two families had been very close and it had been agreed then, and always expected, that the betrothal would be held to, the wishes of the two parties involved set entirely aside. Their plans had gone somewhat awry, however, when the Earl had died earlier than expected and his sickly heir had followed two years later. Lady Celia was now betrothed to the Earl of Comerford. This year, Lady Celia had finally been brought out, and the expectation was that she might enjoy herself for one season, before being married in the early summer and would then be suitably settled with the Earl. She would be a countess. It was a small drop in title, but then that was to be expected given her deformity and, in compensation, the Earl of Comerford would be connected to a duke and have a very wealthy wife.

Laurence bowed. "Lady Celia. I believe I have the honour of this dance?"

Sparkling brown eyes and a ready smile greeted him as Lady Celia swept an immaculate curtsey and held out her right hand to be led to the dancefloor. She wore white elbow length gloves and as Laurence took her hand he could feel that the central three fingers of the glove had been stuffed with something. Her glove, then, had been adapted so that no-one could see the real shape of the hand, even though the *ton*'s whispers had already seen and described it multiple times.

The music began and Lady Celia, a happy smile on her face, proved to be an excellent dancer.

"Are you enjoying your first season?" asked Laurence politely.

"I am," she said. "I love to dance, and my Papa has been generous with my clothing allowance, as you can see."

She was indeed dressed in the very latest fashion, with a delicate silk dress made in a deep crimson which suited her black hair and dark eyes.

"And are you enjoying the season, Mr Mowatt?"

He was distracted by the sight of Frances as they passed her, who was fanning herself, even though the room was not very warm. Laurence wondered if the fanning motion was similar to the rocking and swinging that she seemed to enjoy. Perhaps it was a way to release her pent-up feelings at being forced to attend such occasions.

"Mr Mowatt?"

"I do beg your pardon," he replied. "My eye was caught by an acquaintance. The season is always a pleasure to partake in. Is the Earl of Comerford here tonight?"

Lady Celia shook her head, black curls bouncing. "He is not. I have not seen him for some years."

He frowned. "Some *years*? I beg your pardon, Lady Celia, I thought you were betrothed?"

"He was in the navy, being the second son, but his older brother was always sickly and died earlier this year. He returned at once, but has been much occupied. The last time I saw him, I was twelve years old. It has been six years. But yes, we are indeed engaged to be wed."

Laurence wanted to ask questions, but was aware it would sound rude, too blunt to express surprise that she had barely seen her betrothed since she was a child. Instead, he smiled and said only, "I wish you a happy reunion and marriage."

She nodded and that was the end of their conversation. He thought, with a wry smile, that Frances would not have been so polite, so restrained. She would have made her feelings known, would have asked bolder questions, or, if she were Lady Celia, would have said exactly what she thought of being betrothed to a man she did not know. Although perhaps it was simply a matter of convenience for all involved. The Duke and his wife did not have to fret over the prospects of their daughter, the Earl did not have to concern himself with choosing a suitable bride. All had already been taken care of. Was that not, after all, what he wished for? A marriage of convenience, a wife ready-chosen and pre-approved by his family.

Such a wife would be Honora Fortescue, for it would be an eminently suitable marriage and there could be no possible objection. Lord Barrington might believe in true love somehow appearing in the next twelvemonth, but Laurence knew his duty and was a more practical man. Lady Honora, daughter of Lord and Lady Halesworth, heiress to the Fortescue Hall and estate. His future wife. He nodded to her as he passed one more time round the ballroom with Lady Celia and she nodded back. Yes, it was all settled, if not yet formally then certainly there was a kind of understanding between them. Unless Lady Honora bagged herself the Duke of Buckingham, the deal was as good as done. There was a comfort to that, he felt. Duty taken care of. No need to look further. No need to think of wooing any lady here. His life, once married, would continue as before: he would spend time with the married ladies of his acquaintance, would take care of the estate, but his wife would take care of everything else – the household and children. It seemed a lonely future, but that was absurd of course. Half the married men of the *ton* lived as he did, as he planned to do. They sported in brothels, kept a mistress, or, like himself, kept their eye out for bored ladies of the *ton* who would enjoy a little adventure. It had always been this way. There was no need for his life to be any different.

He could see Miss Lilley, who had retreated even further from the occasion behind a vast potted plant, her fan still fluttering in an agitated manner. Perhaps he would go and talk with her again, after all he owed it to Lord Barrington to show consideration towards his goddaughter, and it would be something to report back to him. Besides, she made a change from the simpering girls here.

Frances could not stomach one more dance. The swirling bodies, the different perfumes all jumbled together, the constant music and chatter were making her head ache and her stomach turn over. She moved along the wall until she was in a corner behind a vast plant and settled herself close to two women, one a fair-headed and amply bosomed woman in a dark pink silk, the other a small-built woman in blue taffeta. They were commenting on various dancers. Frances caught Mr Mowatt's name and began paying attention to their conversation.

"Mowatt." The woman in blue sighed as he danced past with Lady Celia Follett. "They say… well, I believe he can be very friendly, if approached by a married lady…? And – and discreet?"

The fair-haired woman smiled dreamily. "He is… quite magnificent," she murmured. "Every *inch* a gentleman."

The woman in blue caught her breath. "Oh. And… and how would one…"

"A card to his rooms. Perhaps an invitation to the theatre or opera or even the Pleasure Gardens, that is where we… well, never mind."

"And you… still?"

"Oh no. Mr Mowatt's acquaintance is of a short-lived nature, he does not wish to draw unwanted attention. Especially from a lady's spouse."

The woman in blue swallowed. "But it would be… worth my while…?"

The fair-haired woman leant closer. "You will remember it for the rest of your days."

Frances listened behind her open fan. This was what Mr Mowatt preferred, then: to amuse himself with married women rather than seek love in his planned marriage, as romantic Lord Barrington would no doubt want for him.

It was no concern of hers, certainly.

She had enjoyed talking with him, had begun to think of him as a friend, but the women's gossip had made her feel uncomfortable. She was unsure why. He had certainly not behaved inappropriately to her. She was tired from the long evening, she would seek out her mother and beg to go home, even if she had to invent a sudden faintness.

On the other side of the ballroom Laurence was intercepted by Lord Radcliffe.

"Mowatt, there you are. I'm trying to convince Lymington here to come down the House of Flowers with me tonight. They say there's fresh stock. How about it?"

The Earl of Radcliffe was a rake of the highest order and Mowatt had little time for him. The House of Flowers was an expensive brothel and the Earl was a regular customer, but Laurence was not particularly fond of his company.

"Another time, Radcliffe."

"Already taken? One of your married ladies, I suppose. Can't be doing with them myself, too prone to falling in love for my liking and then it's the very devil to get them out of your business, sending love notes and whatnot and weeping in public, not the thing at all."

Laurence was in fact intending to go home alone tonight, but was not about to tell Radcliffe that. "Appointment already made, I'm afraid, can't be undone."

"You're a dog, Mowatt," said Radcliffe with a chuckle. "Don't be getting involved with any duelling-minded husbands, will you?"

"I'll try not to."

Radcliffe turned to Lord Lymington, who shook his head.

"Dull man," pronounced the Earl. "I'll leave you to your paperwork, then. Nothing like coming into your inheritance to make a chap boring. You all need to learn to leave matters of business to your stewards, like I do."

They watched him go, Lord Lymington frowning. "Does he run his estate well, though?"

"No," said Laurence. "He lets parts of it go to rack and ruin, that's what I hear. Don't listen to him. Let's go to the club and have a drink instead."

Lymington looked relieved at the change of plan and agreed, leading the way through the busy throng. Laurence saw Miss Lilley watching him as an attendant helped her into her evening cloak ready to depart, her face thoughtful as she met his gaze. He nodded to her, but she did not nod back.

The Little Season was coming to an end as Christmas was now only a few weeks away. Although supposedly less demanding than the season proper, it was not proving a success for Frances and Lady Lilley was already losing patience after a particularly dismal social call.

"I did *try*."

"You did not try at all!" cried Lady Lilley, her temper beginning to rise at Frances' stubborn insistence. "You were all but mute, Frances, indeed I could see Lady Carlisle beginning to wonder if there was something wrong with you."

"Her perfume was overwhelming, and she would not stop talking."

"Her perfume is from Paris, and she was paying a social

call, of course she would talk! Did you expect us all to sit in silence together?"

"That would have been more agreeable," muttered Frances, not daring to speak out loud for fear of increasing her mother's wrath.

"What did you say?"

"Nothing," mumbled Frances.

"Of course. You never do say anything. One might think you a dumb animal in a frock brought into the drawing room. Dash has more to say for himself than you do in company."

Dash the spaniel, hearing his name, came forward wagging his tail and whimpered with affection when Lady Lilley caressed his ears.

"You see? He speaks more than you do."

Frances held her tongue with some effort. Antagonising her mother too far was not wise when she had a favour to ask. "Might I go and visit Lord Barrington until the season begins in earnest?" she asked.

"How are you supposed to make the most of there being fewer ladies in town during the Little Season if you run away to Margate again? You are not likely to meet anyone worth knowing there… unless you have?" asked Lady Lilley, suddenly hopeful. "*Have* you met someone, Frances? Is there a young man in Margate to whom you have formed an attachment?"

"No, of course not."

"But you said Mr Mowatt was there on your last visit, was he not a suitable person?"

"I'm sure he is suitable," said Frances. "He has no interest in me, however."

Lady Lilley sighed.

"Can I go?"

"I suppose if you were not much seen until the season proper, it might be for the best." said Lady Lilley. "It might make you look… well, anyway, yes, you may go and visit Lord Barrington. Let us hope he remembers you when he dies. You have spent more time with him than any of his other young relations."

To Frances this sounded positively grasping, but she knew better than to say so, instead hurriedly leaving the room and instructing Deborah to pack before her mother could change her mind.

CHAPTER 6
Caught by the Tides

MARGATE IN EARLY DECEMBER WAS COLD, THE SEA breeze no longer gentle but sharp, throwing sand into eyes and chilling the skin. The invalids had all gone home, now there were only the locals, so that the need for bathing houses and bathing carriages was greatly diminished, the beach almost empty aside from a few children or dogs running in the wind, unconcerned by the chill. But Northdown House was still a haven of cosy comfort and Laurence was glad he had chosen to visit before he returned to the family home for Christmas.

"You will not need to attend the Assembly Rooms this time, Laurence," promised Lord Barrington on Laurence's first evening there. "The season here is quite over until the warmer months see fit to bless us once again."

Laurence did not say "thank goodness" out loud, but he thought it. "I had the pleasure of seeing Miss Lilley in London," he said instead. "We danced together at the Halesworth ball."

"Indeed? I am glad to hear it. She will be joining me here in a few days, I hope your paths will cross."

"Yes, Sir, I intend to stay a week, if you'll have me." Having

Miss Lilley join them was unexpected, but he was glad for her sake that she had avoided any more of the Little Season.

"Capital, capital. Then we shall be a merry band."

Frances arrived two days later as dusk came on, the worthy Deborah in tow. Lord Barrington welcomed her in the hallway with a cup of mulled wine.

"Frances my dear, it is wonderful to see you again so soon, I had thought not to enjoy the pleasure of your company this side of Christmas."

"I begged Mama and since the season proper will not start until March she has let me off the Little Season, once I did not take the eye of the Duke of Buckingham."

"Ah, yes, I heard of that. It was a bad business, losing the Duke and then his heir so suddenly, thank goodness he had a younger son. Now, allow your maid to do her duty by you so that you are ready for dinner with Mr Mowatt. I myself cannot dine with you, for my physician will be visiting me this evening and will expect to find me tucked up in bed with a hot mutton broth and nothing in the way of a sweet course. The man has no proper feeling for the joys of this earthly life. But Mrs Norris will not stint you and Mr Mowatt, you will always find a generous table when she is in charge."

"I did not know Mr Mowatt was visiting just now," said Frances, "though he did mention he would try to."

"He is a devoted young man," said Lord Barrington with a smile, turning to Deborah, still waiting with Frances' trunk. "Deborah, I leave your mistress in your capable hands. You have all of twenty minutes to make her ready for dinner."

"Yes, Sir." Deborah bobbed, pointing the footmen towards Frances' trunk and hurrying upstairs to be ready for her.

"Frances, I will bid you goodnight and see you tomorrow. Enjoy your dinner and be sure to eat some of the apple puffs on my behalf, for I shall be missing them dearly."

Upstairs, Frances submitted to Deborah's ministrations, washing and changing her dress and shoes.

"Not the blue silk, it is too elegant, there are only the two of us at dinner. Did you not bring something plainer?"

Deborah shook her head. "Lady Lilley has disposed of most of your plain clothes," she said. "She complained you looked more like a maid than a lady. And besides the blue is not as fancy as the green," she added, pointing to a frothy green confection spilling out of the trunk.

"Oh, do as you please," said Frances, annoyed. "But no ringlets. Or jewellery," she added, seeing Deborah lift out her jewellery case.

She descended the staircase to find Mr Mowatt waiting for her at the bottom.

"There is no need to take me in to dinner," she objected. "I am well aware of the location of the dining room."

"Good evening, Miss Lilley," he said. "It is a pleasure to see you again."

"Is it?"

He offered her his arm and she took it after hesitating.

"Yes. I would have been forced to dine alone and one mouth could never do justice to Mrs Norris' cooking."

The table was laid out with beautiful floral decorations of white camellias and red holly berries, lit up by dozens of candles which made the silverware and glasses shine. Formal seating rules had been applied, so that their places were laid at either end of the long table, but Frances shook her head.

"That is an absurd seating. Benjamin, change the places. I am not about to shout down the table to Mr Mowatt all evening. We can sit closer together."

Laurence watched, amused, as Miss Lilley stood waiting to be reseated. The blue dress she wore was plain, but the colour of it lifted the shade of her eyes, making them more blue than grey, which suited her, he thought. She should always wear brighter hues.

The seating rectified, they were now closer together, on opposite sides of one end, the dishes hastily rearranged to their new positions.

Mrs Norris, as expected, had produced a feast, starting with crawfish soup, which was followed by a roast turkey, the rest of the table laden with woodcocks, ragooed lobsters, fried oysters, mushrooms and beef collops as well as fillets of whiting. Lemon jelly, apple puffs, stewed pears and ginger biscuits would complete the meal.

"I wonder how the people of Margate get on when we visitors are gone for the winter," Frances remarked, as she finished her crawfish soup.

Laurence frowned. "Get on?"

She gestured at the table and its bountiful platters of seafood. "Margate has gone from being a tiny fishing village of no import to a fashionable seaside resort in less than thirty years. Given its proximity to London, it would be even more so were it not that Brighton has the Regent's favour. The population here has nigh on doubled in the last ten years, all to look after the gentry that come here to be taken care of."

Laurence shrugged. "I do not see what is wrong with that.

They have a fine Assembly Rooms, new shops and houses, all manner of activities in which to delight. They must be much better off."

She tilted her head. "They?"

"The locals as well as the visitors."

Frances frowned. "You think a fisherman goes to the Assembly Rooms, that they shop for feathered hats and silk stockings in the milliners, that they can afford a fine town-house? All of the things you mention are for the visitors alone, or for the few merchants of Margate who have done very well from their patronage, but they had money to invest already, so they were not exactly poor before. The fishermen, the dippers at the bathing machines, the maids who clean the lodging houses and do the laundry, anyone of that sort must watch their little houses pulled down to make way for fine new lodging houses, they must pander to the visitors to earn their wage, and come winter – why, we are all gone, we return to our estates and lock up our holiday homes and they must make do without our money during the hardest part of the year, counting their pennies until we return again."

Laurence was surprised to hear a woman speak of matters relating to political economy, it was something men might speak of after the ladies had retired to the drawing room and they were left alone with their cigars and port. But she was right, he had not thought of the ebb and flow of a town like Margate. London might ebb and flow but it was always full enough. "What would you have us do, then? Not come here at all? Surely then they would be worse off."

"I do not think we should stay away. But perhaps spare some thought for whether, when fine new townhouses are built along the promenade, there should also be cottages built for the workers somewhere nearby? Is there a harbour and a beach where the fishermen can safely bring in their catch, or have they been pushed aside for the passenger boats arriving from London and told not to spoil the main beach which is full of fine families strolling and bathing? When Lord Barrington locks up Northdown House for the winter, he takes the staff with him to his main estate, or ensures they are all paid to work throughout the winter, none of them are dismissed till they are wanted again as many other fine houses do – not the footmen and cook, who are harder to come by, but the laundry maids, the kitchen boys and suchlike, who make little enough as it is. He is a thoughtful master to them but it behoves us all to think of these things, and to take action where we may, rather than to think the world was made for us alone to enjoy."

Her eyes were bright as she spoke and Laurence found himself wanting to continue the conversation, even though dinner was drawing to a close. "Does Lord Barrington have maps of the local area?" he asked.

"He does. He is very fond of collecting maps and drawings of how Margate has changed in the time he has been here."

"Perhaps…" He was about to say that he could look through them together after dinner, but he changed his words. "Perhaps you would show them to me?"

She looked at him as though she doubted his sincerity, but then nodded. She took an apple puff, shook her head at the offer of the lemon jelly and, having finished, looked at him expectantly. "Shall we go to the library, then?"

The library at Northdown was better endowed than many great homes, for Lord Barrington was an avid reader and had a fine collection. There was a shelf with a desk nearby set aside especially for the study of how Margate had changed, and here

Frances led Laurence, pulling down a few books and then using little weights to spread out several maps.

"This, you see, is Margate when Lord Barrington first came here," she said.

Laurence leant over the paper. The shape of Margate, with its natural curved bay, was at once recognisable, but as for Margate itself, it was barely there at all.

"Look," said Frances. She pulled out a drawing, a sketch titled Marcoaet, which must have been made from a boat, for it looked across the harbour and towards the town. But again, there were fewer than thirty houses or buildings, including an old windmill up on the hill and the spire of a church. "By a Dutch artist, van Overbeck. It was drawn sometime between 1663 and 1666. As you can see for yourself, Margate barely existed except as a little fishing village. It was probably only the safe natural harbour that drew anyone to live here at all." She picked up a quill and dipped it in ink. "Since I was a child, this is a list of all the new buildings in Margate and the ones I can recall that are no longer standing." She wrote quickly, with an odd letter y to which she gave a curly loop as though it were a whorl on a shell, the list growing longer down the page, an impressive feat of memory.

Laurence was standing very close to Frances and while she spoke had become aware of her scent. Not a perfume, for as far as he could tell she did not wear any, but her personal scent, a waft of salt air and lavender soap, the apples she had eaten and something else that he could not put into words, something fresh and cool. But she was looking at him, waiting for a response.

"Remarkable," he managed. "How did he obtain it?"

She shrugged. "I do not know. He collects such things. As

you can see, there were a few fisherman's cottages, and then further back some farmhouses. Nothing much more. Before that time it was called Mergate or Meregate. Marsh-Gate because it lay between two tidal streams, or perhaps Sea-Gate. Later as it grew it all merged together and became Margate."

Laurence re-appraised her as she spoke. He had thought her plain when he had first met her, but she was not, only not given to all the fripperies and furbelows of her peers. He had thought her topics of conversation odd, and they were, but only for a woman, a man speaking as she did would be known for his scholarly interests. There was something appealing about time spent with her, she was certainly different from any of the women, married or not, that he knew. He had grown to enjoy her company, he realised.

"Show me the later maps," he said, taking a seat at the desk beside her. "Do you have the drawings of Northdown House when it was being planned?"

The three of them spent a few days happily resuming their daily walks by the sea, though for shorter periods, since it was cold, with the rest of their days in the library, gallery or drawing room. Along the seashore Laurence spent part of the time talking with Lord Barrington and part of the time walking alongside Frances, offering her shells that he spotted and listening to her descriptions of them. By the third day he had proudly learnt the Latin names of at least five kinds of shell and felt himself quite the collector.

On the fourth morning Lord Barrington was absent at breakfast, and Laurence was summoned to his bedchamber by a footman. His uncle lay propped up on cushions in his bed, looking pale, though he smiled readily enough at the sight of Laurence and his voice still seemed strong.

"Laurence, my boy, I am weary today, I shall not be fit for much. Be so kind as to drive out with Frances to some beauty spot or other where she can collect shells. You can take the carriage of course, and one or two of the footmen to look after you. Her maid can go with you if she desires a chaperone, though I am sure I can leave her in your care. A morning outdoors will brush away the cobwebs."

Laurence bowed and gave orders that the carriage be brought round but Frances, oddly, hesitated at the idea. They had passed an enjoyable evening together, so he was uncertain of the reason for her reluctance.

"Are you concerned that we might be alone, that it might be remarked upon? Your maid can come with us and I can assure you that –"

She shook her head, impatient. "There is hardly anyone about at this time of year and anyway, who cares what gossips think? Besides, Deborah will only complain about the cold."

"Then you do not wish to go out because…"

"The tide."

"The tide?"

"It is rising," she pointed out as though to a simpleton.

"There is plenty of time," he said, piqued that she should think him ill informed, though truth be told he had forgotten about the tide. "It will be at its highest point by…"

"Half past twelve," she said.

"Well, we will be long returned, wanting sustenance since it is hardly the right weather for a picnic. Fetch your collecting basket, we will have a brisk ride there and an hour or so for your shells."

"I do not wish to bore you."

"I could do with the walk."

She hesitated but then gave a brusque nod and went to dress, returning in a grey dress topped with a pelisse in soft brown velvet trimmed with brown fur, a nod to Deborah's concern that she would catch a chill, for the sun, while bright, was not warm.

Laurence gave orders to the driver that they were to go to Broadstairs, a town close by to the east, from where, at the current low tide, they could walk round to Margate in a couple of hours, which he felt would give them ample time for Miss Lilley to collect shells and for him to avoid any visits from the eager young woman of Margate and their mamas who might have heard he was in town. The carriage could go ahead and meet them in Margate, rather than following them along the coastal pathways above the cliffs.

True to her word, Frances did not bring Deborah, and so once the carriage had been dismissed, they were alone on a windswept beach, walking along at her usual slow pace, eyes always searching.

"I am sure we will be comfortably in time to round Botany Bay before the tide is too high," he said after a while.

It was odd to be alone in the company of a young woman. Laurence was all too aware that it would be frowned on by anyone of good standing and, should they meet anyone along the way, they would be sure to assume the two of them were at the very least engaged. Perhaps he should have insisted on the maid following them, for the sake of appearances at least.

She did not answer, only stooped to pick up a large mussel shell which was lined with shimmering mother of pearl, brushing the sand away from it and tilting it in the light before dropping into her basket.

"It is curious, is it not," he tried again, for there ought to be some conversation, "that the moon should govern the tides?"

"The Greeks believed that the goddess of the moon was Selene," she said, still scanning the sand, "and that her chariot of white horses pulled the tides to and fro. Even without the scientific knowledge we have today, they understood that the moon was linked to the tides. There are many such instances of stories hiding scientific knowledge within them. I believe that is why Lord Barrington likes reading myths and legends from around the world. He appreciates the truths hidden within fiction."

"Are there myths and legends regarding shells?"

She paused from her searching and met his gaze, as though he had finally said something of importance. "Shells have been used as objects of great import all over the world," she said. "Cowrie shells were used as currency in Africa, conch shells are blown for ritual sounds, shells were divine offerings to Aphrodite since she was supposed to have come ashore in one, as well as honouring her as the goddess of the sea. And of course, the scallop shell has been used for hundreds of years by pilgrims travelling to Santiago de Compostela in Spain. They wear one on their person and the way is marked with scallop shells. The scallop is seen as a symbol of renewal and rebirth, of becoming your true self." She gave a shrug. "And of course they are used for decorative purposes, for jewellery and suchlike."

He looked her over. She wore no jewellery at all, not even earrings, unlike most women of his acquaintance, who considered themselves only half dressed without their necklaces and earrings, their bracelets and brooches. "I would have thought you might like pearls," he said. "Since they are found within shells."

She nodded. "They are beautiful," she said. "They remind me of shells when I see them."

"Have you ever found one yourself?"

"Only tiny seed pearls, once or twice. Not yet grown to full size. They take years to grow. Once a bit of grit gets inside a shell, it must be covered in layers of nacre."

"Nacre?"

"The pearlescent coating on the insides of shells. They build up over the piece of grit to make the pearl."

"I believe pearls are a symbol of beauty and love," he said, the gallant words coming automatically, though he immediately wondered if such words were too flirtatious. He was accustomed to speaking in such ways to the married women with whom he spent most of his time, but perhaps he should not have spoken in such a way when alone with a young woman. Pearls, after all, were frequently given to brides to be worn on their wedding day.

She grimaced. "I would prefer to think of them as symbols of wisdom and experience," she said. "A pearl is created over many years, an oyster turning something painful to itself into something bearable. The beauty we enjoy is a by-product of its efforts." She stooped again, selecting a stone which had a hole through it, bored by the sea over many years, and held it out to him. "This is called a hag stone. You are supposed to be able to look through it at a witch and see through her disguise."

He took the stone and looked down at it in his hand. It was tempting to look at her through it, to make a joke about seeing her true self, as he would have done with his sisters. If he had been wooing her, he would have made a seductive comment about seeing her stripped of her disguise, and enjoyed a little banter between them as to what she might therefore be wearing… or not. Neither seemed right. Instead he held it up and looked through it to the sea, then stiffened.

"Is it a seal?" He pointed out to sea.

She turned at once and they watched the spot he had pointed to, where the waves broke offshore and there was foam. And yes, there was a dark brown head, bobbing up and down, steadily regarding them.

"Do you often see them?" Laurence asked, enchanted. He had never seen a seal before and there was something about its curiosity that was endearing, how it stared at them even as they stared at it.

"Sometimes, when there are not too many people. Not on the main beach at Margate, but here, on the quieter shores."

"Perhaps she is a selkie," he said, smiling. "Should I ask her to marry me, do you think?"

She turned away from the seal, regarding him with her head tilted to one side. "Marry you?"

"A selkie is a seal-bride," he said. "There is a story of a man who saw a beautiful woman emerge from a sealskin. When he hid her sealskin, she agreed to marry him and was a loving wife, even bearing his children. But one day she found the sealskin where he had hidden it and she returned to the sea, never to be seen again." He thought. "I never understood why she would be a loving wife but then return to the sea just because she found the sealskin again. Surely, if she loved him, she would have stayed regardless?"

She said nothing for a few moments, and he thought perhaps she disagreed with him or was uninterested in the story, but after a few more paces she stopped and turned to face him, her bonnet ribbons fluttering in the wind.

"I understand why she would go."

"Who?"

"The selkie."

"Do you? Why?"

"It is exhausting not to be your true self, to have to wear a mask to be considered acceptable. It is why I do not much like to be in society. I can wear the clothes my modiste and mother have insisted on, I can make polite conversation, I can sit and sip tea at one house after another until I could scream, but when I get home I will sit alone and in silence for the rest of the day, just to recover." She looked at him, as though judging his expression, then continued. "I know I am not like other people, that you and everyone else finds me odd, but that is the truth of it. I do not know how other women bear the season, though I can see for myself that they can and do, indeed they seem to find pleasure in it." She looked back at the sea, now empty, the seal having disappeared. "Perhaps the man should have allowed the selkie to come and go from the sea, that she might not grow exhausted by the ways of humans. Perhaps then she would have stayed with him forever." She turned away from the sea, began walking onwards. "The tide is rising," she called over her shoulder. "We must make haste."

Laurence stood, watching her walk away. She had shown him a part of herself he had not been expecting, had countered his light-hearted story of a selkie with a truth buried in the story that had never occurred to him, that tinged the tale with sadness rather than mystery, that the man had not been able to see that his bride was unhappy, had not allowed her true self to be known, had made her hide it away until she could bear it no longer and had abandoned what love had been between them, unable to sustain her human form without respite. He looked back out to sea, but the seal was gone, had dived below or returned to its own kind somewhere else. Ahead, Miss Lilley's brown velvet and fur pelisse was the only seal-like form on the beach, and he hurried after her.

Within an hour they had reached Botany Bay, where giant chalk stacks rose up out of the water, but Laurence had forgotten how slow their pace was when gathering shells. The sea was already lapping at the stacks. They would not reach Margate, it would take another half an hour to reach that shore. The quickest way off the beach was just beyond the chalk stacks, but the water was already knee deep and rising. They could not retreat, for the shoreline was rapidly receding behind them. Above them were steep cliffs which were unsafe to climb.

"We may have to wait at the top of the beach there, against the cliff, until the tide begins to fall again," he said. "But it will be a few hours."

"No need," she said. "We will walk through the gap in the stacks to the other side, where we can reach the higher beach. There is a little path cut into the cliffs where we will be able to leave the sands and reach the clifftops. From there we can walk to Margate in safety."

It was an unexpected decision, but he nodded. The water was still only knee high, so he could carry her in his arms. He would be soaked, of course, but it would be safe enough. "I will remove my boots. If you would not mind holding them while I carry you, I think it will be safer than allowing water to get inside, which might weigh them down."

She frowned at him. "*Carry* me?"

He stared back at her, confused. "Well, of course, Miss Lilley, I hardly think you can walk through the sea, it is far too deep. It would be dangerous."

"Nonsense," she said briskly. "I will be entirely unharmed if we are quick about it." "Though," she amended, "my boots will likely be ruined, and Deborah will have plenty to say about seawater on the hem of my pelisse and gown, but she will get over it and my modiste and shoemaker will be delighted to make new ones. Now then."

To his horror, she strode forwards. The sea was already lapping at her boots, but as she reached the curved archway between two chalk stacks, wider than a large door, the top of the arch towering high above her, she scooped up her pelisse as well as her skirts and pulled them upwards. Laurence saw her cream stockings, the pink silk ribbon bows holding them up at the knee, then one shocking glimpse of the bare white skin above, before the water was already swirling between her knees, threatening to wet her thighs. He stood, staring as she walked through the archway and then disappeared to the other side, before hastily pulling off his boots and following her. The cold seawater drenched his legs and lower breeches at once, but he made his way through the arch and through the shallower water up to the beach, where he found her, skirts and pelisse back in place, her little boots sodden, the pale brown leather turned dark. She watched him as he replaced his boots, unable to avoid sand getting inside them.

"I expect your man will be able to remove the sand and dry them out. Now, we had better use the cliff top walk, for we cannot make Margate, the water is already too high. The path to it is up here."

She made her way up the beach, soft sand sucking at her feet, making her walk slowly towards the tiny path at the top, cut through the chalk cliffs, allowing them to reach the upper ground away from the beach. Laurence followed behind in silence. He had expected to carry her, would have seen it as the gentlemanly thing to do, had offered it without any intentions of intimacy, of the opportunity to touch her. But her actions had stunned him, both her bravery in risking the deep wading alone, but also her lifting her skirts so high, affording him that momentary image which would not now leave him, the delicate pink bows and above them that flash of skin, the whiteness of her thighs, how the foam had swirled between her legs. He was breathless with desire both at what he had seen and her lack of coyness. And yet she had not been brazen, there had been no intention to arouse in her actions, only her matter-of-fact solution to the situation in which they had found themselves. If he had been the man in the story who had seen, for one second, the stirring sight of the woman beneath the sealskin, he too would have grabbed at the fur and hidden it away to keep her by his side. As he reached her at the top of the cliff, the sea below them, he thought for a moment of pulling her towards him, of slipping his hands beneath the brown velvet pelisse to find her warm body, looking into her wide grey eyes before kissing her upturned lips.

"The carriage will be a welcome sight when we reach it," she said, looking him up and down. "We are both in need of a warm bath, are we not?"

Her words only brought more images to his mind, the steam rising, the heat and wetness of her skin against his if they were to share a bath together, the pink bows of her stockings lying discarded on the floor… He shook his head, trying to rid himself of the fantasy before it subsumed him.

"You do not think you need to be warmed after that experience?"

"It was nothing," he managed. "But I admire your bravery," he added.

"I am not a damsel in distress in need of rescuing," she retorted. "I have been caught by the tides more than once over the years, which is why I warned you of them. But no matter, there is little harm done. Now, we had better make our way to Margate or the footmen will think us lost."

They walked in silence back to Margate, where the carriage, as agreed, was waiting and returned them at a brisk pace to Northdown House, where Deborah exclaimed over Miss Lilley's wet boots and hurried her away for a bath. Laurence refused one, uncertain that he wished to continue his thoughts about Miss Lilley. He changed into clean clothes and left Roberts to deal with the boots, returning to the drawing room, where he poured himself a drink and tried to clear his head. His thoughts about Miss Lilley were inappropriate, and besides, he had no interest in such an odd woman. No doubt he was missing the charms of his usual bedfellows, that was all.

The evening passed with the usual delicious food, some conversation and an early night for all, but Laurence spent a restless night, thanks to dreams of wide-eyed seals diving through waves which rose ever higher while he searched in vain for someone – he could not see whom – lost in the darkening waters, waking more than once with sweat on his brow.

CHAPTER 7
Christmas

L AURENCE CAME DOWN TO BREAKFAST THE NEXT DAY feeling awkward, but Miss Lilley greeted him at the breakfast table as though nothing had occurred and so he determined to put the event behind him. He had no real interest in Miss Lilley, after all, and that one unexpected glimpse of her legs was not enough to ruin a perfectly amicable acquaintance. He helped himself to coffee and sat near his uncle as the three of them discussed their Christmas plans.

"I will close up Northdown for the winter months, as usual," said Lord Barrington. "I miss it when I am away, but it does not do to leave Ashland Manor with no master for too long, they see little enough of me as it is. And Northdown is always at its best in the summer months. Indeed this year I have tarried longer than usual, generally I am gone by November, the cold makes my bones ache. Frances will be headed to her family. And you, Laurence? Frolicking in London as usual?"

"No, Sir, I am to return home to my father this year."

"Ah. It will be the first year since your dear mother's loss?"

"Yes, Sir."

"It will feel different, of course, your mother was always the heart and soul of Christmas, but your father and sisters will make it merry and they will be exceedingly glad to have you there. They have missed you these past few years. It will do you good to spend time with them. To forget one's ancestors is to be a brook without a source, a tree without a root, according to the old Chinese proverb."

Laurence nodded. "I have enjoyed my visit with you, Uncle, I shall do my best to return in the spring." He turned politely to Miss Lilley. "It has been a pleasure to enjoy your company, Miss Lilley. Will you be in London or at Woodside Abbey for Christmas?"

"Woodside Abbey. My sisters will bring their families and my brother will be there also, so we will be a houseful."

"Ah, the children will enjoy having their favourite aunt to play with," said Lord Barrington. He turned to Laurence. "Frances is wonderful with children, though she does not much care for the grown men and women of society."

"Children are easier," retorted Frances. "And I can always escape to my bedroom to hide from them. One cannot hide from society."

"I am not surprised you like children," said Lord Barrington. "'An honest man is always a child,' as Socrates taught us, and I know of no-one more honest than you, Frances. Indeed, I hope you will both know the joy of children one day." A shadow crossed his countenance. "It is a great sorrow of mine that I never had a family."

"You have us, Sir," said Laurence. "Your nieces, nephew and goddaughter."

"Indeed I do," said Lord Barrington, smiling fondly at the two of them. "And you are all a great joy to me. I am grateful for your time spent with this old man. Now, I shall not keep you longer, you both have long journeys to make and I shall have to travel myself the day after tomorrow."

The carriage was brought round soon after breakfast. It would take them to the nearest staging inn, where they would join separate post-chaises to their respective parts of the country. Frances bestowed a kiss on Lord Barrington's cheek, then he and Laurence shook hands, before the two young people climbed into the carriage while their luggage was securely strapped to the back and roof. They drove away, both waving to Lord Barrington, who sat in his chair outside Northdown House, watching them leave.

Once on the road proper, they settled back.

"I wish you all the compliments of the season," Laurence said as they drove. "Will your family all have gathered already?"

"Yes, it will be very noisy, for my two sisters and their five children will be staying with us. And you?"

"Yes, although we will be quieter. I do not yet have nieces and nephews."

"Lord Barrington was right," she said. "I mostly prefer children to grown men and women. They speak their minds, and do not make polite conversation just for the sake of it. And they love my shells. We play together for hours with them."

"I am surprised they are quiet enough for you," he said.

"Oh, I have to hide away sometimes to rest my ears from their racket," she agreed. "But on the whole, I enjoy their company."

At the inn, Laurence saw her conveyed to her post-chaise with Deborah and her luggage, then stood by the window as they waited for it to depart.

"I will see you when the season begins in the spring," he said.

"Perhaps," she agreed. "Though if you choose your bride swiftly enough you may well be married by the next time I see you."

He could not imagine it. "Perhaps," he managed. "And perhaps you will be engaged also?"

She shook her head firmly. "Not if I can avoid it," she said. "If I can get to the end of the season unmarried it is possible my father will allow me to set up a home of my own at last."

He smiled at her stubborn insistence and bowed. "Then I hope I will be permitted to call upon you one day, wherever your little home may be."

She nodded, then waved her hand as the carriage moved off.

Frances only just made it back to Woodside Abbey before an icy wind delivered drifts of snow and daily fog, but the Abbey was snug enough and the snow a great delight to her nephews and nieces. While her sisters Rebecca and Susan huddled indoors with Lady Lilley, discussing clothes and gossiping about their neighbours, and her older brother Charles spent most of his time discussing hunting with his father, Frances threw herself into the festivities with the children.

They coerced a gardener to come out with them to the woods and dragged back a giant Yule log for the fire as well as so much greenery to decorate the house that they had to make use of a sled to carry it. The greenery, along with bright red ribbons and mistletoe, were hung about the rooms and hallway, making the Abbey festive, and the rest of their days were spent alternately playing outside until their clothes were soaked through by the snow or pulling on the bell to demand more hot chocolate, biscuits and cakes from the kitchen.

In the evenings, Frances brought out boxes of shells and lay on the drawing room floor with the children, turning them over, explaining their origins and making patterns with them, before the smallest ones would inevitably fall asleep in her lap. She liked to stroke their soft hair and watch them sleep, and spending time with them largely removed her from the necessity of partaking in the tedious conversations after dinner, as well as avoiding too many pointed references to her unmarried state and questions regarding the upcoming season.

Sometimes, when she tired of the noise of the children, she retired to her bedroom or the library and read her books on shells or watched the snow tumbling endlessly out of the sky, a sight she found restful, akin to watching flames flicker in the fireplace. She relished this chance to be away from the endless social whirl, which would intensify when they returned to London in the spring, but there were days when she wondered if her plans to remain a spinster would take from her the pleasure she found in the children's company. Would she one day regret the choice she had made to live alone? She was unsure, but the thought of the marriage mart only wearied her, and she could not see her way to one without the other. Being an aunt would have to suffice.

Lord Sabin, a widowed cousin of Lady Lilley's known to them as Uncle Richard, and his daughter, Lady Andrea, joined them for Christmas and Frances found herself wishing that her parents might follow Lord Sabin's approach regarding his daughter's marriage. Lady Andrea had come out the previous year, but her father seemed to show no hurry to have her wed and off his hands.

"Ah, there is plenty of time," he said indulgently, when Lady Lilley asked about Lady Andrea's marriage prospects. "I will keep her close to me while I can, for she will leave me soon enough and I shall miss her when she does, my last to fly the nest. The house will be quiet without her. I have no desire to pack her off to fortune-hunters or young men barely out of their nurseries, so there is no hurry to make a match."

"Do you have someone you wish to marry?" Frances asked Lady Andrea when they were alone.

Lady Andrea shook her head. "There are a few whom I find pleasing," she said. "But as Papa says, why hurry? He took his time choosing dear Mama and they were very happy together for many years. Why does your mother want you to marry in haste?"

Frances shrugged. "I have been out for four years, while she was married to Papa by the end of her first season. And they are happy enough together." This was true up to a point, but even Frances would have had to acknowledge that Uncle Richard's marriage had been a love match, while the Lilleys were no such thing – they were, as Mr Mowatt had put it, respectful to one another and there was some affection or at least contentment between them. By the dictates of the *ton*, theirs was a successful marriage, but she wondered whether Mr Mowatt knew of what he spoke when he said he wanted only a marriage of convenience. Would it make him happy? Still, that was his concern, not hers. He was a pleasant young man, no doubt he would arrange a satisfactory marriage. He seemed clear on what he needed in a wife, which must surely help matters along. Frances had never been sure of what she wanted in a man, she had only identified what she found annoying. Which was most men, their disinterest in her shells, their incessant need to talk, their evident distaste for her blunt way of speaking or topics of conversation.

She smiled as she thought of Mr Mowatt and how shocked by her conversation or behaviour he had been on various occasions, but at least, unlike other men of her acquaintance, he had persevered in talking with her, which was unusual. She had grown to like their conversations, for he did not persist with false flattery as many young men she had met tended to do, instead he seemed to find her half odd, half amusing, yet worthy of his time. He had proven a quick learner regarding her shells, trying to recollect the Latin names of her finds and looking about him to find suitable items to add to her collection. It was pleasant, she admitted to herself, to have someone her age to talk with from time to time who did not always insist on boring small talk and the niceties of polite conversation. In some ways he reminded her of her friend Elizabeth Belmont, who was quietly willing to allow each person to be their true selves, to accept them as they were, a rare skill in a society that demanded all must follow the same rules and be nought but paper doll copies of one another.

She hoped perhaps to see Mr Mowatt again when they returned to London, for there would certainly be little chance of escaping to Margate once the season proper had started. This festive season would be her last respite before plunging back into the marriage mart and she was determined to make the most of it.

Laurence was welcomed home with open arms by his father and his Aunt Constance.

"Laurence! You have beaten both your sisters here, though they will be hot on your heels, I hope. It looks like snow."

Sure enough, only a few hours passed before his two sisters Arabella and Edith arrived in their carriages, husbands in tow. They had married within a few months of one another and now were both expecting, so that all of the household fussed about them, ensuring their every comfort.

"Are we not to enjoy snowball fights, then?" asked Laurence. "It is how we used to pass our winters."

"We shall nominate our husbands to act in our stead," said Arabella cheerfully. "You will get thrashed, Laurence."

"And you will stay cosy and warm and watch from the windows, I suppose?"

"Indeed. Tell your man to be ready to dress you all over again, for you will be quite soaked through by the time they are done with you."

So it proved when Laurence and his two brothers-in-law, as well as his father, braved the snowy-swept gardens to have a vigorous snowball fight, though he put up a fine defence. Roberts only shook his head with a smile, having already prepared a hot bath and warmed clothes for Laurence to change into.

Laurence had dreaded the visit, for it was the first time he had spent Christmas with his family since his mother's death four years previously. That following year, unable to bear the thought of celebrations without her, he had gladly taken up an invitation from a friend to spend Christmas in Scotland and each year afterwards he had found a way to celebrate the season elsewhere. But this year he had run out of excuses and had steeled himself for a Christmas lacking her warmth and sense of fun.

To his surprise, there was still her touch on the days that followed. Her portrait hung in the drawing room where they gathered each day about the fire to breakfast, to play silly games, to read alone or to each other, or to play cards. His sisters' voices echoed her tones and the cook, Mrs Williams, took care to serve dishes he remembered from his youth, including the Maids of Honour and preserved cherries that had been his mother's favourites. He had forgotten, in the unending whirl of social parties of one kind and another that he spent his time attending, that his family were not much given to grand balls and formal dinners, preferring to spend time alone or with close neighbours, some of whom made their way through the snowy lanes to join in the festive cheer, sharing hearty meals and foolish games of charades or Blind Man's Buff, causing much merriment. In the mornings and early afternoons, when the weak sun showed its face, he and his father wrapped up warm and walked about the estate with the dogs in tow, talking of everything and nothing at all.

"It is good to have you with us this year, Laurence, we have missed you."

"I should have joined you sooner, I –"

His father patted his shoulder. "There is no need to explain, Laurence, it is a hard thing to lose a mother. We all of us miss her, but I like to think I see her in the three of you when you are together, a little bit in each of you. It comforts my heart."

"I will join you again next year," said Laurence. "I was afraid it would not feel like old times, but it does, even with Mother missing."

"It is our memories of her that bring her back to us," said his father, his voice wavering. "She loved Christmas. She was not one for travelling here there and everywhere to attend the best parties when she could stay at home and enjoy the family."

That evening, Aunt Constance took Laurence aside. "I hope you will choose a bride soon," she said. "Your sisters are beginning their own families. It would be a happy thing if all your children might be of an age to play together. Do you have a woman in mind?"

"Possibly, Aunt," said Laurence. He meant Honora, of course, but for one moment he thought of Frances, how she had spoken with fondness of her nephews and nieces, had said she enjoyed time with them. Which was absurd of course, since she did not intend to marry.

"Will you tell me more about her?" she asked, smiling.

"Not just yet, Aunt," he managed, confused by the thought of Frances appearing to him in the place of Honora.

She patted his hand. "All in God's time, then, but I look forward to welcoming her into our family," she said kindly. "The right woman by your side will be the making of you, Laurence."

It was almost February by the time the roads were clear and safe enough to return to London and Laurence bid a fond farewell to his sisters, wishing them well in their confinements. He promised to return for a spring visit to his father and aunt, then travelled back to London, glad of the thick coat and furs his aunt had piled onto him, since the weather was still bitterly cold.

For the first time since he had set up in London, Laurence found that his rooms at Albany felt empty. The thought that he might continue on as he had done for the past few years for many more years to come, only with a larger finer house to be his one day, was dismal rather than exciting. He had forgotten the warmth that family brought and now that he was alone again, he felt its absence. Still, he had invitations to spare piling up on the tray in his drawing room, and elite amongst them all was the prized voucher that would gain him admittance to Almack's, indicating him as an eligible young man in this season's marriage mart. There would be some fun to have. But he decided he would visit home more often and keep his father company, for he had enjoyed their time together and besides, he could learn about how to manage the estate that would one day be his. His sisters, too, had been of good cheer and soon they would be delivered of their babies, making him an uncle. Perhaps he might spend time with the youngsters as they grew up. He liked the idea of being a kindly uncle to them, as Lord Barrington had so generously been to him. For now, he must shrug off his feelings of solitude and enjoy his carefree bachelor days.

After a bumpy and chilly journey from Woodside Abbey, Frances awoke to the dripping sound of icicles melting outside her window and a rising dread inside. London's frozen winter was slowly giving way to the first days of March, heralding the return of the *ton*. The men made their way to Parliament, which was promptly delayed, leaving them with little to do for the next few weeks. The women, however, had much to do, for now the season would begin in earnest. All efforts made in the Little Season paled into comparison compared to the dedication that would be committed to the marriage mart for the next twelve weeks.

Lady Lilley was all smiles. "Vouchers!" she said at breakfast to Frances. "Vouchers to Almack's!"

Frances did not reply, only buttered more toast.

"You will need to look more pleasant than *that*," snapped Lady Lilley. "Smile, Frances, and try to look pleased."

"I will smile when I have to," said Frances. "At the ball, and not before."

Lady Lilley left the room in a huff, but the lack of enthusiasm from her daughter did not stop her from booking an appointment with the modiste and the milliner, for last minute adjustments and additions to Frances' wardrobe. In so doing, she made enquiries and discovered to her satisfaction that the Duke of Buckingham did not yet appear to have chosen a bride, although it seemed that his attention was slowly being directed towards Miss Elizabeth Belmont.

"As she is a friend of yours, make sure to spend some time with her," instructed Lady Lilley. "Especially when the Duke of Buckingham is in attendance."

"You want me to steal his attention away from one of my only friends?" asked Frances.

"Not at all," said Lady Lilley, colouring. "But there is no harm in being attentive. He has not made her any promise, therefore he is still entirely free to pay his compliments to any other young lady."

Frances shook her head. "I would never step between Elizabeth and the current most eligible man of the *ton*. It would be a despicable thing to do."

Lady Lilley sighed. "Really, Frances, you seem determined to be a failure. Anyone would think you did not want to marry."

"I don't, as you well know," said Frances.

She meant it, although she was aware of what a struggle she would have to face in making her parents accept her wishes. She had hoped that one more dismal season would make her case for her, but it seemed unlikely. How many more years would she have to wait before she might have the future she hoped for, where she could be mistress of her own fate?

CHAPTER 8
A House Party

A LMACK'S OPENED FOR THE SEASON IN MARCH AND was its usual staid self, full of people feeling superior for having secured a voucher, with little else to recommend them. The dull food and drink on offer was vastly inferior to private balls, where the hosts would at least lay on a decent repast for a young man about town.

"Welcome, Mr Mowatt. You will recall Miss Hervey," said the Master of Ceremonies as soon as he spotted Laurence. "I am sure she would be pleased to offer you a place on her dance card."

Miss Hervey was a newly minted debutante, still wide-eyed at being allowed to stay up past her bedtime and at entering the hallowed halls of Almack's. Laurence whirled her round the floor, taking a weary pleasure in seeing her excitement. Almack's no longer held such charms for him, nor did most of the social events he regularly attended. They were all so very similar. The same decorations, the same faces, the same dances. He hoped this young woman would get married off quickly enough to avoid his own growing boredom.

Miss Hervey was followed by various other young women, all eagerly pushed forwards by their mamas, who saw in him only his current respectability and the lure of a future title. They passed through his arms, one after another, in dances both lively and stately, none of them able to converse in anything but the most stilted polite platitudes, until he began to long for the silent comfort of his drawing room.

"Mr Mowatt, what a pleasure to see you here." Lady Hind, married for ten endlessly dull years to Lord Hind, had never plucked up the courage for an affair, but she regularly spoke with Laurence at gatherings where she could timidly flirt with him before returning to her lonely bed to recall in great detail every titillating moment passed between them.

Laurence took away Lady Hind's glass of champagne and bowed over her naked hand, placing a delicate kiss on the inside of her wrist. "The pleasure is yet to come, I'm sure."

Lady Hind's colour rose and she glanced about her for watching eyes. "My champagne, Mr Mowatt, if you please."

Laurence took a small sip from it, then turned the glass as he handed it back, so that, at her next sip, she would press her lips where his had been. "Would that my lips might taste something sweeter."

Lady Hind's hand trembled as she received the glass back, but tonight she was feeling brave. "My dance card is sadly missing a partner for the next dance."

"I hope it is the waltz?" Laurence asked.

Her colour rose even higher at the idea of dancing such an intimate dance, only recently allowed at Almack's and only between couples where there could be no hint of impropriety. "I could not possibly... the Master of Ceremonies would never..."

Laurence took her dance card from her and shook his head. "Alas, it is only the quadrille," he said. "Still, it is a way for couples to be… *playful* together, is it not? Exchanging partners so frequently."

Lady Hind stared at him in scandalised desire.

"Come," said Laurence, adding his name to the card and leading her to the dance floor, depositing her champagne along the way into the hands of a footman. He enjoyed teasing Lady Hind, knowing full well she would never actually consent to anything more than dancing, but these ways of talking, the constant banter, the suggestiveness, were for some reason, beginning to feel repetitive. He had always been accomplished at this kind of flirtation, finding just the right words to whisper if they were intimate, or to speak out loud if there were hidden meanings to be hinted at but which could plausibly be denied should outrage be forthcoming. But of late these games of words seemed lacklustre, even when they led to other pleasures, which was certainly not going to be the case with Lady Hind. He shook his head. Perhaps he was just tired, since neither debutantes nor mature women were of much interest of late. An early night soon would be wise, though he was engaged for the next six nights at least at various balls and parties.

With Lady Hind left to slow her breathing after their dance together, Laurence deftly avoided a forlorn looking young woman and her pushy mama and headed towards a quieter part of the room.

"Mr Mowatt."

To his surprise he found himself next to Miss Lilley.

"Miss Lilley, how unexpected. May I have the honour of a dance?"

"No. My feet hurt and I have barely slept. I have been

dragged to three balls this week. None of them ended before two."

He could not help chuckling, enjoying her usual blunt honesty. "I am sorry. Perhaps an ice, or a drink?"

She nodded. "Yes please. I am hungry but there is nothing decent to eat here. The ham sandwiches are dreadful. Dry and the ham is cut too thin."

Laurence had never heard a lady confess to being hungry. "I hope the other parties you attended this week fed you better."

"They tried. But if you are a lady, you must only take tiny mouthfuls. A single pea and perhaps a shred of beef. By the time dinner has ended you have only eaten enough to satisfy a mouse."

"Do you have a remedy for this dreadful state of affairs?"

Her lips twitched in a smile. "My maid Deborah waits up for me with a wedge of ham pie, a pot of tea and some gingerbread. Else I would starve."

The idea of her sitting in her bedroom eating ham pie while still in her evening finery made him laugh. "Do other young ladies have ham pie waiting for them when they get home?"

"I hope so, for their sakes. If not, you will find yourself dancing with skeletons by the end of the season."

He found her an ice and a drink, then secured her a plateful of small rout cakes, which, while dry and somewhat tasteless, were enough to stave off the worst of her hunger pangs.

"I am promised to Miss Skeffington for a dance," he said, reluctantly. Miss Lilley's conversation had made a welcome change this evening, but he could hardly leave a lady without her promised dance partner. "I hope to see you again soon," he found himself saying. "Will you be at the Portman picnic?"

"I begged off and Mama allowed it if I would attend tonight."

He hesitated. "Then perhaps our paths will cross in Margate one day."

She sighed. "I long for Margate. But Mama is determined I should stay here for the remainder of the season. I will try to convince her otherwise. Goodnight, Mr Mowatt."

"Miss Lilley." He bowed and watched her depart. A shame. She had made him laugh, which had cheered him. If he could have taken her away to the safety of Lord Barrington in Margate, he would have done, but she was immersed in the season now and there was no way out of it.

Lord Barrington sat in his study and re-read Laurence's letter. He smiled at its contents, but his eyes drifted to a portrait hung above the desk, of two young men in the outdated clothing of an earlier era, posing on a bridge, the Grand Canal of Venice behind them, misty buildings shining along the waterways. He lingered on their happy smiles, then took up his quill and wrote.

> *My dear Laurence,*
>
> *It gave me great pleasure to receive your last and to hear of your progress through the season. I am certain you are regarded with great esteem amongst the families of those young ladies who seek their companion of a lifetime. As for your misgivings regarding the fairer sex and their apparently shallow conversation or interests, I shall refer you to the great poet John Dryden and his words, thus: 'He who would search for pearls*

must dive below'. Dive below, my boy. Do not allow the strictures of our society to bind your actions, nor your words. When you sense something more than mere comeliness lies beneath a young woman's exterior, take the time to understand her true character and do not be shy in divulging your own. It is in this way that two souls come to know one another, and when they do, there is nothing in heaven nor earth that can divide them, nor can any subsequent deed or occurrence take away that joy of true union which I so deeply wish for you.

Believe me always your most affectionate uncle,
Barrington

He thought for while longer, resting his chin on his hand as he gazed out at the gardens and the empty swing which swayed in the breeze, before penning another missive, this one to Lady Lilley.

My dear Lady Lilley,

I hope that Frances acquits herself well this season and that she will find a suitable match soon. I know that this is your most earnest desire as it is mine, to see her happy and settled. May I suggest that for a girl with her delicacy of feeling it might be beneficial to host a house party? In the safety of her home and in the bosom of her family, she might find the necessary courage to more easily converse with appropriate gentlemen of your choice? You will forgive this old man his abominable habit of interfering in the lives of those for whom he holds great affection.

I remain your faithful servant,
Barrington

"Really, Lord Barrington is an old mother hen when it comes to Frances," sniffed Lady Lilley on receiving the letter a few days later. "He indulges her fancies." She sipped her tea, waiting for an answer from Lord Lilley, but she was disappointed in this, as he was buried in the newspaper and made no reply. "Although," she added, thinking over Lord Barrington's point and deciding that there was some possible truth in it. "Perhaps he is right."

Her husband made no reply.

"Lilley!"

He emerged from behind the paper. "My dear?"

"We are to hold a house party."

"Why?"

"So that we can choose a handful of suitable young men and encourage Frances to get to know them better in the comfort of our home. Then we shall pick the most likely and be done with it."

Her husband nodded agreeably. "If you say so, my dear."

And so Lady Lilley set about planning a house party to find Frances a husband. There was to be no more of this shilly-shallying. No more seasons ending in humiliation. She would choose the most likely candidates, invite them all for a week, and then encourage the least offensive to Frances to offer for her hand – and there would be no refusal permitted. There was, after all, only so much indulgence that could be bestowed on the girl. Lady Lilley herself, as a girl, had not been allowed such nonsensical ideas. She had been wed in her first season to the future Lord Lilley, an excellent match approved by all.

And her marriage had not been so bad; her husband treated her with the sort of kindly respect he might have offered had his best hunting dog been combined with their excellent and long-standing housekeeper. He was not tight-fisted, nor inclined to violence when in his cups, so there was nothing Lady Lilley could complain about. Yes. It was time Frances grew up and took her place in society as a married lady, after which her odd ways would be her husband's to manage and Lady Lilley could turn her mind to her son's altogether easier nuptial arrangements. Out of courtesy, since he had suggested the idea, she also invited Lord Barrington to the house party. She hoped he might make a generous bequest to Frances when she married, so it was best to keep him apprised of progress in that quarter.

A week later his reply arrived. She opened the letter, looking over it with growing interest.

My dear Lady Lilley,

You are too kind to me. I regret I cannot attend your house party, for my health will not permit it. May I send my nephew, Mr Mowatt, in my stead? He is my heir, as you know, and will make a charming guest, far more suited to a house party than my aged and infirm person.

I remain your faithful servant,
Barrington

This response was most agreeable and indeed something of a relief to Lady Lilley, for hosting Lord Barrington, with his inconvenient chair, was always difficult, since all the bedrooms of Woodside Abbey were on the first floor. She was well aware of his nephew and heir, who was always seen at the best parties and who had an easy charm about him, always first to dance at balls and a safe pair of hands for young ladies. She *had* heard the odd whisper or two about his escorting married ladies about town, but that was perfectly respectable, after all. What a married lady chose to do was none of anyone's business, as long as there was a veneer of propriety in her manners and no awkward questions about her youngest children's parentage. She added Mr Mowatt to her list of guests and began preparations.

Frances had at first been delighted to be told they were leaving London, then horrified to hear of her mother's plans. A house party would mean her home invaded, guests at every turn, with no escape. Worse, her mother would choose young men who would then be all but flung at Frances. There would be no escape from a ball pleading a headache, instead she would be forced to make dull conversation all day and evening. It was a suffocating thought.

By the time the house party came around, Woodside Abbey looked at its best, for Lady Lilley was gifted at arranging flowers and other decorative touches and Lord Lilley was generous when it came to housekeeping accounts. Frances' two sisters, with their families, had also arrived to help host the many events and were eager to assist in marrying off their younger sister. Frances, meanwhile, was regarding with horror the endless events Lady Lilley had seen fit to arrange. There would be dinner each night, a picnic by the waterfall on one of the sunniest days, and a ball on the last night. To fill the rest of the time there would be card parties, drives to local beauty spots, a few pleasant walks and, of course, in the evenings there would be parlour games, music, perhaps singing. The guests would be well cared for.

Frances' worst fears were promptly confirmed. With Lady Lilley and her two older daughters making a coordinated effort, there was not one moment of the day when Frances was alone, from the moment she arrived downstairs for breakfast until she retired at night. Her only snatched moments of silence were when she must change her clothes for the next activity, and she began to actually look forward to being dressed for dinner each evening, even sitting perfectly still for Deborah to curl her hair, having already begged the maid not to speak unless she had to.

At each activity Frances found herself with one or another of the young men invited, each of them doing their best to engage her in conversation, while Frances did her best to stay quiet. The result was one failed outing or activity after another, with awkward silences becoming more and more common. By the time the last day arrived, and with it the ball, Frances could hardly even bear to descend to the ballroom.

The ballroom was filled with daffodils and pussy-willow buds, as well as hundreds of beeswax candles, so that it smelt deliciously of honey. Laurence looked about him with approval. Even he, who regularly attended balls, thought this one looked particularly charming. The room was pleasantly full of the house guests without being stifling as often happened at public balls and now he spotted Frances.

She stood with her back to the far wall, her demeanour that of a deer about to take flight. Her mother must have fought to have her way as regards her wardrobe, for she was wearing a sea-blue silk which suited her, with white silk roses in her hair and delicate diamond drops in her ears. She was tugging at her long gloves, as though she found them uncomfortable, and not paying much attention to the room, so that when a young man approached her and bowed she startled, jerking backwards and flushing a blotchy pink about her neck and shoulders, then giving a stiff curtsey and reluctantly holding out her dance card for him to add his name.

Since Frances was the daughter of the hostess, naturally her dance card was rapidly filling up, and by the time Laurence reached her she could only offer a quadrille or a waltz.

"Please don't pick the waltz," she added in a fervent whisper when she saw him about to add his name there. "I don't like it. It's too…"

Intimate, thought Laurence, but he nodded and instead chose the quadrille, which was about to start. He held out his hand and led her to take their place amongst the couples squaring up for the dance. Neatly arranged into four couples for each square, they began the repetitive formations required, whereby each person would dance with every other, criss-crossing the square between them and holding hands to turn about. It was not a dance made for much in the way of conversation, nor for paying attention to one's partner, since it called for dancing with the other three ladies as much as with Frances herself. Laurence contented himself with performing the steps well and offering a ready smile to the other ladies, all of whom had pleasant countenances except for Frances, who kept her face free of any expression. She did not miss a step, but showed no pleasure in the dance, her body wooden. Laurence, who enjoyed dancing and was often complimented on his skills in the ballroom, was sorry for her. The season must be hard indeed if neither dancing nor speaking were of pleasure to a person and yet must be endured, night after night, day after day, knowing oneself to be judged and found wanting at every turn, no matter how much effort was expended.

The dance ended with bows and curtseys all round.

"With whom will you dance the waltz?" he asked, before she could step away.

She shook her head. "I will say I am faint and ask someone to take me for an ice instead. If I'm slow about it, I can waste enough time and won't have to dance it at all."

"If you need someone to take you for an ice, I'd be happy to oblige."

She gave one of her shrugs. "If you have nothing better to do."

From another woman, it would have sounded churlish, as though he had offended her and now must fawn over her to make up for his rudeness, but she was only stating things as she saw them; she considered taking a young lady for an ice a boring task and did not want him to waste his time.

"I insist," he said. "I will return to you when it is time. You may tell anyone who asks that you are engaged during the waltz."

She nodded, then turned away.

Laurence kept an eye on her for the next few dances, saw her pass through the arms of each partner without unbending and almost without speaking, could see her mother's pinched look of growing disapproval. The waltz would be the next dance and he was ready to act on his promise to rescue her from the ballroom floor. He was dancing with a Miss Swanson, when he noticed Frances slip out of a side door, almost sliding along the wall to keep from being noticed.

"Surrey is such a lovely part of the world," chattered Miss Swanson, evidently well briefed by her mama that this would one day be Laurence's home county. "I am exceedingly fond of Surrey."

"Do you go there often?" managed Laurence, turning his head to try and see if Frances had come back into the room. She had not. She was still somewhere outside in the darkness.

"I've been there only once," confessed Miss Swanson. "When I was five years old but even then I could see how wonderful it is."

Laurence only just stopped himself from rolling his eyes at her fawning. Fortunately, the dance was coming to an end, so he bowed and moved away from her as fast as was seemly. He made his way across the room, trying not to look too focused on the door Frances had taken, allowing time to nod and briefly speak with one or two other guests.

Finally, he reached the door. It was not the main door, more of a side door such as a servant might use to bring more ices or candles as the evening wore on. Gently, he pushed against it. It opened. He made his way through it as quickly as possible, not wishing to draw attention to himself.

He had expected to find himself in a side-room, where Frances might have gone to have a few moments of solitude, but instead he was in a short corridor, plainly decorated, very much a servant's passageway, at the end of which were stairs leading downwards. He followed them, beginning to think he had made a mistake. These stairs were likely to lead him into the kitchens, where the household staff would no doubt be disconcerted to find a lost guest and wonder what had possessed him to follow the backstairs into what was clearly the staff's territory.

But the stairs were oddly quiet. He could not hear the clattering of pans or voices from below, no-one passed him on the stairs carrying refreshments. From above, he could hear the opening strains of the waltz. Perhaps Frances had returned to the room without his seeing her and was even now thinking that he had reneged on his promise to her. He was about to retrace his steps when he saw that the stairs ended in front of a small, closed door. Curious, he turned the handle and opened the door, then stopped in surprise.

The room might have been built as a convenient storage room beneath the ballroom, for it was not particularly large, with a low ceiling only a few inches above his head. But three candles had been lit, and the flickering light showed a room where every available surface, including the ceiling and a small section of the floor, had been covered in shells. And standing in the middle of the room, startled by his arrival, was a scowling Frances.

"What are you doing here?"

"I—I followed you here," said Laurence.

Her frown deepened.

"I'm sorry," he said. "I thought you had slipped out for some fresh air, and I had promised to take you away from the dancing."

She said nothing.

"What *is* this place?"

Her voice was very small. "It is where I come to be alone. To breathe. When it is… too much for me."

He looked about him. The shells were common enough,

they were those he had seen her collect on the strandline at Margate. But here, in the soft candlelight, they shone. They had been stuck onto the walls and ceiling, in patterns; some were sunbursts, others rippled waves, spirals or floral shapes. "You made this room?"

She nodded.

"Why is it hidden away?"

"I do not want lots of people to see it. It is mine. Besides, they would think me odd."

"It is beautiful," he said, and meant it. Seeing this room was like being granted an entry into a hidden part of Frances, he realised. He had known she collected shells, of course, had even seen them at the rotunda, but this was different, it was a secret place and hers alone, a place of solace to her, a place to give her the courage to continue the evening.

And he was an intruder.

"I should not have followed you," he said. "I will leave you to rest and when you are ready, if you would like me to, I would be glad to have an ice with you and keep you away from any other dance partners, if they are tiring you." He stepped backwards, one hand on the door about to pull it shut.

"Stay," she said.

He hovered in the doorway.

"You may stay," she repeated. "I only needed... time to myself, to rest."

He nodded but remained on the threshold.

"You like dancing," she said. "You look happy when you dance."

"And you do not like it," he observed, trying to be as frank as she. "You know all the steps, but you seem to endure the dances rather than taking any pleasure in them."

She grimaced. "I am always counting in my head, my dancing master used to insist on it."

"It is hard to follow the music when you are counting."

"Follow the music?"

Laurence listened to the waltz coming from upstairs, then took a few steps, his body swaying to the music. "Like that."

"Without counting?"

He gave a chuckle. "Without counting."

"I am not sure I am able."

He held out both hands. "Try."

She hesitated.

"Please."

She took a few steps towards him and he let go of the door to do the same, meeting her in the centre of the small room. Gently, he offered his hands again and she placed hers in his.

He listened again and saw her doing the same. He moved her hands a little, to and fro to the music. "Like that."

She frowned. "But the steps…"

He took a step closer, placed his right hand on her waist and nodded to her to do the same to him. Her left hand clasped in his, he raised it, so that they were now looking at each other through a circle made of their arms. Again, he swayed back and forth to the music without moving his feet. He watched her lips and saw them move silently.

"No," he reminded her. "No counting."

"But…"

"Tell me about the shells," he said, still moving them both slightly from side to side.

"What about them?"

"How you chose the patterns."

Her furrowed brow became smooth. "The sunburst was the

hardest, I had to find shells with a yellowish tint to them and there are not so many, then I found the rose-tinted ones to contrast against them, as an outline for the sun's rays…"

He tightened his hold on her waist and began to move his feet and she, trained in the correct steps to take, followed his lead but she stopped speaking and her lips moved again in silence. Laurence smiled down at her, shaking his head again.

"The shells?"

"I started with the flower shapes, the sunburst came later. The last ones were the ripples, as a border. But I have run out of space and there is nowhere else for them to go that is private. I decorated the rotunda, but I do not like to go there with other people."

"What do you think about when you are placing them?"

Her body softened as she relaxed. "I look at their colour, I feel the shapes and textures of them and think how they would go together, how this shell might look next to another, of shells in the past which would have suited the placement and where I might find more of the same…"

She was dancing. Her body was swaying to the music as she spoke, her feet were taking the correct steps and as Laurence gently steered them in a circle and she could see the shells all around her he could see her taking them all in, both their individual beauty and the shapes and colour shifts they created together. Laurence remembered for a fleeting moment his thoughts, his desires when he had seen her walk through the sea, how he had wanted to put his hands on her and feel the warmth of her body, as he was doing now. There was a softness to her, a gentleness he had rarely seen. Her wide grey eyes contained an expression that was peaceful, even happy.

"… Lord Barrington says he will take me further afield, to

Whitstable, where the strandline is very full of shells. He said we will fill a carriage with them," she went on, with a laugh.

Laurence smiled down at her. She was so wrapped up in what she was saying that she did not realise that she was dancing far better than he had seen her dance all evening, graceful and fluid in her movements, easily following the music.

"You are dancing," he said.

She stumbled at once, but then, to his surprise, regained the rhythm.

"I am," she said, and smiled up at him, a wide, open smile which he had not seen before. "Thank you. When I think of the shells it is so much easier. I will try to remember that when I dance with my next partner."

Laurence suddenly felt uncomfortable, as though, rather than a compliment, she had said something disagreeable. "You are welcome," he said stiffly, lowering his arm and unclasping both her hand and waist. "We should probably return to the ballroom, I would not wish for our absence to be noted and commented on."

"No, of course," she said and walked past him to the door. "You may follow when I have been gone a few moments."

Left alone, Laurence stood amongst the shells. Why had he been so aloof with her just then? He was not sure. Something she had said had bothered him. His eyes wandered across the shapes and patterns, before he gave a quick blow to the three candles, extinguishing each in turn so that the room was plunged into darkness. He made his way back out into the passageway by touch, fingers running across the swirling shapes.

Only when he reached the ballroom again and saw Frances in the arms of one of the other young men did he realise that it was her comment about future partners that had made him feel uncomfortable, the idea of her dancing more gracefully and easily with other men, of taking pleasure in the experience. It was unfair of him to resent something that might help her find a husband this season. Dancing was, after all, a way to grow more intimate with someone, and she could probably do with all the help she could get. He would make sure to offer to dance with her again, to end the evening on a friendly note.

For once, Frances was not counting. She allowed the music to guide her and kept her mind on her shells, surprised that Mr Mowatt's guidance on this had been so effective. When she thought of her shells it was as though her whole body had exhaled, leaving her body loose and more easily attuned to her surroundings, rather than suffering them as an invasion of her senses. It made the dancing feel like rocking or swinging; she could feel a kinship to it which she had never before noticed, despite many hours of practice under the eyes of more than one frustrated dancing master. She would not say it was enjoyable yet, but it was more comfortable. For just a few moments in her room of shells, with Mr Mowatt guiding her, she had glimpsed a joy to it, which had not remained once in the arms of whoever this young man was, she had forgotten his title. But then her shells were not all around her, that was what must be making the difference.

The dance ended and she curtseyed, then swiftly withdrew to a corner of the room, close to where Elizabeth was standing, speaking with Lady Honora. Frances could not catch all of the conversation, but Lady Honora's lips tightened at something Elizabeth had said.

"Mowatt wants to marry me and he'd be a decent catch for anyone," she said.

"Then I wonder you do not hasten to marry him," said Elizabeth, her voice raised from its usual murmur. She turned away, meeting Frances' gaze, then looked over her shoulder to Lady Honora. "You will excuse me," she said. "I must speak with my friend."

Lady Honora opened her mouth, then closed it again. "By all means," she said, and there was something tight in her voice. "I would not keep you from your friend." She turned and walked away, tapping her fan on the arm of Mr Mowatt, who had been heading towards them, and indicating the dining room. He hesitated, then took her arm and they walked away.

Frances watched them go. So Mr Mowatt was all but promised to Honora Fortescue. She had not known that. Not that it made any difference to her, certainly, Mr Mowatt was free to marry where he chose, and he had made it plain that he wished only for a marriage of convenience. Lady Honora would be a good match – she would bring with her a third estate, making Mr Mowatt – or Lord Barrington as he would be one day, extremely rich, for he would have not one but three estates – from his father, his uncle and his wife. Few marriages could be so well favoured. Even Frances' twenty thousand, a most advantageous amount, would pale into insignificance. She would henceforth regard him as already spoken for, if he had already made his intentions clear to Lady Honora and she in turn was sure enough of them to repeat them to Elizabeth. He would marry soon and then would visit Lord Barrington less often, having more pressing matters to attend to, such as the care of his wife. Frances supposed she would miss some of their walks and talks in Margate, as she had found him an easy companion, but after all they were little more than acquaintances, so it was no great loss.

When, half an hour later, Mr Mowatt came to her and asked for another dance, she only said that her dance card was full and turned away. There was little point in raising her mama's hopes when he was already spoken for.

The guests were late to rise the next day and breakfast almost became the midday meal. There was plenty of fuss and bustle as they all began to depart, with servants loading up carriages and repeated farewells as the house began to empty.

Laurence watched as the guests departed, noting that Miss Lilley held back from effusive promises to visit again, to meet in London and so on, instead quietly curtseying when required and nodding her head without much in the way of words issuing from her mouth. He could see that she was both weary from all the social obligations that had been thrust upon her and no doubt dreading her mother's disappointment when it turned out that it had all been in vain, for he had not noticed any particular interest shown to her by any of the young men present.

"Might I trespass on your hospitality one more night, Lady Lilley?" he asked that afternoon. "I am expected back at Albany but there are some minor renovations being made to my set which should be completed by tomorrow." It was the truth, but he was worried about Frances, who looked drawn and had grown increasingly silent. He wondered whether she might speak more when the crowds had departed.

"Of course, of course," said Lady Lilley, looking meaningfully at Frances. "It is a delight to have you with us, *en famille*, a little longer."

But Frances was quiet all evening and despite Lord and Lady Lilley's best attempts, asking questions about Margate, Lord Barrington, shells and more, neither of the two young people seemed much inclined to converse with one another. Frances spent most of the evening showing her young nephews and nieces some of her shells, explaining what made each one distinctive, then allowing them to lay them out in different patterns on a side table, showing them how the differing shades might look best next to one another and ignoring everyone else, until eventually an early night was had by all.

Laurence woke on the day of his departure to shouts of laughter somewhere outside. Curious, he made his way over to the windows to look down on the gardens, where the five children belonging to the Lilleys' two elder daughters were playing with a sizeable hunting dog belonging to Lord Lilley. The dog was currently engaged in dragging a large branch three times its own length across the immaculate lawn, no doubt ruining it in the process. There was a woman with the children, he supposed for a moment it must be a nursemaid, but then he realised it was Miss Lilley, her hair coming loose from its pins and dressed in a very plain grey gown, something even a maid would find dull. But she was more full of life and fun than he had ever seen her, running with the children, pulling at the other end of the dog's treasured branch, then rolling down a small slope with the two youngest children, heedless of her dress getting stained by the grass or the fact that it got ruffled up, exposing her legs to the knee in white stockings. It reminded Laurence of their excursion to Botany Bay, how spirited she had been, without a trace of fear, the lack of modesty regarding her bare legs which had stirred something in him.

It rose up again now, watching her hair come tumbling down altogether, falling to her waist in a cascade of chestnut-brown waves, her face full of laughter instead of its usual stillness. And something else came to him, the odd thought that she would make a kind mother, for her laughter and play-fulness with the children was delightful to watch and clearly they all loved her. The youngest, when falling, turned to her without hesitation for comfort, even the oldest held her hand as they hurried round the side of the house, following the dog, still laughing at almost tripping over the long branch.

He remembered his mother laughing during a snowball fight one wintery day, how she had fallen backwards into the snow but still been laughing as his father helped her up, how they had embraced one another before calling their children to come indoors, where hot spiced apple juice was served and cook was coaxed to provide gingerbread biscuits, hot from the oven to warm them.

He turned away from the window and went through the motions of washing and dressing, his mind elsewhere. Honora had been brisk at the ball, giving a terse assent to the idea of them having a half-understanding, nothing formal as yet but if either of them were still unmarried in a year's time… they would be a good match, no-one would object. He wondered how their marriage would be. Would there be laughter beneath his windows in the mornings? Would there be apple juice and gingerbread in the winters after snowball fights, and lemonade and ices in the summers after swimming in a nearby river? His memories of childhood were full of such days but he was uncertain if this planned union would bring with it such light-heartedness. It was an arrangement, a practical plan, which did not necessarily promise such moments. But he was the only son, and it was nearing time to set aside such childish fancies. A boy might wish for snowball fights and building twig rafts at the river's edge with his mother and father, a man must think of more practical things.

Laurence straightened his cravat and made his way down-stairs to bid the Lilleys farewell. They had gathered, all of them together, in the hall and he spotted Frances towards the back, loose hair hastily pushed under her bonnet, her mother glowering at her dishevelled state. He was sorry for her, but there was little he could say in front of everyone that would not have been thought odd and he did not want to give her mother false hope when he had no intentions towards Frances, so he only bowed, murmured her name amongst the others and took his leave.

CHAPTER 9
An Offer of Marriage

L ADY LILLEY WAS SUNK IN DESPONDENCY. DESPITE the promising idea of the house party, nothing had come of it. The young men had arrived, danced, spoken with Frances and then, one by one, had left, even Mr Mowatt who had stayed an extra day, about which she had been hopeful. No-one had shown real interest, no-one had asked to speak with her or Lord Lilley privately. None of them had even asked for permission to visit again, or expressed hope that they would meet Frances soon in London or elsewhere. Another season was proceeding dismally. It was now late March and in just three short months it would all be over and Frances would be headed for her fifth season. *Fifth*! It was not to be borne. The word spinster echoed in Lady Lilley's head. Perhaps it was as best to acknowledge it. Perhaps Frances could look after herself and Lord Lilley in their old age, although Frances did not have the most appealing bedside manner. Still, it would be her duty as an unmarried daughter to care for her aged parents.

"Hosmer's coming for a visit," announced Lord Lilley at breakfast one day.

"Whatever for?" asked Lady Lilley.

A distant cousin of the family, elderly Lord Hosmer had married three times and outlived each wife, though he was without an heir. Two of his wives had died in childbirth, the third had died of some wasting disease, no doubt bored to death by her husband who lived in the far reaches of Wales and was not inclined to mix with society.

"How should I know? On his way to London, stopping in along the way. Feed him dinner, give him a bed for the night and hope he makes it a short visit. Man's a dreadful bore."

Lord Hosmer really was a dreadful guest, in Frances' opinion. He drank his soup and coffee with slurping and gulping noises that made her want to commit violence involving the silverware. He would not stop talking about his views on the best way to do everything from schooling a horse to laying out formal gardens, and his eyes slid over her face and figure in a manner she found objectionable. She tried to keep out of his way, but he found her no matter where she went on the estate. He frowned at the shells on the ceiling of the rotunda, appeared vexed at the sight of her rocking in the library with an atlas balanced on her knees, shook his head whenever she spoke, as though her views were entirely unacceptable. On the third evening of his visit, Frances hastened away with her mother to let the men smoke and drink alone.

"Mama, when will Lord Hosmer be leaving?"

"I am not sure," said her mother, from behind a magazine. "A day or two, perhaps. He said he was only staying a night in his letter, but he seems to have grown fond of the place – and of us."

Frances sighed. "I hope he leaves soon."

In the dining room Lord Hosmer and Lord Lilley drank port and puffed on cigars, speaking mostly of estate management and politics until Lord Hosmer made a startling change of topic.

"Your youngest daughter is still unmarried, I see."

"Yes, it's a damned thing. She's odd in her ways," said Lord Lilley, allowing himself to be frank, since he was speaking with a member of the family. "But not peculiar, you know, just won't mind her tongue and speaks her mind far too often for polite society. Probably spoilt her, being the youngest," he added, taking another gulp of his port. "Can't be helped now, will just have to find some chap to take her off our hands or give her up as a bad job and have a spinster in the family. Her older sisters were never this tricky, easy enough to marry off."

Lord Hosmer coughed. "Perhaps I might be so bold as to offer for her hand."

Lord Lilley choked on his cigar, then regained control of himself. "Frances? My dear chap, she's forty years younger than you if she's a day."

Lord Hosmer shrugged. "No matter. Young enough to bear children. Old enough to be taken in hand. Perhaps what the girl needs is a firm husband. I can assure you she'd be well provided for, both while she's my wife and in the event of her being widowed. Never managed to get an heir so far, it's a regret of mine. But there's still time, if I have a young wife."

Lord Lilley was silent for a few moments, pondering this extraordinary offer. The reality was, Frances was not going to attract any other proposals of marriage, he was fairly sure of this. His wife's resigned air after the house party had been obvious even to him and here was Lord Hosmer, a marquis and part of the family, asking to marry her, undaunted by her odd ways. Why, Frances would actually be marrying upwards and have the opportunity to provide an heir to a decent estate, even if it was in the darkest depths of Wales. Certainly, there was a considerable age difference, but perhaps Lord Hosmer was right. Perhaps, being the youngest, the girl had been spoilt and a husband who would impose his will on her would be more successful than her parents had been in making her fit for society. Lord Hosmer was known for disliking parties and other social gatherings, which might actually suit Frances. And if she should dislike her husband, well the truth was he was likely to die while she was still young and she would likely be left with children and a goodly estate and income to provide for her. He, Lord Lilley, could certainly make sure of that through the marriage contracts that would be drawn up. She would also have her marriage portion, which was ample and would mean she would not be reliant on Lord Hosmer for her own wants, should he turn out to be tight-fisted. The notion had seemed absurd at first, but he could see the benefits of it. It was worth considering.

"I will discuss your offer with Lady Lilley," he said.

Lady Lilley spluttered into her morning hot chocolate, but slowly came round to the idea. Lord Hosmer was not the husband she would have chosen for Frances, but then Frances was *so* difficult and perhaps, as her husband suggested, an older husband would be right for her. She was not enthusiastic with her consent, but her consent was given nonetheless. All that remained was to inform Frances.

"No!" Frances, appalled, got up from her chair in the morning room and began to pace the room, heart pounding.

"But consider," said Lady Lilley, "Lord Hosmer is titled, he is a marquis. You will be a marchioness. Think of that, you will rank higher than your mother!"

"I don't care! He is old. And ugly. And he smells."

"Frances, really!"

"It's the truth. Tell me that's not true."

Lady Lilley opened her mouth before closing it again. She took a fortifying sip of tea before trying again. "Lord Hosmer has a delightful castle in Wales –"

"Wales? I am not living in Wales!"

"There are beaches in Wales," tried Lady Lilley weakly. "I am sure you could collect shells there…"

"He has already told me that he thinks shells only fit for children!"

"Ah, children," said Lady Lilley with some relief. "Yes. Lord Hosmer is very keen to have children, so you will have children to care for, with whom you can of course gather shells and so on. You enjoy spending time with your nieces and nephews, do you not?"

"Yes," said Frances reluctantly.

"Well then, think what a joy it will be to be a mother."

"Not if Lord Hosmer were my husband."

Lady Lilley sighed. "Frances, it is not a choice. Lord Hosmer has offered for your hand and we – your parents – have given our blessing."

"You would force me to marry Lord Hosmer?" She could not believe what she was hearing, could not believe her matrimonial choices had suddenly been taken away, replaced with an unthinkable certainty.

"It is not *forcing* –"

"I do not wish to marry him. You say I must. That is forcing."

"Well then so be it," said Lady Lilley, standing up, her voice wavering. "Frances. You are to marry Lord Hosmer. There will be no more said about this. I have a headache. I will be in my bedchamber." She swept from the room.

Frances sat for a few moments, before she was startled by a tap on the door. "Enter," she said without thinking, then hurriedly rose as Lord Hosmer entered the room. "I was just…" she began, seeking an escape, but Lord Hosmer closed the door with a firm motion, then advanced on her.

"Miss Lilley, I would like to speak with you on a matter of importance."

"My father…" began Frances.

"Your father and mother are already aware of my intentions and fully supportive of them."

Frances backed slowly away from him as he advanced, then, finding the backs of her knees against a chair, sank into it, keeping her eyes on the floor. The tips of Lord Hosmer's shoes came into her view. She did not lift her face.

"Miss Lilley, it is my intention to marry you."

"I thought it was customary to ask," said Frances quietly.

"I beg your pardon?"

"You have not *asked* me if I wish to marry you."

There was an icy silence before Lord Hosmer spoke again. "I was warned of the defects in your character," he said. "Let us begin as we mean to go on. You will raise your face and look me in the eye when you speak to me."

Frances kept her face down.

"Miss Lilley. Raise. Your. Face."

Slowly she looked up, her darting eyes meeting his for a brief moment, before looking over his shoulder at the closed door.

"You will look me in the eye when I speak to you."

She fixed her eyes on his, discomfort growing in her, meeting eyes with this stranger impossible to maintain.

"Better," he said. "Will you marry me, Miss Lilley?"

She struggled to keep his gaze. "No, Sir, I will not." She looked away, the relief almost breathtaking before something hard was thrust under her chin, her head jerked back up by his walking cane.

"You will marry me, because it has been agreed," he snarled. "And damn it, Miss Lilley, I will teach you to be a well-mannered wife, whether by fair means or foul. I have trained hunting dogs and horses and a woman will be no different. If it takes a beating to make you follow my orders, then so be it. You *will* meet my eyes when I speak to you, and you *will* marry me. I shall depart tomorrow morning and before I do so I will inform your parents that we are betrothed. I will leave your mother to make whatever foolish arrangements a woman believes necessary for a wedding; trousseaus, flowers and a gown, I care not. I will return to marry you before two months are up and then we will travel to my home in Wales, where you will learn the meaning of the words in the marriage service, 'to *obey*'. I will not take any pleasure in training you with harsh methods, Miss Lilley, but neither will I be so remiss as to fail in my duties as a husband by allowing your stubborn will to prevail. So were I in your shoes, I would submit, and do so gracefully. Your life will be the better for it. You need only be obedient to my will and produce at least one healthy heir and I will be satisfied. It is not much to ask of a wife." He stopped, wheezing with rage.

Frances sat very still, face still held forcibly up to him. There was a brief silence before he lowered his cane and she bowed her head, hands shaking in her lap though she tried to clench them together.

"Do you have anything further to say, Miss Lilley?"

She shook her head.

"Then I will bid you good day for now and make plans to depart. I will return soon and expect to find you a willing bride."

Frances said nothing, only clenched her hands tighter, trembling as he made his way out of the room, the sound of his cane tap-tapping sharply into the distance.

Frances sat alone in her rocking chair for a long time that day, but the rocking motion gave no comfort. She had thought that her parents would grow weary of their efforts to find her a husband and instead disburse her marriage portion with which to set up the life she desired, a spinster but happy. But that was not to be the case.

Lord Hosmer was old, that was the one thing in his favour. He might die, and then she would have what she had always wanted: a home, perhaps there would be children, which she had little objection to, but at any rate she would be able to manage her life as she saw fit. But what if he lived to a ripe old age, and she had to stand his company for decades to come? The thought was unbearable. But to whom might she turn who could help her escape the future she now faced? Only one name came to mind, though to even contemplate the thought was scandalous. But she had run out of choices.

Laurence had spent another dismal evening at a ball. He did not know what he regretted more, that he had spent a tiresome few hours in the company of young women who had bored him witless, or that he had turned down not one but two invitations from ladies of his acquaintance. The truth was that neither of the invitations had appealed to him. He had enjoyed these women's company in the past, but the shallowness of their intimacy was beginning to weary him. There was physical pleasure to be had, certainly, but it left a hollow feeling afterwards, when they hurried home to their husbands while he returned to his empty bed in Albany. He imagined what it would be like to wake with a woman who did not need to go anywhere, who would stay in his arms, what it would feel like to know that she loved him. The half-formed image gave him a pleasure greater than the titillating touches and whispers that had filled the past few years.

"A card from Lady Salisbury, Sir."

Laurence sighed. Lady Salisbury had been a brief dalliance, an agreeable evening as well as the night that followed, but she had grown overly fond of him, sending her card with what was now becoming an alarming frequency. Laurence had always maintained a careful distance from such women, for they were a risk if they could not make a show of indifference or at least polite acquaintance in public. Once or twice a lady had grown fond of him, and he had been flattered but gently detached himself from them. The easiest way to clarify his position was to be seen with another lady, thus signalling that the previous liaison was well and truly over, but when Laurence cast his mind about for a suitable woman, the options were unappealing. Lady Maurice was too talkative. Lady Harrington too fond of being seen in public with her beaus. There was Lady

Lewis but... his heart was not in it. Nor his loins, oddly. None of them were appealing, even though they were all considered beauties.

"Will you be going out tonight, Sir?"

There was no shortage of options. He had barely shown his face at Boodles of late, so an evening at the club was a possibility. His friends would welcome him and he would enjoy an evening of drink and talk, perhaps gaming, a tasty meal in pleasant company. Or he could choose one of the ladies he had mulled over and attend them as their companion for the evening. Or there was a pile of unopened invitations on the silver tray left on his desk. There would be balls and dinners, theatre and opera, he need only choose a diversion and the evening was open to his pleasure. And yet... the thought of any of them bored him. Instead he thought longingly of stretching out on the sofa with an interesting book and a good dinner, a glass of wine in hand and afterwards, the comfort of his bed and an early morning ride in the park, not to see and be seen as everyone did without fail on Rotten Row each afternoon, but only for himself, for the pleasure of riding and the fresh air that always made him feel like a new man.

"No, Roberts," he said, and a burden lifted from him as he spoke. "I will be staying in tonight. Choose a wine, nothing too heavy, and throw together a meal, I'll dine alone."

"Very good, Sir."

He felt relieved at the decision, but when he closed his eyes he had a better idea.

"Roberts?"

"Sir?"

"Book a post-chaise to Margate tomorrow morning and pack my bags. I believe I'll visit Uncle Barrington."

"Of course, Sir. Will we be staying long?"

He shrugged. "A week or two, depending on the company."

Miss Lilley would probably be there. She would surely have coaxed her mama into escaping the *ton* once again and he had to admit she made interesting, if odd, conversation. If he found her there, he might stretch his visit a little longer. Miss Lilley would make a refreshing change from society in London, with her direct gaze and her outspoken opinions.

The journey was tedious as usual but Laurence eagerly anticipated his arrival at Northdown House, which looked at its best in the spring, the gardens filled with all manner of flowers, from daffodils and crocosmia, and the fresh green of newly-opened leaves. Uncle Barrington would not mind his arriving unannounced, if he were still awake, and so it proved.

"Laurence, my dear boy! What a pleasure it is to see you here again so soon. Are you staying?"

"For a few days at least, Uncle, if you'll have me."

"Always, my boy, always. Andrew, make haste and let Mrs Norris know there is a hungry young man to feed, she will take it as a challenge. I have already dined, for late dining does not agree with my constitution, but you need a hearty meal inside you to make up for the long journey here."

They made their way to the dining room, where Mrs Norris managed to conjure up a remarkable meal, including a rich onion soup, a hearty beef steak pie, potted partridge, cardoons, Spanish peas and a large portion of trifle. Laurence tucked in while Lord Barrington drank tea and nibbled on some gingerbread which he claimed was beneficial to his stomach.

"Frances, sadly, is not with me, as you see. Her mother

insists on her staying in town now that the season proper has begun, I hear she has vouchers promised for Almack's. Poor girl, she will not like it one bit, but her mama will not rest till she is married off."

"I will confess that I had hoped to find her here, Sir. She is… odd, but her company has grown on me, I have found our walks…" Laurence groped for the right word and stumbled on one that seemed wrong, given their many disagreements, and yet which somehow was also right, "…peaceful."

"Those who look for seashells will find seashells; those who open them will find pearls."

"Sir?"

"Al-Ghazali. A Persian polymath of the eleventh century. Frances may appear odd, but she has much to offer those who take the time to know her."

Laurence nodded. A pearl was too romantic a word for Miss Lilley, with her stubborn nature, unsuitable topics of conversation and her blunt words, but he understood his uncle's metaphor.

"I do not think she enjoys the season."

"No, but she does not have a choice in the matter if her parents have enforced her attendance."

"They might let her choose her own path," ventured Laurence.

"Not marry at all? Why, Laurence, I never thought to hear such words from your dutiful self."

Laurence shrugged. He disliked the idea of Miss Lilley being forced into a staid marriage, one where her oddities would be flattened and eventually lost altogether. He preferred to think of her as she was now, strange ways and all, and if that required her not marrying, well, it would suit her nature better, even though the *ton* would find it objectionable. "I should not like to think of her being unhappily married," he mumbled.

Lord Barrington smiled. "Quite right, Laurence. Quite right. We should all hope for the happiness of our fellow man, or in this case, woman. More port before we retire for the night?"

The next morning dawned sunny and with the promise of warmth.

"Should we follow our absent friend's ways and take a stroll along the beach?"

Laurence assented and rode the amiable Hippomenes alongside his uncle's carriage, down to the promenade, where they spent a happy morning strolling to and fro. Laurence enjoyed the salt air and the peaceful nature of their conversation. As they went along, he spotted odd shells that took his fancy and stooped to collect them, putting them into the pockets of his breeches, an activity which his uncle did not refer to, only speaking of the new fruit trees he had planted in the orchards last autumn and how they were now showing their first new leaves.

"There is even blossom on one or two of the strongest, though fruit in their first year might be too much to hope for. But I am a patient man, and besides, I do not plant for myself, Laurence, I plant for your future."

Later that day, having changed for dinner, Laurence recalled that his breeches from earlier in the day were heavy with shells. He took them out and laid them on his bed, examining their ridges and whorls, their delicate shades of cream, pink and grey. A thought came to him and he scooped up the collection and made his way out of his room and along the corridor, to the Green bedroom, where Miss Lilley always stayed. The room was empty, some of the furniture draped with holland covers, the bed stripped. It was cold and stark, but he fancied he could still smell her here, a faint memory of her skin. Carefully, he deposited his assortment of shells on the broad windowsill, then spent a few moments aligning them into a pleasing pattern, smiling at the thought that on her next visit here she would find them and wonder at who had placed them there for her. Lord Barrington would deny all knowledge and besides, he rarely ventured to the upper floor. She would know, then, that they had been left here by Laurence, that he had thought of her in her absence, had continued her work of gathering shells and had left them here for her collection. He hoped that this would bring a smile to her sober face, that she would think of him kindly when she took up the shells into her hands, understanding them as a gift.

The next afternoon, while Lord Barrington took his usual nap, Laurence rode out on Hippomenes, taking the road down to the clifftops and then riding along them for some miles, enjoying the brisk breeze, the steady sound of the waves breaking on the shoreline, the cries of the gulls wheeling above him. He returned late in the afternoon, full of energy. As he dressed for dinner he thought that he might offer to call in on Miss Lilley in London, to see how she was faring and perhaps take a letter from Lord Barrington to her, for he knew they corresponded regularly. Yes, it would be the gentlemanly thing to do, to call on a lady of his acquaintance and pass on the regards of his uncle. He might even stop off at Brown's and order some of their iced biscuits for her, they were practically works of art. Perhaps he could even bespoke her some biscuits decorated as shells, as a nod to her passion for them. He strode down to dinner in an excellent mood and spent some time describing his ride to his uncle, who seemed pleased that Hippomenes had received exercise and that Laurence was exploring the neighbourhood.

"I have received some news from Lady Lilley," said Lord Barrington after dinner, when they were enjoying port together. He pulled from his waistcoat pocket a folded piece of paper, on which was written, in a lady's hand, a lengthy message. "I thought, since we both have a connection to the person in question, that you might wish to hear it."

"Indeed, Sir?"

"It seems Frances is to be married."

Laurence's stomach lurched in a quick dip downwards, almost giddy, but it quickly turned to a leaden weight. There was no reason for this, of course. Miss Lilley was only an acquaintance, perhaps slightly more than that only by virtue of her connection to his uncle, and therefore they had spent more time together than might have been usual with other young ladies of his social circle, but there was no reason why he should...

He swallowed, realising that his uncle was watching him, waiting for an answer. "In-indeed? My felicitations, Sir, I know you are very fond of her, you must be delighted on her behalf. To – to whom is she engaged?"

Lord Barrington gave a half smile and referred to the letter before him. "A Lord Hosmer, apparently."

Laurence tried to bring to mind a Lord Hosmer from amongst the members of the *ton*, but the only person he could think of was… "The Lord Hosmer of whom I am aware is a marquis," he managed at last. "But he is – or was – at least sixty years of age, which is, not meaning to offend you, Sir, far too old for Miss Lilley. Is it his son?"

Lord Barrington's mouth twitched again. "No, no, it is the gentleman to whom you refer who is to marry her. Lord Hosmer has no heirs, I understand."

Laurence leapt to his feet, unable to keep still. He felt a need to walk about the room, or perhaps strike something or someone, though he was unsure what or whom, only that his hands had become fists and that his jaw was clenched hard. "She cannot possibly marry someone so old. You must forbid it, Sir!"

"I cannot do any such thing," replied his uncle. "Lord Hosmer has made her an offer, which it appears she has accepted, Lord and Lady Lilley are delighted."

"But it is – absurd – unacceptable – unthinkable that a young lady should marry a man in his dotage and be happy!"

"Perhaps she has decided that an older gentleman would suit her best after all. It appears Lord Hosmer is keen to have a young bride, as he has no heirs. She can look forward to the comfort of children and will be a companion to him in his later years, once there are no more… expectations of her."

The idea of Lord Hosmer, whom Laurence had once met at a ball, who had abominable breath, gnarled hands and a stooped back, having… expectations of Miss Lilley, as his uncle had so delicately put it, was more than he could bear, the very idea was disgusting. Laurence turned first one way and then another, pacing about the room. "You surely cannot think she would be happy Sir, that the marriage would be in any way suitable. It is a monstrous suggestion."

Lord Barrington leant back in his chair, his eyes following Laurence as he paced the dining room. "Your consternation in this regard leads me to ask whether you yourself had any intentions of marriage towards Frances."

Laurence stopped, stunned. "No, Sir."

"None at all?"

"She does not wish to be married, Sir, you know this yourself, it has been the subject of discussion between us more than once."

"I did not ask about her intentions, but about yours. Is there a part of you that had considered her as a possible bride?"

"No," said Laurence promptly. "She is… not…" He fumbled for the words he needed, but none of them were readily at hand. "She does not wish to marry, and for myself I would require a wife who is well versed in all social niceties, which Miss Lilley, begging your pardon, Sir, is not."

Lord Barrington nodded. "Quite so. But then it should not really concern you whom she marries."

Laurence swallowed. His uncle was right, of course. Every year, all kinds of unsuitable matches were made across the *ton*, and though some had raised eyebrows in the past, he had not felt this rush of emotions in regard to any of them. He had not known outrage, or anger, or despair or… or *jealousy*. And that was what this feeling was, it was jealousy. He did not want Frances married off to Lord Hosmer because he wanted her for himself. Odd, blunt, stubborn Frances. He wanted her. He stood silent for a few moments, then sank back down into his chair, legs weak at the realisation. Lord Barrington watched him closely, then poured him a glass of port, which Laurence downed in one gulp.

"Have you had a change of heart, dear boy?"

"I – I think so, Sir, I... had not realised it before but... yes."

Lord Barrington leant back in his chair, a warm smile on his face. "Well done. I am proud of you. An excellent choice."

"But..."

"But?"

"*Is* it an excellent choice? She is... very odd, Uncle. Would it be wrong of me to marry a woman who may not be able to fulfil her duties as Viscountess Barrington?"

"In what way might she not be able to fulfil her duties?"

"She will need to be a hostess, she will need to attend social occasions..."

"And do you doubt her ability to do so?"

"She does not care for small talk, she does not like balls. She..." He tailed off, remembering her unhappy face at Almack's. All that arose in him at the thought of it was the desire to comfort her, to take her away from whatever might cause her discomfort and instead bring serenity back to her countenance by whatever means necessary, and truth be told by comforting her he meant clasping her to him, brushing her lips with his and then... He shook his head. "She would shy away from company."

Lord Barrington nodded, his face grave. "When you imagine being with her, what do you think of?"

Laurence must have looked shocked, for Lord Barrington corrected himself. "I do not mean in the bedchamber, Laurence. I mean when you imagine your life together, what do you think of?"

Laurence opened his mouth and then hesitated, for he had been about to describe a *ton* marriage: the annual season in London, the summers hunting, with formal dinners and balls held at both Northdown House and the Surrey estate. But what had he really thought of? He had imagined…

"Holding her close," he managed at last, the words coming slowly but more surely as a smile grew on his uncle's face. "Our children about the fire at Christmastide, walking with her on an empty Margate beach when all the invalids have gone elsewhere, watching her when she is happy with her shells. Reading together, riding together, talking of what interests us. Sitting together in companionable silence with her head on my shoulder. Rowing with the children on the lake."

"There do not seem to be many other people in what you describe," observed Lord Barrington. "I do not hear mention of balls, of formal dinners. It seems to be you and Frances and your children, happy together at home. Is that what you long for, Laurence? After all your years in London?"

Laurence swallowed again at the wave of emotions that had risen up in him as he described their imagined life together. "Yes," he said quietly and then, more decisively, "Yes. I long for Frances and me to be together, quietly. I do not care if she does not want to be a hostess for grand dinners or balls, she need not force herself. I want only that she be happy at my side."

Lord Barrington's eyes shone and his voice came out hoarse. "Then go to her, my boy."

"What can I say to her? She has already made her choice."

"I very much doubt it was her choice."

"Her choice was not to marry at all, she told me so herself."

Lord Barrington leant forward in his chair. "Tell her what you just told me. Tell her how you saw the two of you. Ask her to imagine her future with Lord Hosmer and then with you. She will choose you, Laurence, I am certain of it."

"Over her own desire to be alone?"

"Few of us in this world truly wish to be alone, Laurence. We may choose to be so when the other options are closed to us or are made too difficult for us to bear. But all creatures of this world desire affection, to find safe harbour in the arms of someone who loves them. Frances may have seen no other option but to be alone. If she were allowed to be her true self, I think you would find that she would be a loving wife. Go to her, Laurence."

Laurence stood again. "I must tell Roberts. We will leave on the first post-chaise I can secure to London, Sir."

In the cold light of dawn Laurence climbed into Lord Barrington's carriage, which would take him to the inn where he could hire a post-chaise back to London. He looked out of the window to where Lord Barrington sat in his chair by an open window, his hand raised in a farewell which looked like a blessing.

CHAPTER 10
A Letter

L AURENCE ARRIVED BACK IN LONDON, STIFF IN BODY but excited in his mind. He had spent the eight hours of jolting carriage ride unable to sleep, instead gazing out of the window, going over and over his newly-found feelings for Frances. He revisited every moment of his acquaintance with her, from the first glimpse of her on the beach, when he might have thought her a maid, his startled surprise at her topics of conversation, which even now brought a smile to his lips. Her simple understanding of his uncle's romantic past and her fearlessness when caught between the tides, both of which made him admire her character. And between these recollections were other memories that stirred different emotions in him, that made him realise why he had grown weary of the married ladies of the *ton*, why none of this year's sparkling debutantes had managed to make any kind of impression on him. Her wide grey eyes framed with dark lashes, her chestnut hair tumbling down her back while at play with the children, her face, uplifted and eyes closed, while on her swing. And her bare legs, white against the dark rocks, strong against the swirl of water rushing across her skin. The things he could do to her once they were together, the pleasures they might share and then wake in one another's arms, no hurried secretive flirtation this but instead a deeper satisfaction.

Once inside his set at Albany, Roberts busy with preparing dinner, Laurence washed and changed before sinking down in a chair in the drawing room and pouring himself a port. On the sideboard was the post tray, with a letter on it. Glass in hand, he stood and made his way to it, picked the letter up. The writing looked feminine; he wondered if it was one of the married women he had dallied with over the past years, but something about it was not right. He lifted it to his nose but there was no perfume. As he lowered it, he caught the oddly shaped letter y and suddenly knew it for a letter from Frances. That oddly curled y, so like a shell, was her hand, he was sure of it, though he had seen it only once. But an unmarried young woman would never write to a young man, it would be impropriety of the highest order. He must be mistaken. He put the port down, carefully opened the letter and began to read.

Sir,

As it is your intention to marry soon, I will be so bold as to ask you, in the name of our friendship, to choose me as your wife.

Laurence's heart thudded. He took a step backwards, fumbling behind him for the chair. Finding it, he sank down onto it. His hand was shaking and he lowered the letter onto his knee, then continued reading in shocked disbelief.

You may have heard, perhaps from Lord Barrington, that I am engaged to Lord Hosmer. It was not my choice to accept him, it was forced on me by my parents who cannot imagine that a woman might not wish to marry and so have insisted upon this engagement. I acquiesced, thinking that such an old man might well die, leaving me a wealthy widow and able to live the life I would have chosen myself, alone and free.

He could not help it, he let out snort of laughter at her bluntness. No doubt many women had made just such a calculation, but they would have kept it to themselves. Not Frances. She was too honest for that, she might even have told Lord Hosmer to his face.

But as the day of our nuptials approaches…

When was the day? How much time was there left? Had he received the letter too late?

I find myself unable to bear the idea of becoming Lady Hosmer. We have nothing at all in common, which I might be able to bear, only that he has already said that he will "take me in hand" and force upon me such parts of life to which I am least suited.

And she might not even know, thought Laurence, what other things Lord Hosmer might force upon her. His stomach had settled into a lead weight.

And so I ask if you will marry me. I see now that I

cannot remain unmarried. I must marry, but I would rather be your wife than Lord Hosmer's.

Warmth rushed through Laurence, a sudden happiness. She loved him! She had realised it only recently, just as he had, but now that they had both realised their true feelings… He read on.

I know that you wish for a marriage of convenience, that love would not be part of our marriage, and this I willingly accept. I know that you think me odd, as most people do, but I can assure you that I am not without practical abilities. I will be able to run your household as you would expect, I am willing to bear children and care for them. You will not find me ungrateful. I will also fully understand should you spend much time away from the estate and maintain friendships with ladies of your acquaintance. I will not draw attention to such liaisons, nor in any way reproach you for them.

The tingling warmth was replaced with a sudden cold. She did not love him. She believed, as he had told her, that he wanted a loveless marriage, and she too wanted only a marriage of convenience. She would not care if he were to dally with other women, would in fact expect it and turn a blind eye. She offered a marriage, but not the one he desired.

If this arrangement were to suit you then I beg that you make haste and offer for my hand. I cannot break the engagement to Lord Hosmer without an alternative suitor, but if you are willing to marry me then I will curtail the agreement and we can be wed at once. I have begged to be sent to Margate on the tenth of this month to tell Lord Barrington the news as my parents hope he will be generous on the occasion of my being wed, but I am to be married soon after I return. Come to Margate. If I see you there, I will know you agree to my proposal. If I do not see you there, I will know it cannot be and will submit to becoming Lady Hosmer, but I beg you as a friend not to abandon me to such a fate.

I am yours,
Frances

The tenth… she had been in a carriage on her way to Margate even as he had come to London in search of her. Their paths must have crossed. If he had but stayed in Margate one day longer…

I am yours… but she was not. She would be his in name only. He did not doubt her word, honest to a fault as she was. If he married her, she would undertake to run his household well, to bear him children and to all lookers-on appear a devoted wife. She had accurately described all he had believed he wanted from a woman, from a wife.

But now he wanted more. He wanted tenderness and passion, he wanted love. And cruellest of all, he wanted those things with her, Frances. What would it be like to live side by side with a woman he desired and cared for and yet receive only dutiful obligation in return?

Unbearable. He would not do it, it would be a sham and a torture of a marriage. Even to lie with her… yes, certainly, he would do so, for she had agreed to bear him children, but he did not wish to lie with a woman who submitted to him out of wifely duty. He wanted his wife... he wanted *Frances* to welcome him to her bed with open arms, to seek him out, eager for the touch of his hands, his lips on hers, he wanted to hear her sighs of pleasure, he wanted to love her entirely and be loved in turn. No. He would not go to Margate. He would stay away, she would be married off and he would learn from this that a marriage of convenience was not what he wanted after all. Yes, his heart would be broken for some time but no doubt one got over these things. After some time he would find someone else to love and the sentiment would be returned. There were love matches amongst his acquaintances and his own parents had loved one another, it was not impossible. He would stay away, and she would marry Lord Hosmer.

She could not marry Lord Hosmer.

The thought utterly disgusted him.

Not only was Lord Hosmer old, and ugly, but he was not even kind. Frances would, apparently, be "taken in hand," as though she were a hunting dog to be trained by the master of the hounds, to be schooled to his command and punished for failures. Hosmer would shape her or, more likely, break her. He would not tolerate her bluntness, her rocking, her shells. He would beat them out of her, whether through words or the back of his hand or worse. Laurence would see her again one day at some social gathering and barely recognise her, a puppet on strings, moving at the will of her puppet master. The Frances he had grown to love would have gone, never to return. Even when Lord Hosmer died, which one could only pray would be soon, it might be too late. She would have been broken beyond repair, beyond rescue.

But he could rescue her now. He could save her from the dark fate hanging over her head. And if she could not love him, then she could not, but he could love her. He could love her and be close to her and perhaps, perhaps, she might grow to love him in turn. She had reached out to him, after all, she had turned to him in her hour of need, seen him as someone who might be relied upon to care for her.

He would not fail her.

"Roberts!"

"Sir?"

"Do not unpack my bags. We return to Margate tomorrow morning at first light."

CHAPTER 11
A Promise and a Bequest

FRANCES STOOD IN HER ROOM AT NORTHFIELD HOUSE and ran her fingers across the shells left on her windowsill. Lord Barrington had never collected shells in her absence, and anyway he was mostly confined to the ground floor. Who had placed these shells here in her absence? Could it be Mr Mowatt? Had he visited and thought of her, collected these and deliberately left them here for her? She ran her fingers over them one by one, held a few in her hand. There was something touching in the idea of his having done so. She had asked him for a marriage of convenience because she knew that was what he wanted, but if he had not been so certain on the subject she might have offered something more… not that she knew precisely what that might be, but she would have made the offer to explore what it might consist of. She liked him. Love? That she was not sure of, no, for surely it was supposed to be something wild and passionate, something all-encompassing. That was how people spoke and wrote of it. She had read Byron, she had heard the maids gossiping and even young ladies of the *ton,* sighing over beaus.

But she liked Mr Mowatt. She had found his company on their walks pleasant; he talked but not incessantly, and he listened to her with interest. Sometimes she shocked him, she knew that, but rather than be outraged or dismayed, he had asked more questions, like the day when she had told him of Lord Barrington's romantic past and he had given it some thought, she could see that. He had not treated Lord Barrington differently afterwards, which pleased her. When she had opened up about her feelings while they discussed the selkie women, he had looked at her strangely and after that walk had often seemed to pay her closer attention, but he had not refuted her feelings, had not chastised her for being odd and unable to behave as the *ton* would wish and expect.

Laurence. She turned the name over in her mind. Laurence. What would it be like to be closer to him, to call him by his Christian name, to spend their days together? To grow closer physically, as well, for the marriage would need to be consummated and she had a vague understanding of what that would entail. But they would walk together, talk together, he might hold her hand when helping her, they might be arm in arm. They might... kiss, she supposed. She wondered what that would feel like. She wondered if she should, if he did respond to her letter and come to Northdown, offer more than a marriage of convenience. She could say that she enjoyed his company, that she would be willing for there to be something more between them.

But she did not want to frighten him away. If he came, it would be in answer to her letter, and she had laid that proposal out very clearly. She had offered a marriage of convenience, no more or less, and he would accept or reject her based on that assumption. She must hold to what she had offered. If he came, the deal would be done. And then they could tell Lord Barrington. He would be pleased, she thought. He had been willing for Frances to be a spinster all her life if she so chose, but he was a romantic man; he would prefer to see her married, even if it were a marriage of convenience.

Lord Barrington had received Frances with every appearance of delight, but when dinner was served, he sat back in his chair and looked her over.

"To what do I owe this unexpected pleasure, Frances? I usually receive word from you that you wish for an invitation."

"You don't mind?"

"Of course not. I am always happy to see you. But these circumstances seem different than usual. I hope you have not run away from home? Your parents know where you are?"

"I have not run away," said Frances.

"I am glad to hear it. But?"

"But I have been made an offer of marriage which I am anxious to avoid."

"You could refuse the man…"

She shook her head. "My parents have decided I am to marry. If I refuse him, they might find someone worse… if there is such a person."

"Lord Hosmer is not to your liking?"

"You knew already?"

"Your mother wrote."

"Have you met him?"

"I am… aware of him. He is not a man I would ever choose for… anyone."

"He has been chosen for me and it seems I do not have a choice. Unless… unless I marry someone else."

"Is there someone else?"

She swallowed, nerves rising up again at the audacity of what she had done, what she was doing. The scandal of every part of it. Writing to a man was bad enough. Writing to a man to ask him to marry her… there could be no greater forwardness. Mr Mowatt would probably never speak to her again, outraged by her conduct.

"There might be, but I cannot speak of it until… until he has made his feelings plain on the matter."

"Yet you are here," said Lord Barrington. "Do you expect to meet him here, or to receive correspondence here?"

"I – cannot speak of it, Sir."

"Never mind, then," said Lord Barrington. "Eat, my dear, you look pale and thin. I cannot have your potential suitor believe you ill. Eat, and we shall speak no more of this until you wish to."

She picked at the food, unable to eat much when her stomach was balled up tight. By the end of dinner she had barely spoken nor eaten. Lord Barrington watched her rise and waved his hand towards the gardens.

"Perhaps you would like to spend time outside, my dear? It is too chilly for me still, but you younger souls are more robust. I will retire early, if you will forgive me."

Frances wandered the gardens in the gathering dusk, saw the delicate white cherry blossoms shining in the darkness, their petals brushing her hair as she walked beneath the branches. All around her was the scent of spring, the warming earth, the fresh grass and leaves, the delicate fragrance of flowers, all flavoured with the salted air. It should have calmed her, but even the swing could not manage that task tonight. Her hands shook, and little shivers ran up and down her despite the warm evening. She was desperate for Mr Mowatt to arrive and yet the idea of him being here was terrifying. It would mean she had to let go of all her plans for a happy future alone and bind herself to him, out of fear of marriage to Lord Hosmer. Had she been mad, to write to a man and ask to be his wife? What if he had read her letter and set it aside, scandalised at her brazen behaviour? If he had, then she was doomed to a marriage she found both disgusting and frightening. If he had decided to save her, however, he would come here, would tell her that he agreed to her rash proposal and then what? Would he marry her at once? He wanted a marriage of convenience; might he leave her here at Northdown and go about his life elsewhere? He had not arrived today; how many days would she have to wait before she knew that his answer was a no? She had told him the date by which she was bound to return to marry Lord Hosmer, but she did not know whether he would reply at once or after some time of consideration... or not at all? Perhaps, shocked once too often by her behaviour, pushed too far by the outrage of her writing to propose, he would simply not answer her at all, sever all connection between them and go about his life, scandalised at the very idea of marrying a woman who could do such a thing.

The dusk turned to night and still she sat in the gardens, unable to retire to her room, where she would feel even more locked into her swirling thoughts. At least out here, in the silent darkness, swinging to and fro, she could try to still her fear at the prospect of being forced to marry Lord Hosmer.

She was interrupted after an hour or so when a footman appeared bearing two lanterns. He did not speak to her, only hung one in a nearby tree and laid one near the swing.

"Thank you. I will put them out before I retire."

"Yes, Miss."

And he was gone again. The lanterns flickered, dimly lighting the small space around her swing. She supposed Lord Barrington had sent him out, a sign that she might stay out as long as she pleased. Why could he not have been her father? He would not have forced marriage on her, would have found a way for her to be a spinster if she so desired. She sighed. If Lord Barrington had been her father he would have let her remain unmarried, as he had, or else would have set his romantic mind to finding her a husband, and it would not have been Lord Hosmer. It would have been… She tried to think of any young men of her acquaintance whom Lord Barrington would have offered as a suitor. A young man, a man with prospects, a man with a kind heart and enough curiosity and open mind to consider an odd girl as his future bride, someone who would walk and talk with her along the beach, someone indeed like Mr Mowatt, but more romantically inclined, for Lord Barrington would not be able to stomach a marriage without love. In marrying Mr Mowatt, she would at least be marrying someone of whom Lord Barrington was fond, and she trusted his judgement. There might not be love in the marriage, but there might be affection, some care of one another and trust, a shared delight in their children? These things might be possible.

"Miss Lilley?"

She jumped to her feet, startled by the tall shadow approaching her.

"Mr Mowatt!"

He had come, he had come, he had come to her, had come here to Northdown, did that mean…

"I received your letter." He came closer, stepped into the

light. His clothes were rumpled from the journey, he looked weary, but his eyes were bright, there was an intensity to his voice.

She stood, the swing pushing gently at the backs of her knees, uncertain of how to proceed. "I knew of no-one else to whom I could turn," she managed at last. "I – I thought only of you. You have been – friendly – to me and so I believed that you might consider my offer, that you would not allow me to be forced into a marriage with Lord Hosmer."

"I would not allow that to happen to you," he said and there was emotion in his voice, something like anger at the idea, which emboldened her.

She stepped closer to him, so that they stood face to face, within arm's reach, looked up into his face.

"Then you will marry me?"

He hesitated and that frightened her.

She spoke again, anxious to secure him, to escape her looming future with Lord Hosmer. "As I said, I know that you wish only for a marriage of convenience, and I am happy to abide by that choice. I will be a good wife."

He opened his mouth to speak but she could not let him refuse her, she must make her plea now, or risk a lifetime of unhappiness.

"I know that I can be odd in my manners at times, but I will try harder, I will not disgrace you in the eyes of the *ton* or of our neighbours. I am willing to bear children, you have seen me with my nieces and nephews, I am fond of them. Our marriage will be everything you wanted to achieve." She stepped closer and now they were only a hand's breadth apart, she could feel the warmth of his body. Summoning all her courage she placed a hand on his chest where his heart was beating hard and fast below her palm. She did not want to be too emotional, he might not like it, but there was too much at stake, she must plead her case. "Marry me, Laurence." Her voice shook. "Please."

He looked down at her and slowly raised his hand, placed it over hers, warm over her cold skin. There was one last moment of hesitation and then he said, "I will marry you, Frances."

Relief swept over her, and she sagged. Her movement towards him was met with him pulling her into his arms, holding her stiffly as though surprised at the turn of events. He looked down at her, frowning, then lowered his face to hers and kissed her. It was a soft kiss, and then he drew back, looking into her face as though seeking something there. Frances only gazed back up at him, uncertain of what to do. The kiss had been tender and gentle, she almost wanted him to kiss her again so that she could experience that unexpected touch again and better understand it, better explore all the sensations it had stirred in her. But she had agreed to the marriage being one of convenience, and tender kisses were not part of that. Perhaps the kiss was intended only to seal the agreement between them, she did not know if that was a custom, something a man would be expected to do to agree a betrothal.

She stepped back and at once he loosened his arms, letting her go. She was right then, it had only been an acknowledgment of the agreement between them. Even though she had liked it, she must not expect such intimacies regularly, for this was an arrangement, not a love match. She would speak and behave more formally, so that he would know she was not trying to change his mind.

"I am grateful to you, Mr Mowatt. I am certain that our

marriage will be a good one, you will not regret your decision. And now I will leave you, it is growing late and you have had a long journey. I will ask the servants to bring you a tray for your dinner, so that you can be comfortable. I will see you in the morning. Goodnight."

He opened his mouth as though to speak but then closed it again and bowed. "Goodnight, Miss Lilley."

She walked through the house, checking more than once that she had behaved correctly. She had repeated her intentions to be a good wife. She had secured his agreement and accepted a kiss as confirmation, without in any way suggesting that she would expect further intimacies, returning to using his surname rather than his first name. She had thought of his comfort, withdrawing so that he might rest and arranging for him to have something to eat after his journey here. These were all the actions of a reliable wife, she thought. She had done her duty. There was a lingering sensation of disappointment, of something just out of reach but she supposed that was only because of her planned life as a spinster, which was now gone from her future. That was to be expected. She would set the feeling aside. It was better to be married to Mr Mowatt than to Lord Hosmer. She must make her peace with the sense of disappointment; it would fade, she was sure of it.

Laurence stood in the garden for some moments after Frances had left him. One of the lanterns, burning low, sputtered and went out, the other lantern flickering as a chill wind passed, leaving him in deeper darkness.

He was engaged to the woman he loved.

A reckless joy rose up in his chest, making him want to

shout out with happiness, but it was balanced by a cold chill that sank to his stomach like a lead weight. What had he agreed to? He was to marry a woman he loved... but with the agreement that there should be nothing romantic between them, that the marriage was to be only one of expediency: he had saved her from a wretched future, she was to provide him with a suitable wife and, one day, with heirs. That was all. Nothing more.

But her lips.

He had watched her from the door before he had approached her, seen her swinging back and forth, her face set with a worried frown. She had startled at his voice, then come to him, put her hand on his chest, made her case in a shaking voice that made him want to sweep her into his arms and hold her tightly, to promise that she would be safe with and loved by him, always. But that was not what she had offered. She would have been shocked by his change of attitude, might even have withdrawn the offer. He knew the life she wanted: to be left alone to gather her shells, the days passing in solitude. She did not really want a husband, she was simply afraid of the one being forced upon her. His only chance of having her by his side was to agree to what she had offered, to save her from a barbarous future.

He made his way back into the house and was met by the footman, who assured him that Miss Lilley had made good on her word, a tray was about to be sent to his room. She had asked for hot water that he might wash, and for one of the maids to put a bedwarmer in the bed to take off any chill.

He stood in his room and watched the steam rise from the water in the jug and basin. Frances was keeping her word, being a thoughtful wife. She would stick to her word, he was sure of it, but in that moment he would have given up the warm bed, the hot water, the fine meal, for one more kiss in the garden, just one.

She had moved towards him when he said he would marry her and it had made him reach out for her, take her in his arms and kiss her. He had not been able to help himself. But when she pulled back he had hastily let go of her and now he regretted it. He should have held her, have asked gently if she would in time consider something more between them.

Too late. The quick kiss would stand only as a token of their agreement, not the start of something more. Could he now begin a conversation to change the terms of their agreement, would that be unwanted? He considered going along the corridor to her room, to softly knock and say... but no, that would be ungentlemanly in the extreme, would frighten her and make her think him a liar and a breaker of promises.

No. He would leave it as it was for now. Once the marriage was done, he would try, perhaps, to suggest that there could be more. He would tread gently, he would not startle her with new demands. It was possible, after all, that after their wedding night, when intimacies had been shared in which she took pleasure, she might reconsider their agreement, might open up to his suggestion that there could be love and pleasure in their marriage. Yes. He must tread with care. He would behave with more formality, so that she could trust his word.

The next morning, Laurence woke late and found that Lord Barrington and Frances had already headed to the beach. He refused breakfast, taking only a cup of coffee, and then mounted Hippomenes, urging the horse to a gallop to the shoreline.

There he dismounted and found a boy to watch the horse, all the while scanning the sands.

He spotted them with ease. Frances, head down, the breeze playing with her skirts, making her way along the beach, which was full of visitors old and young. Some way off, Lord Barrington sat in his chair, his carriage nearby, the footmen in attendance. Laurence would go to him in a moment, but first he must see Frances, must touch her and speak with her, know that she was truly his betrothed, that he had not awakened from some strange dream.

"Miss Lilley!"

She turned at once and her face lit up with a smile that made his heart swell. He hurried across the beach to her, making his way past people. "Excuse me, good morning, excuse me..." until he stood before her. She was dressed in a pale frothy green dress, as though newly risen from the sea, her cheeks and lips pink, eyes bright, meeting his gaze directly, unlike that first time when she had kept her eyes lowered even when speaking to him.

"Mr Mowatt..." she began.

"Please call me Laurence."

She swallowed. "Laurence," she repeated, voice low. "Good morning."

It was not a dream. She had called him by his name.

"Frances," he said, panting with the dash of getting to her and the rush of emotions. He looked down at her lips and badly wanted to kiss her again, but her wide grey eyes seemed anxious and instead he took her hand and pressed it. He wanted to shout out loud, tell the whole world that she was promised to him. She was to be his bride and that was all that mattered. He wanted a witness of what had been agreed, wanted to make it real as soon as possible.

"We must tell Uncle, he will be very happy with the news."

Frances nodded. Her cheeks were flushed and when Laurence offered her his arm she took it without question. They walked along the beach, feet slipping occasionally in the soft sand. It took them a few minutes to reach Lord Barrington, whose head was reclined on a small pillow made for this purpose, eyes closed, resting in the bright sunlight. One of the footmen had been dispatched to Northdown to bring back a picnic for the midday meal.

"Uncle Barrington?" Laurence said.

"My boy?" he replied, eyes still closed.

"I – that is we – have something to tell you."

Lord Barrington opened his eyes and looked up at them. "Have you indeed?"

"Yes, Sir. We are to be married."

Lord Barrington's eyes creased into a deep smile and he stretched out both hands, taking a hand of each of them in his own and clasping them tightly. "Ah, this is happy news. I confess I had hoped for such an outcome when the two of you first met. As Sophocles said, one word frees us of all the weight and pain of life, and that word is love. I hope love will always smile upon you both and on your marriage."

"Thank you, Uncle," said Laurence.

"Thank you," murmured Frances.

"And it will be soon? The wedding?"

"Yes, Sir. I will visit Lord and Lady Lilley and then my father, there is no need for a delay."

Lord Barrington chuckled. "I believe my goddaughter is looking forward to getting rid of Lord Hosmer, Laurence, and quite right too. Besides, when your parents know that Laurence has asked for your hand, Frances, they can have no possible objection. He's younger and richer and a great deal better looking. And he may not have a title yet, but it will happen soon enough. I am an old man, and a tired one at that."

"There is no hurry on that front, Sir," said Laurence. "We hope you will be with us for many years yet."

"You're a good boy," said Lord Barrington fondly. "You will make an excellent husband to Frances here. And she will make you happy, I know it. Now, finish your shell walk for the day. This evening, we shall celebrate with some excellent champagne to toast you both."

Frances squeezed his hand and stepped away, walked a few paces from them and then stooped to pick up a shell. Laurence stayed by Lord Barrington, both of them watching her.

"You chose with your heart, and the heart is never wrong, Laurence, though it may seem it sometimes. The heart always wins."

Laurence nodded. "Can I push your chair, Sir?"

"No, Laurence, walk with your intended. I shall rest here for a while, enjoying the sunshine and the knowledge that the two of you will soon be wed. I am a contented romantic today. I shall bask in your reflected happiness."

Laurence gave him a bow. Let his uncle believe it was a love match on both sides. It would give him joy and there was no harm in it, after all. "We will not be long, Sir, the tide is coming in, the strandline will soon disappear."

"Like as the waves make towards the pebbled shore, so do our minutes hasten to their end."

"Shakespeare, Uncle?"

"Very good, my boy. Sonnet Sixty by the great bard. Now

go along, your future wife is waiting for you." He raised his hand and Frances waved back. He sat smiling, watching them as they moved slowly along the beach, before he leant back against the pillow and closed his eyes again, the sun shining down on his pale skin.

"He was happy," said Frances, as they walked on.

"He was," agreed Laurence. "I think perhaps he has been playing matchmaker to us for the past few months."

"Has he?"

He nodded. "Asking me to stay when you were already his guest, suggesting a house party to your mother and then sending me as his representative. And we had a conversation…" He trailed off, remembering how Lord Barrington had teased out of him what he really wanted, rather than what he had believed a marriage should be.

"He believes we are in love," said Frances, stopping to collect another shell. It clinked against the others in her basket.

"Yes," said Laurence. He looked at her pink lips, the curve of her dark lashes as she continued to look downwards, always seeking.

He thought of the kiss in the garden, how soft her lips had been. She had not been cold, there was warmth there, he was sure of it. She had looked up at him, lips parted and for a moment he thought she might lean towards him for another kiss but she had not. Perhaps she had been shy, it would have been her first kiss, after all, and she could not know he would be gentle with her. Perhaps he should say something now, to indicate to her that it was not his will that they be nothing but convenient spouses to one another. That he felt more for her, that if she felt the same, they could see what might grow between them, they could –

"Should we tell him it is a marriage of convenience?"

He swallowed, her bluntness hurtful. "Perhaps it is kind for him to believe it is a love match, if it makes him happy."

"I have never lied to him." She stopped, looked up at him, her grey eyes uncertain.

"It is not exactly a lie," he tried, uncomfortable under her direct gaze, unable to think of the right words to say. Why was it so easy to utter witty words of seduction to a married lady who desired him, but impossible to find words of real affection for Frances? He did not want to frighten her away by suddenly declaring his love for her, when she believed there was to be only a cool agreement between them. He must proceed gently, to see if she would come closer to him, would learn to love him in her own time. "We are… friends, are we not? We are… fond of one another?"

"Yes," she said, then looked down again, moved a few steps further along.

He watched, drinking in the sight of her, her steady gaze, her total attention to the search, heedless of the breeze playing with her bonnet ribbons, the way her skirts ruffled about her. Any other woman would have kept up a constant stream of chatter, mostly about herself: her hair, the need for a parasol, fear of the gulls, and other such nonsense. But Frances walked as though in her own world and Laurence had a great desire to find a way into that world, to walk within it at her side, even if in silence. He lengthened his stride to reach her and took the handle of her basket, eager to offer some assistance, to find some way to be part of her activity.

"Let me carry them for you."

She looked up in surprise, but then nodded and let go of the basket, even as a shout came from behind them and they both turned to see the footman Benjamin running across the beach, trying to get their attention.

"Come at once! Lord Barrington is unwell!"

Laurence shoved the basket of shells back into Frances' hands and set off at a run, his feet struggling against the soft sand. He reached the chair and the slumped figure of Lord Barrington and bent over him, touched his face and then held his wrist.

"He is dead, isn't he?" he asked, already knowing the answer.

Benjamin nodded, speechless.

Frances appeared by his side, her breath short with running. She looked down at Lord Barrington's face, his eyes closed, his face peaceful. "His heart was growing weak, like his legs."

"How do you know?"

"He kept saying he was tired."

"Did our news... was it too much?"

She shook her head. "He was happy. He died happy."

There were tears in Laurence's eyes, real distress at the loss. She put one hand over his, uncertain of how to comfort him, but wanting to show that he was not alone.

He nodded at the gesture, then cleared his throat and addressed the footman. "Benjamin."

"My lord?"

Laurence stared at him, then realised. He was Lord Barrington now, the title had left in his uncle's dying breath and drifted across the sands to him, before the footman had even seen what had happened and called for him. He tried to gather his thoughts. He must take care of everything now, there would be a funeral and a will, an estate to take over, many responsibilities that would fall on his shoulders. One thought above all others shone out. He must take care of Frances. It was not necessary for her to attend the funeral, few women attended such an unpleasant event, and he would be occupied for some time. The wedding would have to be postponed while he settled into all that the new title and position would demand of him; besides which it would not be appropriate to marry too soon after his uncle's demise. He would ensure she was safe and cared for until he could claim her. She must not be troubled by anything, must stay with her family where she could be looked after until he could return to her side. There were already too many busybodies along the shore, staring and whispering; he had no wish to subject her to further discomfort.

"Benjamin, take Miss Lilley back to Northdown and arrange for her safe travel back to London."

Frances stared at him. "Back to London?"

He nodded and took her hand. "I will have many things to do here and then at Ashland Manor in Surrey. It will be best if you are with your family."

"But I –"

But Benjamin had already waved over the driver, who swiftly brought the carriage close to the promenade and, apprised of the situation, made haste to let down the steps, while the footman stood waiting, his hand held out to help Frances in. She looked to Laurence, but he was speaking with the second footman, Andrew, directing him to secure the services of a funeral director at once, while he stood guard over his uncle's body. Slowly, she stepped into the carriage. He came to the window as the footman took a seat next to the driver.

"Benjamin will take care of everything," he assured her.

"You will be safely back with your family in no time, and I will take care of everything here."

He touched her hand where she clutched at the window frame, then bowed and stepped away, gesturing to the driver, who cracked the whip, the carriage moving smartly away from the promenade, the horses urged to a brisk trot.

The next few hours passed in a bewildered daze for Frances. Deborah exclaimed over the death of Lord Barrington and swiftly packed. Benjamin kept the carriage waiting to take them on the first stage of the journey, to where a post-chaise could be secured that would see them arrive in London late that night, the longer days thankfully allowing for later travel. For most of the journey Frances feigned sleep, for her thoughts were a jumbled whirl of confusion and distress and everything about her – the noise of the wheels, the chatter of Deborah, the endless rocking and jolting, all caused wave after wave of nausea which she was hard-pressed to swallow back.

Lord Barrington was dead. Her kindly godfather, in whose eyes she could do no wrong, was gone and she had seen him only for a moment, had not been able to bid him a proper farewell, although she was glad to have seen his face peaceful. And now Laurence had sent her back to her family with unseemly haste, hurrying her into the carriage and now back to London with barely a word. He had said only that he would "take care of everything here," but what did that mean? They had made no firm plans as yet – he had not said when he would call on her parents to make a formal offer for her hand in marriage. Was she to break off the engagement with Lord Hosmer when she reached home, which might not even be accepted without proof of another suitor for her hand? Or wait until Laurence made her a formal offer?

Halfway to London a sudden horrible thought struck her. No-one but the two of them knew of their agreement. Lord Barrington had known, but he was now dead. None of the servants were aware of it. They would not be able to confirm her claim that she was now engaged to Laurence. There had been no betrothal gift, she had no ring or other item to show from him. Had Laurence regretted his promise, and then seen a possible way out of it? By bundling her back to her family he could, if he wished, now avoid the entire question, for a lady could not simply claim that a gentleman had proposed to her without any evidence to that effect, nor any word from the man in question.

London was a continuing whirl of social events and Frances was hard pressed to avoid most of them, for even grief did not excuse her from as many occasions as she would have liked. Lord and Lady Lilley were very sorry to hear of Lord Barrington's death. They had considered him a trustworthy influence on Frances, and he had treated her well. But he had been an invalid for many years now. It was to be expected that he might meet an early end and therefore they were not about to halt all their plans for mourning, and that was an end to it.

Frances kept away from them, from their well-intentioned pity and comfort which she did not find comforting in the least. They asked briefly after Laurence – now Lord Barrington of course – and she did not know how to tell them what had been agreed. She could not bring herself to say that she had written to him, that she had proposed marriage to a man she barely knew, that he had met her at Northdown House and agreed to a marriage of convenience between them. It would sound like a concoction, a fairytale, in fact an outright lie to save herself from Lord Hosmer, for Laurence had sent no word back with her, had made no public promise except to a man who was now dead.

Her parents would be appalled at the idea that she had done such a thing and would demand proof – and what proof could she offer from Laurence? She would have to wait for him to come to her, to visit her parents and declare himself. She could only hope that he would come soon, while her mother talked of the trousseau for the upcoming wedding to Lord Hosmer and Frances tried to stall her, claiming a headache so that she did not have to attend a fitting, coming late to break-fast so that there was little time to discuss floral arrangements. But the preparations continued, for Lady Lilley was not about to allow Frances to avoid them altogether, and so she had no choice but to discuss lilies of the valley and roses, with no in-terest in either.

The sweet smell of white lilies filled the gallery in Northdown where Lord Barrington had been laid out. Neighbours and local acquaintances had visited to view him and in a few short minutes his body would be taken away by the funeral directors, for the funeral would take place the next day. Laurence stood, looking down at the white face, the gnarled hands clasped to-gether in a saintly pose.

"Are you ready for the coffin to be sealed, Sir?" The funeral director hovered behind him.

"Yes," agreed Laurence. A sudden thought came to him.

"No," he added abruptly. "One moment more, please, I must fetch something…"

He hurried from the room and into what had been Lord Barrington's study. Sat at this desk in the last few days, Laurence had found something in a small locked drawer, which he now removed, placing it carefully in his pocket and returning to the gallery.

"If I could have a moment longer alone?"

"Of course, Sir."

Alone, Laurence removed the miniature from his pocket and looked at it. Lord Hyatt in the bloom of youth, a happy smile on his face, warm brown eyes alight with love for Lord Barrington, for whom the miniature had no doubt been a gift. Now he placed the tiny portrait between the cold hands where it could not be seen, in memory of the happiness the two young men had known together. Tears rose unbidden in his eyes. He had to clear his throat and compose himself again before summoning the funeral director and watching the coffin being sealed, Lord Barrington and his true love hidden from the eyes of the world for the last time.

"Barrington's funeral's taken place," said Lord Lilley at breakfast when Frances had been back two weeks. He looked through the letter he had received. "In Margate, a small affair, which is what he wanted, apparently."

Frances looked up, heart thumping. "How do you know?"

"Letter from the new Lord Barrington."

"He wrote to you?"

"Yes. Says reading the will is next and he will be sure to let us know if there are any bequests concerning our family, that he will try to deliver them in person if there are, as he wishes to call on us, to pay his compliments."

"So kind," murmured Lady Lilley. "He seemed a most gentlemanly person, very attentive and polite."

Frances sat in silence. He would call on them, he meant to come soon. She would wait then, she would wait longer so that he might come and explain everything. She would be safe.

She did not feel safe. The wedding was fast approaching, and her mother had decided she should be married from Woodside Abbey. They were to leave London and travel there, travel further away from Laurence and towards the bleak future that had been planned for her with Lord Hosmer. Time was running out fast and still no word, no visitor, no further communication came.

Laurence threw another crumpled piece of paper to the floor in disgust. How was it that he, who had always had a ready quip for a lady, who had written dozens of Valentines and other love notes (always, of course, discreetly anonymous), could not pen a letter to Frances, his future wife, whom he loved and cared for? Everything he wrote seemed either plain and business-like, which he did not want to be, or else too like a lover, which might frighten her. He had started and crumpled a letter to her almost every day since they had parted.

The first had been a tender letter, to share her sadness about their beloved Lord Barrington, mentioning the gratitude that filled him for his uncle's kindness and his bringing them together that they might be happy, ending by promising to come to her very soon. But that had seemed overly sentimental and of course he was coming to her as soon as possible, that went without saying. He had written on other days – of the sadness of the staff at Northdown House but their happiness in knowing he and Frances were to be wed and that she would soon be their mistress, for they were all fond of her. Of neighbours and family who had shared warm reminisces about Lord Barrington, his kindness and generosity to all those who came within his circle of influence. Of the day when he had watched the coffin being sealed, having done what he could to honour Lord Barrington's love story.

But every letter had something wrong with it and while he was searching for a better way to express himself some interruption would come – a request to meet with the steward, visitors proffering condolences, his man of business, even his family – and so another day would pass without a letter being sent. His days, once so leisurely, were now not his own, for as the new Viscount Barrington there was much to be done. No sooner had the funeral in Margate taken place than he'd had to set off for Ashland Manor in Surrey, the main estate, to meet staff and steward, look through accounts, answer questions, receive neighbours, and more. He barely ate breakfasts, snatching only a coffee from the waiting hands of a footman, perhaps some bread and ham at midday and by the evenings he was too tired for a fine meal, preferring a tray sent to his room.

But he thought and planned for Frances. He told the staff they would soon have a new mistress and spoke with the housekeeper to see if she were an easy-to-manage person. Finding her a kindly and experienced woman, he explained that Frances would need her support in learning to run a household and that all should be done as she desired, but without taxing her too much, especially as a new bride. His rooms had been Uncle Barrington's and they were comfortable enough for now, but the rooms which should belong to the Viscountess must be refurbished in the very latest style for Frances. He had a fashionable married cousin whose opinion he trusted come to stay and asked her, as a gift to him, to make the rooms as comfortable and luxurious as possible, but everything should be done in haste, for he must visit Frances soon to claim her hand.

He read his uncle's will and nodded at the various bequests that had been made, giving orders that Frances be told at once.

His father came to visit him at Ashland Manor. "I am proud of you, son," he said, when Laurence explained all the work he had been doing. "It is good to know you'll do the same when I'm gone."

"Don't be in a hurry, Father," said Laurence. "I'll be needing your advice and guidance. I'm to marry as soon as I can arrange it. Wait until we have given you some grandchildren, at least."

His father patted him on the back and cleared his throat huskily. "I have something for you," he said and pulled out a tiny leather box, in worn red leather. Opening it revealed a simple gold band. "Your mother's. She wore it all her life, but made me take it from her hand in her last days when she was unwell. She said your future bride should wear it."

Tears stung Laurence's eyes as he took the little band out of its box. It was such a simple thing, but he could not recall his mother's hand without it.

"Perhaps she would like something grander," said his father.

"She is not a grand person," said Laurence. "I have never seen her wear any jewellery. This is perfect, Father. Thank you."

His father smiled. "Your mother was not grand either," he said. "A shy little soul when I first met her, but she came out of her shell over time, and I loved her more each time another part of her emerged."

The letters Laurence did manage to write were sent mostly to the docks of various ports, making requests for shells from any part of the world, large or small, and promising generous payment for them to any sailor who could oblige him in creating a collection worthy of Frances' approval.

The young man he had engaged for the task did not seem very prepossessing to Laurence. A slight stoop, watery eyes peering anxiously through thick glasses, feet never quite still, so that he seemed to be constantly swaying.

"You are to correctly label and display a collection of shells which I have accumulated. They are currently still in the boxes and packing crates in which they were delivered. My footman James will show you the room they are stored in and be at your disposal in unboxing them and placing them correctly. The display cases have been commissioned and are almost complete, there is only a final coat of paint to be applied. I will be away for a few weeks but will expect to see all in readiness on my return."

"I will do my best," said the young man. "Are you yourself an expert in shells?"

"I know nothing about them." Laurence smiled. "They are a wedding gift."

He would have stayed longer to discuss his plans, but he had to meet with Mr Morling, the solicitor managing the bequests of his uncle, one of which was to be delivered to Frances. Laurence had wanted to take it himself, but there were other urgent matters of business and being absent for several days would not be advisable. He tried to pen her a letter, but once again the words seemed wrong and he did not wish to detract

from Lord Barrington's final words to her. It seemed disrespect-
ful. He comforted himself that she must know he would be
with her as soon as he could and that, by discharging all his
business matters and having everything at Ashland Manor in
readiness for her, he might bring forward the wedding despite
the mourning period. It would have to be a quiet affair, but he
did not think she would mind that.

A week later, Deborah woke Frances earlier than usual.

"A Mr Morling is here with news of your godfather's will.
He came by carriage."

Frances washed and dressed in haste and made her way into
the drawing room, where her parents sat expectantly gazing at
a soberly clad man, who stood and bowed to Frances as she
entered. "Miss Lilley."

She took a seat between her eager parents, both leaning
slightly forwards.

"As goddaughter to the late Lord Barrington, may I first
proffer my condolences."

"Thank you," Frances murmured. Her voice was very small
in the large room.

"You should know that the estate and title have naturally passed on to his chosen heir, the son of his sister Cecilia.
Laurence John Charles Mowatt has changed his name in
honour of his uncle as planned and is now Viscount Barrington.
He has taken control of his estates, chiefly comprising Ashland
Manor in Surrey, as well as other properties and lands further
afield, such as Northdown House and Park in Margate."

Her parents nodded. Frances waited. Was this how she
would receive confirmation that Laurence still intended to

marry her? By a black-dressed solicitor? She had agreed that the marriage would be one of convenience, but this seemed formal even by the terms of their agreement. She swallowed.

"However, the late Lord Barrington also left certain bequests which I have carried out as his representative. Naturally each has been read and approved by the new Lord Barrington, and he has made no objection to any of them. There were sums of money to loyal servants, and so on, but also some larger gifts to those for whom the late Lord Barrington had a particular affection. His two nieces have received five thousand pounds each."

Frances could all but hear her mother's mental calculations. Was Frances, not being connected by blood, to be given a smaller amount? Or a larger one because she was a particular favourite, visiting him so often?

"The late Lord Barrington made special mention of Miss Lilley in his will. He left her ten thousand pounds."

There was a sharp intake of breath from Frances' mother.

"Very decent of him," declared Lord Lilley. "A very generous gift."

Frances knew her mother was practically dancing. She had already been promised twenty thousand by her father. A total of thirty thousand pounds would make Frances a very wealthy bride. As a married woman she would have one thousand five hundred pounds a year. There were minor male members of the *ton* with less money to call their own.

"There was another gift," went on the solicitor. "It is a more personal gift."

At last. Word from Laurence. Frances' shoulders dropped with relief.

Mr Morling hesitated. "It comes with a, er, poem."

Lord Lilley frowned. "A poem?"

"A poem from the late Lord Barrington to be read to Miss Lilley on the occasion of the gift being placed in her hands."

Was this the declaration? Was it a betrothal gift from Laurence? But no, the gift was from her godfather, Mr Morling had just said so, and so was the poem.

From his satchel Mr Morling withdrew a large round flat black leather box as well as a folded thick sheet of cream paper. Lady Lilley stiffened. The box was undoubtedly a jewellery box.

"May I have your permission to read the poem aloud, Lord Lilley?"

Her father nodded. "Certainly."

"Ahem. 'For whatsoever from one place doth fall, Is with the tide unto another brought: For there is nothing lost, that may be found, if sought.'" He checked his notes. "Edmund Spenser, *The Faerie Queen*." He passed the box to Frances. "Miss Lilley. This is now yours."

Carefully, Frances undid the clasp of the box to reveal, laid out on blue velvet, a magnificent pearl parure. A gleaming tiara was shaped into repeating scrolls which looked like the waves of the sea, each one holding a beautiful round pearl, the central one in a teardrop shape. She touched one of the scrolls and the delicate movement set off a trembling of the dangling pearls so that the tiara seemed to come alive, as though the waves were in motion, the pearls being brought to the shore.

There was a necklace, made up of three strands of white pearls, with an extremely large teardrop pearl pendant hanging in the centre. Earrings echoing the teardrop shape of the pendant, and two triple-stranded pearl bracelets.

"It is exquisite," breathed her mother. "Perfect for a wedding."

Frances knew she should say something effusive, but the words would not come. The beauty of the jewellery and the generosity of the money had all been obscured by the crushing disappointment that Laurence had not come to her, had only sent this formal obligation, this dutiful carrying out of a will. She tightened her grip on the box to stop her hands shaking. "There was nothing else?"

Mr Morling looked surprised at Frances' question, as much as at her seeming lack of enthusiasm. "Were you expecting a particular bequest? An item you had been promised?"

She shook her head. There was a ringing in her ears and her throat was very dry. "There was nothing else?" she repeated. "Nothing at all?"

"Frances, really," hissed her mother. "You have been granted a most generous bequest, far above anything we might have expected." She addressed Mr Morling. "We are most grateful to his late lordship as well as to the new Lord Barrington for his generosity in following his uncle's wishes. We will write to him to express our gratitude, won't we, Frances?"

Frances stood and the pearls fell out of the tumbling box, landing on the carpet, exciting gasps and exclamations behind her, a scrabbling to find and return them to their protective lining as she left the room in a daze, unheeding of her name being called behind her. She made her way into the hallway, where a footman hesitated as she turned first towards the stairs to her room and then towards the front door, springing to open it for her as she chose the door. She walked outside and then, her feet knowing her better than her mind, began to run, stumbling at first and then, grabbing at her skirts, faster and faster, every footstep painful, the gravel pressing against her kidskin slippers until at last she veered away from the path and onto the lawn, running and running until she came to the waterfall and the temple, falling to her knees to climb the steps, then rolling onto her back to stare up at the ceiling, at the spiralling shells, desperate for their soothing nature to bring her comfort.

But the swirling shells became the sea and her godfather's choice of poem went round and around in her head, confusing and yet containing something within it she could not make out. *For whatsoever from one place doth fall, Is with the tide unto another brought: For there is nothing lost, that may be found, if sought.*

What did it mean? Something falling and coming to another place with the tide? But then it referred to something lost and to be able to find it, if one *sought*. That something lost could be found if one would only seek it out. Like her shells, of course, the way she sought them out, brought to her on the tides. Perhaps he meant only to poetically refer to her love of shells in offering her a parure of pearls, which were found in shells. Lord Barrington had always been poetic. But there was something about the poem that seemed to refer to more than the shells…

There was little point dwelling on the poem. Lord Barrington was dead and buried, his generous bequest would have been made long ago in a study with a dry old lawyer in attendance, the poem only intended as an extra flourish, a nod beyond the grave to Frances' passion for shells. He would have smiled to have found a suitable quotation, for he had prided himself on such things.

No, the pain was because there was nothing else. There was the money. There was the exquisite jewellery, for even Frances, who cared little for such things, could see its delicate shining beauty. There was the poem, a kindly-meant last nod from her godfather.

But nothing from Laurence. No letter. No word. Not even a verbal message from the lawyer to say that he would follow soon, or even the promise of a letter or visit as soon as his affairs were more settled. Nothing. Only the money and the jewellery, his uncle's wishes carried out to the letter. He would have listened to the will and heard her name and felt... what? Nothing? A sigh at the additional task that must be carried out to complete the terms of the will? A resentment at the generosity of the bequest to someone who was, after all, not even a blood relation? Or perhaps a twinge of guilt at the hastily made promise of marriage to help out a friend... no, only an acquaintance... later regretted. Perhaps he had felt the smallest of twinges and then decided that such a generous sum of money, as well as the jewellery, would amply ease his guilt in the matter.

He had not meant it.

He had not really wanted to marry her.

That was the cold hard truth, and it was a truth Frances must face now. The cold shiver that ran across her skin had nothing to do with the marble floor beneath her. He had said yes out of gentlemanly politeness, perhaps even out of duty to his uncle, and then had regretted it, would have been relieved when Lord Barrington died that there were no witnesses to their pledge. He was a viscount now, heir to not one but two estates, one of which had immediately become his. A rich viscount who would only grow richer when his father died. Plain Mr Mowatt, who had been a pleasant young man with excellent prospects, was now Viscount Barrington and the mamas of the *ton* would be falling over themselves for his attention. He would be presented with an endless parade of young women, vastly better suited to the position of Viscountess Barrington than Frances. Women who could converse with ease, who enjoyed social occasions and could arrange them. Who would appear at parties on the Viscount's arm, elegant and polished, who would dance without counting under their breath and not creep away mid-evening to a space under the stairs where they could be soothed by their odd collection of shells, sheltered from the chatter and lights and perfumes of the ballroom.

Slowly Frances sat up, cold humiliation seeping into every part of her. So be it. Laurence was gone. She had lost him and, she thought bitterly, the poem was entirely wrong in this regard, for she had sought him out and believed herself saved and yet now he was lost to her after all. So much for Lord Barrington and his fanciful notions. So much for friendship. She was alone, must face marriage to Lord Hosmer and a life she had so far evaded, a life she had thought herself clever enough to have escaped by calling on the only man of her acquaintance who might be in a position to save her. She had risked her reputation, she had reached out to him and he had failed her. She would not trust in him again, nor trust any man to rescue her. She would not endure the humiliation of writing to him again, to be met with silence or an outright rejection of her claim that they were engaged. Lord Barrington was gone and Mr Mowatt had taken his place but not honoured their agreement. She was alone. Only her godfather had stood by her. Even in death, he had given her an escape plan which she now intended to put into action.

Dinner that evening was silent, as Lord and Lady Lilley considered Frances' behaviour dreadful and Frances was too busy thinking, but the next morning brought the unwelcome sight of Lord Hosmer, descending from his carriage.

"Would you like your best frock on?" asked Deborah, trying to keep up appearances.

"No," said Frances. "My worst."

"But Lord Hosmer is here…"

"Exactly. The brown."

Deborah looked appalled. The brown cotton was a dress Lady Lilley would only countenance if Frances was going to play with the children outdoors. It was a plain dress in an ugly colour and did nothing for Frances' looks, making her appear like one of the under maids rather than the daughter of the house. "Are you sure, Miss?"

"The brown," repeated Frances. "And no ringlets."

All too soon a footman came to inform Frances that her parents had gone out for a walk in the gardens and that Lord Hosmer was waiting for her in the drawing room.

Frances took a deep breath and went downstairs, rehearsing her words carefully, so that there could be no doubt whatsoever of her meaning.

Lord Hosmer stood in the drawing room, his walking cane in hand, tapping it impatiently on the floor. At the sight of her, his grey brows folded into a deep frown.

"Is this the way you present yourself to your husband, girl? Devil take it, that is not how you will dress when we are married. You look like a maid, and a slovenly one at that. You'll be dressed in silks when we marry, and wear the Hosmer jewels, or I'll know the reason why. I expect a marchioness to look like a marchioness. I know your mother didn't tell you to dress like that, for she turns herself out well enough. Done it to spite me, have you? Insolent girl." He gave a huff. "Well, no matter,

I promised to take you in hand and I shall. You'll not get away that easily." He waved a piece of paper at her. "Special licence. Your mother has been drivelling about a society wedding but I'm glad I said no, looking at the state of you. No. We'll be married tomorrow morning in your chapel and that'll be an end to this nonsense. We'll travel to my home without stopping for a wedding breakfast. It'll take us three days as it is. Your parents have gone for a walk in the gardens, no doubt to allow me to court you, but there's no need for all of that sentimental claptrap."

There was a rushing sound in her ears, a thumping beat in her chest, but Frances licked her dry lips and opened her mouth, the first of her planned words coming out as a whisper so that she had to start again. "There will be no…. There will be no wedding. I refuse to marry you, Lord Hosmer. I never gave my consent to begin with and I do not give it now. If you drag me before a clergyman I will protest that I am unwilling and I will not repeat the vows." She had said the words, had remembered them all, had stood her ground and now it was done.

Lord Hosmer's face turned crimson with rage. "How dare you, you insolent slip of a girl? You will do your father's bidding and mine and there will no more of this disobedience!"

Her legs were shaking under her but she stood her ground. "I will not marry you."

He struck out at her with his cane, catching her in the knees. "I will teach you a lesson! You *will* obey me!"

She stood still, staring at his red face, hearing his angry breathing, her legs stinging from where he had struck her. And then she lunged forward and snatched his cane from his hands. Startled, he stepped back and half-lost his footing. His cane came whistling down on his shoulder, hitting it with a solid thump and a cracking sound. He cried out, then stared in amazement as Frances let go of the broken cane, turned and grabbed a vase full of flowers. She tore out the elegant arrangement, throwing it to the floor, before dousing him in the face with the cold dirty water inside and then hurling the vase to the ground, where it smashed, splinters of glass scattering across the room.

"What is the meaning of this?" he roared, but Frances hardly heard him, the rushing sound was all around her, she could not see anything but the piece of paper held in his hand, the dreaded document that would see her sworn to this man, and she wrested it from his hand and flung it into the fire, where it flickered for a moment before a quick flame rose and the special licence was gone, falling into ashes as they both stared at it.

Lord Hosmer turned to shout at her, but Frances was already screaming at him, stepping closer and closer until she was barely a hand's breadth from him, standing on tiptoe to make herself taller.

"You are a monster! A vile beast with the manners of a guttersnipe, whose wives died because they couldn't bear life with you – what makes you think I would ever – *ever* – be one of them? No woman in her right mind would marry you, no woman would want your stinking breath on her face and your clawing hands on her body! Get out of my sight. Get OUT!"

He reached out to grab at her shoulders but again she was too quick for him, putting both hands to his chest and shoving him backwards, then turning and running to the door where she looked back for one moment, taking in the sight of Lord Hosmer, soaked and red-faced, fallen back on the sofa near the ashes of the special licence in the grate, the carpet wet where he had stood, the floor scattered with shards of glass and crushed flowers. Then she ran to her room and slammed the door behind her, clambering onto her bed, clawing at the covers. She pulled them over herself entirely, covering her head so that she could shelter in the darkness.

From below she heard raised voices, then angry feet, a door slamming and the wheels of a carriage driving away. Then a silence that lasted hours. Her breathing slowed at last and her eyes closed as exhaustion claimed her.

It was dusk when Deborah crept into her room, after a tentative knock at the door which Frances had not answered.

"Are you alright, Miss?"

She crept out of the rumpled sheets. "Has he left?"

"Yes, Miss." Deborah closed the door behind her and hovered over Frances, her face anxious.

"Has he given up on the marriage?"

"Yes, Miss. He told your father he wouldn't have a lunatic like you as a wife, that you'd taint his family line. Begging your pardon, Miss."

Frances sat up in bed. "He said I was a lunatic?"

Deborah lowered her voice to a nervous whisper. "I heard him talking to your parents, Miss. He said that you were quite mad and should be locked away. He even gave the master the details of a Doctor Morrison and said he was a doctor who was experienced with lunatics and would take care of you somewhere private without any scandal to the Lilley family name. He said he's sent a sister of his into Doctor Morrison's care and she was much better for it."

A chill ran down Frances' arms. "They did not listen to him?"

Deborah looked uncertain. "Lord Lilley put the card in his pocket," she whispered. "Should I try to find and destroy it, so he don't try to use it?"

It was like a fog, trying to think. Frances shook her head slowly. "I don't want you to get into trouble," she said. "But I must speak with my parents before they think about what he said for too long. Thank you, Deborah."

Deborah nodded, her face still anxious. "I did have hopes about that nice Mr Mowatt," she said. "He seemed gentleman-ly, and you spent so much time together in Margate. I thought perhaps when he was made Lord Barrington –"

"Thank you, Deborah," interrupted Frances, unwilling to hear anything complimentary about Laurence Mowatt at this moment.

She made her way downstairs to the drawing room, which had been tidied, although a damp mark still indicated the area of carpet where Lord Hosmer had stood. She sent a footman to find her parents and when they came to the drawing room she sat opposite them, took a deep breath and said, "I need to speak with you both. It is about the money from my godfather."

CHAPTER 12
A House by the Sea

LORD LILLEY WAS IN A FOUL TEMPER. HE HAD ALREADY consulted his lawyer, but that had made things worse, for the lawyer had agreed with Frances, saying that the money from the late Lord Barrington was now hers to do with as she pleased, and that as she was of age she could indeed set herself up in a small house by the seaside, as she had always wished to do, and there was really very little Lord and Lady Lilley could do about it. Lord Lilley could, of course, hold back the money that would have come to her on her marriage, forcing her to live on only five hundred pounds a year, the interest from Lord Barrington's ten thousand pounds, and indeed he was minded to do just that, but an objection arose in the unexpected form of Lady Lilley.

"She cannot live possibly on five hundred pounds a year," Lady Lilley had wept. "She will have only two servants and will not be able to keep a carriage. She will be laughed at. *We* will be laughed at. It will bring the Lilley name into disrepute. People will think she is a mad old maid in a hovel."

"She *will* be a mad old maid in a hovel," stormed Lord Lilley.

"Not if she is rich," countered Lady Lilley, showing a finer understanding of human nature than her husband. "If she is rich, they will think she is eccentric, but they will respect her. If she has her marriage portion as well as Lord Barrington's bequest, she will have a fine townhouse and be able to keep a carriage and six servants, including a footman. It will be far more respectable."

"So I am just to give twenty thousand pounds to her so that she may be a rich old maid? We should have married her to Lord Hosmer when we had the chance. Damn Lord Barrington and his meddlesome ways." Lord Lilley fumbled in his waistcoat pocket and frowned. "Where's that doctor's card Hosmer gave me? I swear it was here."

"That is unthinkable," said Lady Lilley, shocked. "Lock her up in a mental institution? Your own daughter?"

Lord Lilley grumbled something under his breath about it being the best place for such a harridan, but the spirit had gone out of him. "Surely with thirty thousand you can find someone for her?"

Lady Lilley nodded miserably. "But she has been through four seasons and no respectable young man will want her by now except for her money alone and what sort of young man would that be? A gambler? A drunkard? One who cannot manage his own affairs?"

"Could try abroad," grunted Lord Lilley.

Lady Lilley looked appalled. "I would not want her married to a foreigner. They wouldn't understand a word she said."

"That might be for the best," said Lord Lilley, but his temper had lost its force and Lady Lilley, sensing defeat and the subsequent acquiescence to come, only sighed and said that Lord Lilley must do what he thought was right. She further hinted that having Frances settled would mean they could turn their attention to a bride for their son without constant comments about their unmarried daughter, which put Lord Lilley in a better mood.

There followed a week of heavy silence at mealtimes and all three members of the family keeping their distance from one another in-between. Frances rocked in her chair and lay under rotunda's shell ceiling, but none of it brought any solace. Lord Hosmer was gone, which had lifted one burden, and it was likely that, at some point, she would in fact be allowed to become an official spinster, but still a heaviness sat over her, weighed her down, her thoughts turning grey each time she tried to gaze into the blue skies above and hope for better days to come. Laurence had forsaken her, and though it should not have hurt her heart, it did. Had she loved him? She was unsure. But she had hoped. She had allowed hope to rise up in her as they had spent time together, at the touch of his lips to hers. Each of these had led her to believe that there could be, might be, something between them one day. That something tender might grow. And she had wanted that more than she had thought, had hoped for it, only to find the promise turned to nothing in her hands, his true character revealed in the cold light of day after that twilight kiss.

When her father sent for her at the end of the week, she braced herself for yet more haranguing. Instead, he waved her to a seat, face bitterly determined.

"I have found you a house in Margate," he said heavily.

"Since you have spent so much time there, I assume you will want to be located there."

Frances' stomach clenched. Margate was forever tainted for her now, partly with sad memories of losing her godfather, but mainly because of Laurence. If she lived there, would she meet him unexpectedly and have to act as though they were only acquaintances, with no mention of what had almost been between them? But her parents knew nothing of that; they would probably expect herself and the new Lord Barrington to be amiable neighbours. Carefully, she inclined her head.

"Very well. It is called Belle Vue Cottage, a newly built house, very respectable and well made. It has been furnished simply for now, enough to be lived in while you decide what furnishings you would wish for it to have. Your mother will choose your staff and naturally Deborah will go with you. It will be rented at first, in case you should come to your senses." He sighed. "If you persist in wishing to live there, it can be bought." He stopped and waited for her to react.

"Thank you," said Frances. "I am grateful to you for arranging it."

It was true, but it was no longer exciting. She had imagined this moment for the past few years and always it had seemed thrilling, a new start, a life of her own, free of restrictions and other people's disappointments in her. Now it was a cold inevitability, the only possible course for a woman like herself, a woman unable to behave as the *ton* demanded.

Her father waited, as though expecting more, then sighed again and said that Lady Lilley would travel there with her to see her settled in. "It will be best to get it over with."

It was not a grand house, but it was smart enough to satisfy her mother, a newly-built square townhouse in an empty field, set back from the main town.

"You will need a gardener," her mother said, surveying the space from the safety of her carriage. "A proper lawn, some hedges, a rose garden…"

Frances said nothing, watching the footmen carrying in such limited items of furniture as she had chosen. It looked bleak even to her eyes. When she had imagined having her own garden she had thought of the gardens at Northdown House, full of fruit trees and flowers, the swing under the majestic oak. Not this patch of wild grasses and churned up soil from the building of the house. Inside there were empty rooms, one after another, each one more echoing than the last. A morning room, a drawing room, a dining room. Downstairs, a kitchen. Upstairs there were bedrooms, the servants' quarters. Lady Lilley twittered about wallpapers and fabrics, about the right kind of furnishings, until Frances could bear it no longer. She had already chosen the plainest possible items presented to her, shaking her head stubbornly at Lady Lilley's sighs of disappointment, insisting that no, she did not want a dining table that would seat ten, that she did not even wish to furnish two of the four bedrooms, leaving them empty and bereft of any decoration.

"I suppose you will keep your shells there?" tried her mother but Frances only shrugged. She had very little enthusiasm for her life as it was to be here, in spite of all the years she had spent daydreaming of it. And meanwhile there was gossip that Northdown House was closed up. It seemed the new Lord Barrington was spending all his time at the main estate in Surrey. So there could not be any chance meetings, even if she had wanted them. Clearly Laurence wanted nothing to do with any memories of Margate.

Trunks of clothing were unloaded, as well as a few crates of essentials: china, kitchenware, bedding. She would have a gardener, a footman, a cook, Deborah, two maids of all work and a groom-driver to go with her small carriage. Laundry could be sent out or extra girls brought in to help on wash day. This was enough to satisfy Lady Lilley that Frances would not be laughed at or made fun of, but the truth was she would still be an oddity in the area. There was no getting around that.

And the move was done.

Lady Lilley shed tears as she left, but Frances remained dry-eyed as she watched her mother's carriage leave, standing at her bedroom window until the road was empty. Then she sat down on her bed and wondered what should happen next. She had lived all of her life in a house where she was told what to do, what to wear, what to say, and now all those choices were hers to make. She tried to feel elated, but there was only numbness. It had all happened so fast. Just as she was beginning to have feelings for Laurence, he had been swept away from her and now she would be alone for the rest of her life. She had not thought, before, how lonely that would feel.

Deborah was of little comfort, for she was evidently sulking, her face set in a permanent scowl. This bare house and silent life must seem a distinct come-down in the world to her. She would have hoped as much as Lady Lilley for Frances to make an advantageous marriage, for it would have elevated her, as lady's maid, from the attendant to the younger daughter of a grand house to the place of the mistress' personal maid, one of the highest positions she could attain.

"It's dreary, Miss, if you don't mind my saying," she said one evening as she helped Frances to undress. "There's to be a ball at the Assembly Rooms next week. I saw the notice in town. Wouldn't you like to attend and make some friends round about these parts, if you're intending to stay? Unless you've changed your mind," she added hopefully.

Frances shook her head. "I will stay here," she said. "But I do not wish to make acquaintances. I wish for a quiet life." She would make this new life work. She would start, and it would develop as she had always planned.

The days went by very slowly. She would rise, breakfast, then take the carriage down to the beach and look for shells, return for a midday meal, spend her afternoons looking over or cleaning the shells, sorting them into types, reading about them. Then she would dine early, refusing to dress for dinner, which made Deborah pout, and then read some more before retiring. It was the life she had planned made real, it was everything she had dreamed of and it was... dull. It was too quiet, too repetitive. It was... lonely. She tried to think what else she had imagined that she had forgotten to incorporate into her days, but all that came to mind were the walks in the gardens at Northdown, with Lord Barrington speaking of philosophy. Or... or Laurence. Their walks and talks together, his occasional shock at what came out of her mouth. But he had never turned away from her. He would be shocked, and then reapproach her, ask questions, perhaps challenge her or agree with her. Her days were now spent in silence to such an extent that her voice was hoarse when she spoke for lack of usage and Deborah urged her to drink a warming tonic.

Frances had been there two weeks when she received a letter from her cousin Lady Andrea, asking if she could come and visit, as she would be travelling nearby to visit an aunt in Whitstable before returning to her father Lord Sabin. Frances sent back an eager letter inviting her to tea, and on the appointed day spent much of the morning fussing about the arrangements, which she usually left to the cook.

Lady Andrea sat in the drawing room and looked about her as Frances poured the tea.

"I hope your new life suits you?" she asked.

"Yes," said Frances promptly. She passed Lady Andrea her cup and sipped from her own in silence. Then, setting the cup back down, she shook her head. "No. I thought it would but I am – I am lonely." It had come out too fast, without her being able to stop herself, the cold truth of her new life.

Lady Andrea set down her cup, her wide eyes anxious. "I am so sorry," she said. "But it is not too late. You could still marry…"

Frances shook her head. "No-one would have me," she said flatly. "I am a spinster now and I have chosen my path." She swallowed. "It is not so bad. I have servants, I have a house, I have a carriage. I can gather my shells. I have the things I always wanted."

"But they do not make you content?"

Frances shook her head, a slow doleful movement. Swallowed, so that the brewing tears would not fall. "It is not how I thought it would be. I thought I wanted this, but I…" *I thought for a moment that I had glimpsed something else, another future, but it disappeared, like water trickling out of my hands.* "It was not to be," she managed at last, and kept her eyes low so that she would not have to see the pity in Lady Andrea's kind face.

Laurence had sent word of his arrival at Woodside Abbey a few days prior to his arrival, so he was surprised at the coolness of his reception. There was much formulaic politeness, of course. Condolences on the death of his uncle, congratulations on his new title and estate. Inquiries as to the health of his father and two sisters, who had both recently given birth to healthy babes. Tea was served. Lady Lilley was an attentive hostess, Lord Lilley was affable. But Frances was nowhere to be seen and neither of her parents were treating him as their future son-in-law, only as a pleasant acquaintance.

"I have been remiss in making my way here," he confessed at last, hoping to prompt them to be more forthcoming. "There was so much to be done after Uncle Barrington died, you understand. The funeral, the estates... but that has all been managed now and so I was free to fulfil my promise and come here."

Lord and Lady Lilley looked baffled by this declaration, but both nodded politely.

Laurence looked about him. "Is Frances here?" he asked at last.

Lady Lilley frowned. "Do you mean Miss Lilley?"

Laurence was lost. Surely he was allowed to refer to his betrothed by her first name? Perhaps Lord and Lady Lilley were peculiarly strict. He sat straighter. "Yes, I beg your pardon, of course I meant Miss Lilley. Is she... will she be joining us?"

"My daughter has recently... set up home," announced Lord Lilley.

Laurence stared at him. "Set up home?"

"Yes."

Lady Lilley tried to make this odd decision seem more acceptable. "Our daughter is very fond of the sea," she began, trying out a well-rehearsed speech for the first time. "And she has preferred... that is, she chose to establish her own household by the sea, so that she might benefit from the health-giving benefits of – of the sea air." Her cheeks grew pink with the effort of making this seem normal behaviour.

"But…" Laurence could barely form the words, he was so thrown by this information. "She never told me that she would be doing such a thing."

"Why would she tell *you*?" asked Lord Lilley, leaning forward and frowning.

"Because I do think as her future husband that I should have been told of this decision, even though I cannot claim to understand it at all."

There was a long silence.

"Am I to understand you correctly, Sir," said Lord Lilley at last, "that you believe yourself betrothed to my daughter Frances?"

"I… asked her to marry me," began Laurence, deciding it was best not to reveal that in fact it had been Frances who had proposed to him, "and she agreed. We told my uncle; he knew of it before his death." He swallowed, thinking of the sudden turn of events. "He died soon after, and I did not think it suitable for her to attend the funeral. I sent her home where she would be taken care of while I put his affairs in order and took on the responsibilities of the title…" He came to a stumbling halt as the truth dawned on him. "She did not *inform* you of our betrothal?"

Lord and Lady Lilley's stunned expressions and slowly shaking heads confirmed he was correct.

"But – but where is she?" A sudden horror took hold of him. "She did not – you said she set up her household – you did not allow her to marry Lord Hosmer?"

Lord Lilley shook his head and Laurence let out a sigh of relief. "Then where is she?"

For a moment they all stared at one another again, before Lady Lilley spoke. "In Margate, of course."

The Lilleys and Laurence spent a further hour in hurried and disjointed conversation, attempting to understand one another. From this Laurence came to understand that no, Frances had told them nothing of their agreement, that she had appeared upset and distracted, had then lashed out at Lord Hosmer when he had come to claim her before insisting that she be allowed to take the late Lord Barrington's bequest and set up home alone.

"I must go to her at once," he said at last. "I do not know if she has changed her mind. But my offer stands. I wish to marry her."

The carriage ride from Woodside Abbey back to London, the restless night he spent in his Albany rooms and the subsequent day's journey to Margate were the longest two days of Laurence's life. Unhappy thoughts chased around and around his mind. Had he not been clear enough with her? Had she thought him so shallow as to retract his word to her? Had she been too afraid to tell her parents? He reproached her a thousand times in his mind, but under it all there was reproach for himself, too. He had hurried her away without clear instructions. He had not written to her, however much he had tried. He had been gone from her side too long with no word, not even a letter to her father stating his intentions. It was clear that she had not trusted him, had waited and waited, before giving up on him. She had been brave enough to refuse Lord Hosmer and then she had taken what little of her pride she could, along with her bequest from Lord Barrington, and gone to live the life she had always dreamt of.

For the last few miles to Margate, Laurence carried a dead weight of dread in his stomach. Frances now had what she had always wanted. She was a committed spinster, her dowry had been disbursed, she was free to live entirely alone for the rest of her days. What if she no longer wanted him, no longer needed him? She had begged him to rescue her and he had failed. Perhaps she had decided she was well rid of him and would close the door in his face, refuse to speak to him, their betrothal null and void.

"Do you wish to stop at Northdown House, Sir, and freshen up before seeing Miss Lilley?" Roberts asked at the last staging post they came to.

"No, I must see her at once," said Laurence. "And besides, the house is closed up, there will be hardly any staff there."

"As you wish, Sir."

"You will drop me at Belle Vue Cottage, then take the carriage up to Northdown House, rouse the staff and tell them to make ready for me."

"Yes, Sir."

The sunny day had faded to twilight and Frances had come back from the beach and spent an hour or so reading, although she had not turned many pages. Her eyes wandered from the book, looking about the room, before she tried again to pay attention to Donovan's fourth volume on shells, which was failing to have its usual calming effect on her.

A sudden pounding at the door made her jump. It was an ill-mannered way to announce oneself, more suited to the back door for deliveries of coal or vegetables than the front. Who could it be? She did not have many visitors, especially after the dreaded Mrs Pagington had insisted on paying her a call in her first week and they had sat in chilly silence for half an hour, after which social calls had noticeably diminished.

The pounding came again. Frances had been used to dozens of servants, the door would never have been knocked on more than once. But here, with only half a dozen servants, sometimes callers had to wait longer. Idly curious after a boring day, she made her way into the hallway, but there was still no servant to answer the call. Sighing, she pulled it open herself.

Laurence.

He stood before her, his clothes rumpled from the journey, hair dishevelled beneath his hat brim, eyes red-rimmed with tiredness.

She stared at him before he broke the silence between them.

"Frances. Why didn't you trust me?"

Unable to speak, she took a step backwards, but he followed her, coming close to her.

"I promised to marry you and you never told your parents, you set up –" he stared about him, "this – a – a home of your own without telling me, without…" He stopped. "Do you want to marry me, yes or no?"

A wave of relief and joy rushed up inside her and she nodded, a silent acquiescence, before bursting out with rage. "You – you did not write! You sent me away without our promise being made public – no-one knew of us, I could not claim you were my betrothed without proof. What would people have thought of me? And I – I waited and waited and you did not come and I thought –" She gave a little sob as the distress came pouring out of her. "I – thought you meant to forget all about me."

Laurence stood before her, chastised. "I am truly sorry, Frances," he said. "I did not think how it would seem to you, how it would feel to you. But I thought of you every day – I tried to write to you but it always went poorly – and I planned for us, for our marriage, I went to Woodside Abbey to claim you –"

"You went to Woodside? To my parents?"

"Yes. It was dreadful. They knew nothing of me, they treated me as if I were a madman."

Frances uttered a tiny gasp of laughter and he seized the opportunity. "I am sorry, Frances, I humble myself to you. You will still marry me, fool that I am?"

She nodded again and he dropped his hat and gloves and pulled her towards him, kissed her lips softly and whispered, "Thank God. I thought I had lost you."

She pulled away, straightened her back. "I stand by my promise to enter into a marriage of convenience with you. I am sorry to have doubted you." She must make it plain that she had not simpered and pined for him, not let her feelings show, the overwhelming relief, the desire to have the kiss last longer, else he would think she expected more than had been agreed between them, and she had come so close to losing him once, she could not risk it again.

He stiffened, then nodded. "I am glad we are agreed," he said. "I will go to Northdown House now, and expect to meet with you in London in a week's time, to arrange our wedding."

She watched him go from the window, then sank into an armchair, trembling with the violence of emotions coursing through her, understanding for the first time, but too late, that she had fallen in love with Laurence and yet was now bound to a marriage of convenience.

CHAPTER 13
Viscountess Barrington

THE WEDDING PREPARATIONS WERE UNDERWAY. A RE-
lieved Lord Lilley was determined that his youngest and
final daughter to be married should have a sumptuous wedding. Lady Lilley, both delighted and amazed that Frances was
finally to be wed, and to someone as eligible as the new, young,
rich and handsome Lord Barrington, was equally determined
that the wedding should be magnificent, as much a reproach to
any who had doubted her daughter's prospects as any desire to
celebrate the marriage itself.

"I don't want…" became Frances' useless refrain, as her
mother ordered yards of white silk and Brussels lace for the
wedding dress, flowers in absurd quantities to decorate everything from Frances to the wedding breakfast table and the
dining room itself, as well as a bride cake of vast proportions,
to be decorated all over with shells moulded from icing and
then gilded.

"But you love shells! And besides, it is too late now. It has
been ordered and they have carved the moulds for the shells
just for your cake."

Then there was to be a flower girl to scatter rose petals, "at least six" bridesmaids and Laurence's carriage would be repainted for the occasion, his new coat of arms proudly displayed on it.

It all sounded too much to Frances, but she was so overwhelmed with relief at Laurence having come for her, for his promise having been kept after all, that she bowed her head and allowed the preparations to whirl giddily around her, even though none of it was what she wanted. She would have been glad of a simple wedding, she and Laurence in a quiet chapel, silence around them so that she might listen to the sacred words that would bind them together, to have the opportunity to pray that he might, in time perhaps, come to love her. This huge bustle seemed very much the marriage of convenience that they had agreed on: full of show and pomp without any true meaning at all and it made her fearful that, having begun this way, it could only ever stay that way between them. Her worry was made far worse by a talk that Lady Lilley delivered, late one evening, coming to Frances' bedroom and telling Deborah to leave.

"Now, Frances, I must speak with you," began Lady Lilley, her pale cheeks blushing pink. "About your wedding night and... and future intimacies between you and Lord Barrington."

Frances thought of how he had kissed her twice, how both times she would have liked more, how warm his hands were, his heart beating when she had laid her hand on his chest and begged him to marry her.

"Yes, Mama," she said, hopefully leaning forward, ready to receive any guidance that Lady Lilley might be able to bestow which might bring her closer to Laurence.

Lady Lilley swallowed. "So, you must submit to your husband whenever he sees fit," she began, clearing her throat twice before continuing. "That, you see, Frances, is how children are... begat," she managed, reaching for a suitably biblical word to help her.

Frances nodded. "I would like children," she said. "And Lord Barrington will expect them."

Lady Lilley looked relieved. "Indeed," she more confidently. "Quite right and proper. So, on the night of your wedding, and on any other night, your husband will come to your bedchamber, and you will... submit to him."

Frances nodded, hoping that more details would be offered.

"And it is most important," said Lady Lilley, swallowing and then clearing her throat again, "that, as a well-bred lady, you should not in any way behave... wantonly."

"Wantonly?" Frances was not sure what was meant by this word. The only time she had heard a woman described so was a maid who had promptly been dismissed.

"You need not worry," Lady Lilley assured her. "You need only keep very still and silent, and all will be well. You can close your eyes."

"Still and silent?" repeated Frances uncertainly.

"Yes," said Lady Lilley. "Submit to your husband and stay still and silent throughout the... the act. That way he will know that you are a true lady and be pleased with you. Then he will leave the bedchamber and you... well, Deborah will come to you and help you clean yourself."

"Clean myself?"

"Yes," said Lady Lilley, standing up with evident relief at having got through the entire explanation. "Goodnight, Frances."

Frances was full of questions but they did not seem suitable, so she only nodded. "Goodnight, Mama."

The door closed behind Lady Lilley and Frances sat and thought for a while. She had received no real guidance, but one phrase stood out to her. That Laurence would be pleased with her if she remained still and silent. She wanted very greatly to please him, to make him happy, to perhaps make him love her. She would do as her mother had instructed.

Laurence was excited. All the turmoil and sadness, the nonsense and misunderstandings of the past few months were about to be swept away, leaving him with a fresh new start and a happy life to look forward to. He was a viscount and his estates were all in sound order. He was about to marry Frances and, if he could persuade her, their marriage might become more than one of convenience. Yes, there was the fuss of an overly lavish society wedding to be got through, but once that was done, he could make Frances happy, he was sure of it. In quiet moments, alone, he thought of her wide eyes, her soft lips and that shocking but erotic glimpse of her thighs. He would teach her all he himself had learnt in the bedchamber for their mutual pleasure.

On the morning of the wedding, Frances was roused before dawn to be bathed and dressed, her mother hovering over the servants, making even her accomplished lady's maid nervous, while faithful Deborah was demoted to an assistant, fetching and carrying. Frances submitted to being dressed in a gown of white silk trimmed with Brussels lace, topped with a pelisse in white satin trimmed with swansdown. The cold pearls were slipped around her neck, her wrists, the earrings poked into her ears, the weight of them pulling at her lobes. Her hair must be curled. Hairpieces would not do for so important an occasion, Lady Lilley decreed, and so she must sit still while the ringlets were carefully teased into position, then topped with the magnificent tiara, from which a delicate veil was draped.

The carriage took her to St James' church in Piccadilly, for no society wedding could fail to be held there and Frances wilted at the noise and bustle of dozens of carriages, followed by the whispering rustles as everyone took their seats, the overpowering scent of vetiver, the stylish perfume of the moment, bringing on a wave of nausea.

She barely heard the words spoken over them, managed a faint, "I will," when a silence fell and she was stared at expectantly, held out her hand as the ring slipped over her third finger, then wrote her name. She would have liked to have clung to Laurence, but that would indicate too great an intimacy between them and she did not want him to think her presumptuous. Instead, she only lightly rested her hand on his arm as they accepted well wishes and returned to her new London home in Grosvenor Square, Barrington House, for the wedding breakfast.

More than sixty diners gathered together in the ballroom, which was decorated with flowers and a table laden with every agreeable dish suited to the occasion, from rolls, butter, tongue and ham to hot chocolate and buttered toast, cakes of every kind, the bridecake itself sitting, gold and white, in the very centre. There must be cutting of it and tasting the heavy fruit cake, while many toasts were drunk to their health and to the marriage.

And then it was over.

All the fuss, all the endless noise and smells and tastes, the constant kissing and shaking of her hand. All gone. Now she was alone and at last she could rest.

Except that she was not alone. She was in a strange house, full of unknown servants and, above all, a husband.

"Deborah can take your bonnet and pelisse," said Laurence. "Then we can go to the drawing room."

Silent, she nodded and Deborah hurried to undo the bonnet and lift it away from the precious ringlets, unbutton and remove the pelisse. Frances would have liked her to have removed all the pearls as well, but that would be thought of as odd. She followed Laurence into the drawing room.

"We will travel to Margate in a few weeks' time," he began, and saw her face light up. He gave an anxious laugh. "Although I should warn you, we have also been invited to a ball held in our honour."

Frances stiffened. "A ball?"

He nodded. "At the Assembly Rooms, it is themed to be a Pearl Ball." He might as well tell her the worst of it. "There will be over a hundred guests and our hostess is Mrs Pagington."

A vast ball at which she, as a new bride, was to be the guest of honour. A ball at which everyone would stare at her and expect her to be the perfect Viscountess Barrington, would judge her manners and behaviour, her grace or lack thereof. Laurence watched her downcast face. He had failed her, though it would have been impossible to have refused without causing offence. He wanted to make light of the ball, to find some humour in their hostess' overbearing manners, but the look on Frances' face left him silent.

They ate a small quiet nuncheon, neither having much appetite after the lavish wedding breakfast, before climbing into the carriage to drive to the Surrey estate, a matter of four hours. For much of the journey Frances closed her eyes and pretended to be asleep, for any familiarity or friendliness between them seemed to have gone, lost in polite formality.

Ashland Manor was a grand old building. Once a Tudor castle, its various owners down the years had updated it and added to it, so that now it was comfortable and elegant inside, if something of a hodge-podge of styles on the outside, but it had a charm of its own and vast gardens which spoke of the late Lord Barrington's love of nature. Frances thought she might be happy living here for the greater part of the year, once she had grown used to it.

Laurence helped her down from the carriage and past the overwhelming sight of over a hundred staff waiting to greet them, his hand tightly clasping hers as they entered the manor, for which she was grateful. He led her up the grand staircase and along a corridor.

"These are your rooms," he said eagerly, throwing open a door.

Frances looked around the bedroom, which had a dressing room and parlour off to the side. She nodded. The room was freshly decorated, she could tell, but it was too much for her tired senses. There were strong colours and patterns, as well as the overpowering smell of perfumes and soaps set out on her dressing room table. It was not a restful suite of rooms.

"It is... lovely," she managed. "May I see downstairs?"

"Of course," he said, excitedly. "There is something special I had arranged for you."

She waited, silent. Her sisters would have made squealing noises, would have gasped or begged to know what it was. To them, receiving a gift was always exciting. But gifts made Frances anxious. She did not know what they would be and she often did not respond appropriately to them if she did not much care for them or was uncertain. She had seen the disappointment from gift-givers too many times, when they looked at her blank expression and frowned or seemed put out at her lack of enthusiasm, an enthusiasm her sisters always displayed, even if afterwards she would hear them dismiss a gift they had declared "delightful," or "enchanting".

"Come, it is downstairs."

She trailed behind him to the drawing room, which was very large and decorated in a pale duck-egg blue, a light and airy room with delicate furniture and a sumptuous fireplace in white marble. This room was not too overbearing. More full of trinkets than she would have chosen herself, but the colour was restful to her eyes. She hoped she might rest here for a while, in silence and peace, for the day had been exhausting.

"There."

Laurence gestured behind her. She turned and was confronted by a vast cabinet which took up most of the wall. It reached as high as the ceiling and the upper part was glass fronted, while the lower part had many small drawers.

Frances stared. In the uppermost tiers, safe behind the glass, were all manner of huge shells, each larger than a man's hand, some as large as her head, of many colours and shapes, all of them clearly from foreign shores.

"Open a drawer," said Laurence.

She reached out in a daze and pulled at the closest handle, which caused a wide but shallow drawer to open, displaying, beautifully presented, row upon row of pink-tinged shells, from those smaller than her little finger's nail to ones almost as large as her hand.

"And another," said Laurence.

She pulled at another, hardly able to see, dizziness coming over her. This drawer was arranged by shape, focusing on those shells which curled inwards on themselves, creating whorls and spirals.

"I spoke with sailors from all over the world," said Laurence. "I had them bring me anything they had to add to the collection and have commissioned more to come."

Frances stood silent. A wave of tiredness swept over her. The shells were... they were... she did not even have the words, only that she could not bear any more of these surprises, new experiences, new expectations. The burden of being the new viscountess was building higher and higher above her, about to come crashing down. She had a desperate need to be alone, to have silence around her, to have no-one looking at her, least of all Laurence, whom she loved and wanted to make happy, yet could not seem able to do so.

"Do you like it?" he asked, a note of anxiety creeping into his voice.

She did not answer.

"I thought having a collection like this would be a talking point for you when guests visit us," he tried again, explaining. "Is it – do you not like it?"

"No," she said.

"Why?"

She swallowed, found the words she had been searching for. "My shells are... private. They are not for others, they are not... a pastime or fashionable accomplishment. They are..."

she could feel herself growing dizzy again, could feel, shame-fully, tears welling up, her voice wavering, "… mine. They are *mine*."

Laurence's face showed nothing but bewilderment. He half-gestured to the towering cabinet. "They – they *are* yours, I had them brought here, the cabinet made – all for you. They are yours."

The tears overflowed, drip-dripped onto her cheek and then the floor before Frances ran, out of the drawing room, through the hallway and up the stairs, mistakenly turning first left and then right along the corridor to her rooms, the door slamming behind her into Laurence's face who had followed her.

He stood silent outside, then put his hand on the door.

"Frances? Frances!"

He could hear her sobbing, followed by an incoherent speech in which he heard the word shells more than once, but it did not sound as though she were even speaking to him, rather speaking to herself, repeating what had upset her.

"Frances! I am coming in."

He heard a wavering, "No," from inside and hesitated, but then turned the handle and entered the room. Frances was slumped on the floor, face resting on her dressing table chair.

Frances buried her head still further into the chair. How to explain to him? Even in the whirl of other emotions there was the hot flush of shame. Laurence had spent not just time and money but care in collecting such extraordinary shells and having them placed inside the beautifully made cabinet. He had tried to do something to make her happy and she was weeping. It was ungrateful, but the desolation came from him not understanding her at all. The shells were her world, her passion and comfort. They were not, never had been, a pretty pastime to flaunt to the world. They had never been something others understood the way she did. People would exclaim over how pretty they were, before their eyes glazed over and they would pass on to something else, some other more important topic of conversation, the latest fashions, the latest gossip. The shells were a secret part of herself and Laurence did not understand. Why was his lack of understanding so painful? After all, she had never cared whether her father and mother understood about the shells , nor any of her siblings, and so it had not hurt when they did not.

But there was something about Laurence, she now realised, that had made her want to share the shells with him. He had walked the beaches with her, had offered shells he had found, had listened. He had, during the house party, understood something she had not even known herself, which was that if she thought about shells she could dance, could find grace and rhythm within herself without the constraint of social rules and the niceties expected of her. He had made her his wife and she had thought happiness might lie within her reach. But this kind gesture brought the illusion crashing down. The shells he had collected and displayed for her were a talking point, a pretty, fashionable pastime for a viscount's wife, something to impress visitors, not part of her private world. And she did not know how to explain it to him, how to reject his gift in a way that he would understand. How could he? He had done what he thought was kind, and generous, and he was right, would have been right had Frances been any other woman. Any other woman would have embraced him, would have thanked him and shown off the gift as a mark of her husband's care of her, his love for her.

The heat of shame flooded through her again, the inability to be as others were. She had failed again. And now he was her

husband. A husband who would shortly expect her to… Lady
Lilley's worried face and paltry lack of details when explaining
how Frances should behave on the wedding night and indeed
what was to occur, had not been in the least reassuring, but
Frances was determined to do her wifely duty, such as running
the household and bearing children and if bearing children
meant lying still and allowing the new Lord Barrington to do
as he pleased, then that was what she would do.

She sat up. "I am sorry. I am just… very tired." Weary to
the bone was what she wanted to say, but Laurence was trying
so hard to please her, she did not want to distress him further.

His face cleared at once. "Of course. Of course. I should
have thought. It has been a very long day and what with the
travel and everything… Shall I have them send up a tray for
your supper? Deborah can attend you and then you can sleep."

"But…"

"But?"

She swallowed, her cheeks turning hot. "It is our… wedding night…"

He shook his head, smiling. "It can wait, Frances. We have
all of our lives together. You need rest."

The next day progressed more smoothly. Appalled by how
badly the first day of their marriage had gone Laurence had
given strict instructions not to wake Frances, to allow her to
get as much sleep as she needed. He inquired of Deborah what
kind of breakfast her mistress would most like and had hot
chocolate and buttered toast sent to her room as soon as she
wakened. He hovered downstairs until she presented herself,
when he had hurried her away from any staring servants and

instead took her for a walk around the gardens, which she seemed to enjoy. They ate a light midday meal outside, the better to enjoy the warm spring day, and then he took her in an open-topped carriage for a drive around Ashfield Manor's estate so that she might get her bearings and see her new home. He carefully suggested she might like to rest again in the afternoon, before welcoming her to dinner, ensuring there should not be the overly-formal seating she had once objected to, the two of them instead seated opposite one another at one end. There were rabbits with onions and collared mutton, an asparagus soup, stewed celery, roast chickens, French beans, lamb cutlets, orange jelly and raspberry puffs.

Laurence made a point of asking Frances about her shells, promising they should spend some time collecting them in Margate after the Pearl Ball, and she seemed in good humour. At the end of the meal she hesitated, looking about her as though expecting a signal which would once have come from her mother.

"Perhaps you would like to retire to your rooms now," Laurence suggested carefully, "and I will… join you there in a while?"

She blushed at once, her cheeks growing rosy and murmured some kind of assent, before disappearing upstairs.

Laurence waited a while before ascending, hoping to find her comfortably lying in bed, but instead she was sitting stiffly at her dressing table, wrapped in a dark blue robe, from which he could see her bare feet peeping out. He himself was naked under his silk banyan robe, and he sat on the bed and patted the covers beside him.

"Come, Frances. Make yourself comfortable."

She rose at once and made her way to the bed, where she removed her outer robe, revealing her long white nightgown, trimmed with fine lace. Peeling back the heavy covers and sheet, she lay down cautiously on the bed, her ankles neatly together, her hands folded over her stomach, eyes closed.

Laurence almost wanted to laugh at the sight of her, but she must be shy. He would be gentle with her and soon she would willingly be in his arms, he was sure of it. He had waited for an eternity since he first realised his feelings for her and now they were together at last.

He lay on his side next to her and gently kissed her lips. She lay, unmoving, her eyes still closed.

"Frances?"

She opened her eyes and gazed at him, her expression telling him nothing at all, then closed her eyes again.

He stroked the curve of her neck and bent to kiss her there, then gently pulled away her nightgown from her shoulder so that he might kiss her there also, his lips tracing the curve of her collarbone. Her skin was like warm silk and he slowly unbuttoned her nightgown, exposing her breasts. Her eyes remained closed, she did not even turn her face towards him, her expression blank. Perhaps she was too exposed. Perhaps she would prefer to be held close, a more intimate position. He put an arm about her and pulled her lightly towards him, that he might hold her in his arms, close to him. She moved obediently but then lay still in his embrace, almost as though she were asleep.

Laurence frowned down at her, uncertain at her odd behaviour, then redoubled his efforts. He caressed every part of her, all the while holding her to him, kissed her soft lips and breasts, revelling in the beauty of her. He desired her, but she seemed so… absent. So silent, so still.

"You are beautiful," he whispered to her, thinking her perhaps uncertain of her appearance. "I have been desperate for this moment with you to come." Slowly, he let his hand slip down her nightgown, pulling it upwards so that he might touch her most intimate treasure.

It took all the willpower Frances had to obey her mother's instructions. She was shy at first, trembling as she waited for Laurence to join her. Once on the bed, though, his touch was so gentle, so blissful, that she longed to return it, not that she knew what to do but she wanted to return his kisses at least, to lay her hands on his bare skin and feel it warm beneath her. He touched her in ways that made her want to gasp with both shock and delight, but she tightened her lips and remained silent. She also kept her eyes shut, as instructed, but when he began to move above her she was unable to resist and tried to look at him through her lashes, saw his face lost in passion and wished she might hold him closer to her. Even when there was a little pain, it was entwined with a delight that was tantalisingly out of her reach. If only she could touch him, hold him tightly, a greater joy would be hers. But her mother had been very certain and this was a marriage of convenience, after all. Their purpose in this bedchamber was to make a child, an heir, and so she steeled every part of herself only to lie still and make no sound. When it seemed to all be over she lay quietly as Laurence kissed her again and then fell asleep beside her, even though Lady Lilley had assured her that he would return to his chamber. When she was certain he was asleep, she dared to lay one hand upon his bare arm, enjoying the warmth of his skin, hoping that she had brought him pleasure.

Laurence awoke early the next morning. He turned his head to look at Frances, asleep beside him. Her long dark hair fell over part of her face and her expression was peaceful, one bare arm resting close to his hand. He wanted to wake her, to try again to bring her pleasure, but the thought of last night made him draw back.

A cold fish.

She was a sea-creature, a chilly siren who had lured him with her wide eyes and her unusual ways. He had believed that there was softness inside, that if he found his way into her heart she would open up to him and him alone, that there would be an intimacy between them. He had thought they could grow closer together, that there would be love between them and the warmth he had been longing for these past months. But she had lain there without moving, without any expression, had not uttered a sound, had kept her eyes closed as though the very sight of him was offensive to her. He was a skilled lover, able to indulge different women in ways that achieved gratification for each, for he had been a willing apprentice in the past. Now, with his beloved in his arms, he had expected to give her whatever she desired and yet he had failed. She had been utterly unmoved, and his own pleasure had been the lesser for it. He would try again, of course. They were married and they must have heirs, but how was it that the delights he had hoped to share were now to be denied him, impossible to achieve? Truly it would become only a marriage of convenience. He sat on the edge of the bed, head in hands. Was he to return to the married women of the past years? His shoulders sagged at the idea. He had enjoyed them, certainly, but now, with his love for Frances, he had hoped for more, he had hoped that he might enjoy her intimacies and bring her pleasure. Now it seemed to him that the dream he had cherished was only a foolish notion.

CHAPTER 14
The Pearl Ball

THE PEARL BALL WAS ONLY TWO WEEKS AWAY. Laurence had the uneasy feeling they should not attend after all, but of course it would be impossible to do so when it was being held in their honour. Frances was pleasant and accommodating in every way, but still, there was something wrong.

Things were not right in the bedchamber, that he was sure of. He could only hope that matters would improve over time, but it hurt him to go to her rooms and be received with such silent stiff solemnity. Nevertheless, he persevered, trying different things each time, hoping for some sign of enjoyment, some hint of what might give her pleasure. As yet, he'd had no success, which was humbling.

Perhaps he had not understood Frances, as his attempts to please her in other ways had failed too. The shell collection – well, that had been a disaster.

There was something different about her rooms, as well, which he could not put his finger on, until one night when he realised that the many expensive and exclusive perfumes and soaps he had ordered for her from Floris and D. R. Harris were nowhere to be seen. Paintings had been removed from the walls, which made them look bare, and the curtains had been taken down and replaced with ones that were plain pale blue, almost white.

He propped himself up on one elbow and looked down at Frances. "You changed the rooms. No perfumes, no paintings, the curtains are plain."

She looked back at him, face troubled. "You object?"

He shook his head. "Of course not. They are your rooms. Why did you change them, though? What was not to your liking?"

She swallowed, looking uncomfortable under his questioning. "I do not like strong perfumes. I am sure the ones you chose were lovely, but I prefer plain soaps and I do not wear perfume. And there was…" She shook her head. "Too much. There were too many patterns and pictures and I could not look restfully anywhere. I am sorry. I prefer plain things, otherwise I feel… overwhelmed."

He nodded, then was silent for a few moments. "If there is any other room in the house that you find… overwhelming… you may decorate it however you please. This is your home now."

She took a breath and let it out as though in relief. "Might I change the dining room and the drawing room? We are there a great deal and they are… exhausting."

He had never thought of them as exhausting, the dining room a rich red with grand portraits of long-gone ancestors. The drawing room a delicate blue, filled with ornaments and paintings, floral arrangements and furniture.

"Frances, please do as you wish with them."

"And if you do not like them afterwards?"

He shook his head. "I rarely think about what rooms look like. I doubt I will notice. If the decor bothers you, it should be changed."

"Thank you." Her voice was a whisper, but she put out a hand to touch his shoulder and Laurence, eager for any sign of warmth from her, placed his hand over hers.

The ancestral portraits were moved to other parts of the house and the dining room was repainted to a woodland green, with little in the way of decorations but some very fine chandeliers and candelabra. The drawing room retained its colour but lost most of its ornaments and at least half of its paintings, while the floral arrangements increased, making the room less cluttered and more in keeping with the view out of the windows into the gardens beyond. Laurence found the changes agreeable and said so, at which Frances seemed to grow in confidence. She had found her way with the housekeeper and the household was well run, to a strict timetable, so that he could be sure that breakfast would be served exactly at nine, tea at three in the afternoon. Frances seemed to like this regularity, the certainty of knowing what would happen. He was beginning to understand her better, though he still wished to give her a gift that would truly please her.

The gangly young man was sent for again and stood awkwardly in front of him.

"You understand the assignment?" Laurence inquired, anxious since his first gift had gone so badly. "This section of the library is to be entirely devoted to books and other papers or subscriptions… everything that is available on shells. You can place orders in my name, spare no expense. If you need my carriage to travel to London or further afield to collect such items, or require the assistance of a footman, both are at your service."

"Of course, Lord Barrington."

"And it must be done quickly. You have one week and one week only."

"Yes, Lord Barrington."

In the days that followed, the young man took his task in earnest. A stream of boxes and parcels were delivered to the house, the carriage went out a few times and more than one footman was kept busy with errands. Meanwhile, in the library, there were new shelves to be built and the delivery of a new chair. Finally, all was in readiness and, his nerves rising, Laurence sent a footman to ask if the Viscountess would be so good as to join him downstairs.

Being summoned by a footman was a formality Frances associated with having done something wrong, again, and being lectured by either her father or her mother. Reluctantly, she made her way down the stairs a week before the ball, where Laurence was waiting for her.

"I have something to show you, Frances," he said.

She followed him through the hallway and into the library, which was larger than the one she had grown up with and filled with beautiful books on all the walls, in shelves which reached as high as the ceiling.

"This – I thought this part of the library might be especially for you," he said, gesturing awkwardly towards a niche. He looked anxious, probably thrown by her dislike of the shell display, now perhaps regretting this gift also.

She looked. By a large window was a niche, the width of her outstretched arms. The shelves here were also amply filled, and next to them was placed a rocking chair with a delicate Chinese screen by the side, creating a partly-enclosed area, obscured from the rest of the room. She smiled at the sight of the rocking chair. A book on the shelf caught her eye and she reached up to it. "Donovan's *Natural History of British Shells*!"

Laurence's expression grew more confident. "Yes. And... others... I had a man procure you a small library dedicated to shells."

She let go of the book, leaving it half-pulled out on the shelf and turned to him, her face lit up. "Thank you."

He smiled, his shoulders losing their tense posture. "I am glad you like it."

She hesitated, then moved closer to him and put her arms about his waist, leaning her cheek against his warm chest. She could hear his heartbeat. "You are a very kind husband."

His arms came around her at once. At first his embrace was too tight, too much, and she was about to pull away, but then something else settled upon her, a strange peacefulness and instead she pressed closer to him, the tightness a release, her breath growing slower, as though she were about to sleep.

They stood like this for some moments and only when Laurence moved to look down at her face, did she step back. He let go of her at once, but his eyes were warm and Frances almost wanted to step back into his embrace, but she was uncertain. Would it be odd, to simply want to stand in silence, arms about one another? Instead she sat down in the rocking chair and rocked gently, smiling up at Laurence, eager to show that she was grateful for this gift, that this space was right for her, that he had better understood her desires than when he had given her the towering display of shells.

Buoyed up by this small success, Laurence sought out an altogether different sort of help. The burly foreman whom he instructed seemed confused by the purpose of the work he was to oversee, but Laurence impressed upon him that it must be completed as soon as possible, and paid handsomely to ensure its urgency was understood.

The night of the Margate Pearl Ball was upon them. It was a full moon, lending a twilight glow to the gardens. The Assembly Rooms were glittering with hundreds of candles as well as the decorations made especially for the occasion, including three chandeliers made out of shells. In the tea room were three giant ice sculptures, one of an open clam shell on which had been laid out hundreds of oysters waiting to be eaten, one a seahorse and one a mermaid, the two of which overlooked a table loaded with brilliantly coloured jellies and iced biscuits, many of which were shaped like shells.

The guests, well briefed on the theme of the ball, had taken the idea to heart. The ladies mostly wore white and their pearls, the gentlemen dressed in black but added pearls here and there to their cravat pins, the studs fastening their cuffs, some even attaching a few dangling teardrop pearls to their watch fobs.

But all eyes were on Frances, whose white silk gown was overlaid with a net into which had been worked tiny seed pearls. She wore the tiara and pearls left to her by her godfather. Laurence gazed at her as he led her in.

"You are utterly lovely," he said. He felt the warmth of her body against his, thought again of how impossible these moments seemed, when there was closeness and yet no pleasure in their marital bed, wondered if he could bear the ache it left in his heart much longer. How was he to break through her reserve?

"I feel overdressed."

He looked down at her and shook his head. She could not see it for herself, but the shining white of the silk and the pearls made her dark hair and grey eyes stand out in contrast. No doubt many of the ladies present thought her skin too brown, but Laurence thought she looked far healthier than most of them. He could see the sunny beach and smell the salt air when he looked at her, rather than the powders and perfumes of dressing rooms. It made him want to hold her close to him, to stroke her dark hair and kiss her long dark lashes, but that would be unseemly and already he was beginning to avoid such moments, for fear of her cool rejection.

Mrs Pagington had spotted them and hurried across the room to greet them.

"My dear Lady Barrington," she exclaimed, "I do declare it is a great pleasure to meet you at last. The late Lord Barrington was a dear friend of mine and the very least I could do was hold a ball to welcome the new Lord Barrington – and when I was told he had a new bride – well, it called for a double celebration! Now come, my dear, I must introduce you to everyone!"

There followed an unbearable half hour during which names and faces were presented in such a rapid fashion that Frances began to feel dizzy. When Mrs Pagington said she must tell the musicians to strike up Frances turned to Laurence in dismay.

"We must dance with our hosts and the other guests," Laurence said reluctantly. "I will return to you when I have done my duty."

Frances felt the weight of what she had agreed to as she danced with first one gentleman and then another, did her best to make small talk and not be her usual blunt self. She could feel the strain of the effort building up in her, had a desperate urge to run home to the gardens at Northdown and sit on the swing, to feel, in its motion, a release of the tension inside her. But that was not what she had promised; she had promised to be Lord Barrington's viscountess, to be a good wife to him. These sorts of events would be part of that agreement. So she must find a way to bear it.

She danced with a seemingly endless array of guests, if only to escape the smothering attentions of Mrs Pagington, when at last she turned to find Laurence by her side.

"Will you accompany me?" he asked.

She took his arm. "I would like a jelly and a drink." What she really wanted was to escape the Assembly Rooms altogether and go and stand in the cool dark gardens of Northdown House, under the old mulberry and cherry trees, but no doubt that was unsuitable behaviour for a viscountess; she had got away with it only occasionally as a girl. A wife could not be permitted such liberties. A drink of something cold and re-freshing was all she could hope for.

He shook his head. "No time for that."

"No time for it? What else is there to do but eat and drink or dance?"

"That is for everyone else. We have something better to do."

She thought he meant the bedroom and her cheeks grew warm at the idea of his hands touching her, but he did not steer her towards the hallway and front door, but to a small door leading to a side street. She followed, confused, then stopped and stared at the sight of a phaeton and two horses, a groom standing holding their reins, little lanterns dangling from it. "Where are we going?"

"It is a surprise."

"A surprise?" She was uncertain. If he had said home, she would have gladly gone, but a surprise? Anxious dread grew inside her stomach. Was he going to do something kind but which she did not like again? She would try to seem grateful but she was a poor actress.

"Get in." He held out his hand and she took it and climbed in with difficulty, trying to avoid the net of pearls from being damaged.

Once in, Laurence joined her and nodded to the groom, who handed him the reins.

"Are you warm enough, or shall I send for a shawl for you?"

She was so bewildered that she could not feel anything, so she only shook her head in silence.

"Very well then." He shook the reins and the carriage moved through Cecil Square and onto the street that would lead them out to the main road. The full moon was their only pale source of light and deep shadows surrounded them. Laurence guided the horses to a comfortable trot when they reached the main road, heading upwards towards the centre of Margate. Frances sat, trembling at the oddness of Laurence's actions. What sort of surprise required them to leave a ball held in their honour and drive a carriage through the dark night? More than once she looked at Laurence's face, trying to make it out in the shadows but his expression was carefully serene.

"Here we are."

Frances peered into the darkness and saw Belle Vue Cottage. Laurence sprang down from the carriage and held up his hand to her, but she stared at the dark outline of the house, a sinking feeling in her stomach. Had she failed so utterly as a wife to him already that he was returning her here, to live alone? Would he set her up here as she had been living before, his wife in name only? Did he find her company so repugnant that he believed they must live separately? Must she live here, lonely as she had been before?

"Come, take my hand."

How eager he was to return her here. Had the ball been only a moment to show her off, a façade for the world, before taking her back where she belonged? There was a faint glimmer from the windows. Perhaps the servants had not waited up and she would have to make her way upstairs to the cold room that she had thought she had escaped. She would have to remove this dress by herself, trapped in its pearl nets, a dress suitable only for a successful viscountess, not for a failed wife, a spinster-wife. Slowly, she climbed out of the carriage, stood before him, waited while he tied the horses to a tree and then turned back to her, his face serious.

"I do not want this marriage, Frances."

The cold dread grew in her. She was right. He did not want her, he had never really wanted her. She hung her head. The weight of failure again, the knowledge that she was unwanted by everyone, that she was never enough, never how others wanted her, always a disappointment.

"Frances. Look at me."

It was hard to look into his eyes. But she did it, held his gaze with difficulty, waiting for the verdict, the judgement. He would say that they must keep separate homes, that he could not live with her, that it was not even a marriage of convenience.

He gazed into her eyes and when he spoke his voice shook. "I cannot live like this, Frances. I do not want a marriage in name only."

Divorce? He was going to ask for a divorce? Beyond failure then. Utter humiliation and disaster, scandal, shame. Her eyes burned with tears, but she held his gaze, her chin raised up high. Better to hear it straight, no falsities, no half-truths now.

"I love you, Frances."

She stared at him. She had not heard correctly. He must have said that he did not love her, that much was plain, there was no need to state it. She waited to hear the rest of what he had to say to her, eyes glazed over, unable to bear his gaze.

"Frances? Do you hear me? I love you."

She blinked and frowned, tried to focus on what he was saying, to understand, but suddenly he was holding her close to him, his face only inches away, speaking urgently.

"I do not want a marriage of convenience. I want you to be my real wife. I do not want you to hide yourself from me, to run away one day like a selkie bride because you cannot be yourself. I need you to be happy, so that you will stay with me forever, because I love you. I –"

He broke off and grabbed her hand, pulling her towards Belle Vue Cottage, then turning the corner before they reached the door, pulling open the wrought iron gate that led to the garden, his hand gripping hers so hard it almost hurt, her dancing slippers encountering hard pebbles beneath her feet, stumbling in the shadows.

He stopped, at last, panting, by a large flat rock Frances had not seen before in the garden, let go of her hand and bent to lift it, sliding it to one side with a grunt, revealing a large hole in the ground, from which light dimly glowed, the shape of a ladder disappearing downwards. She stepped back, startled.

"What is down there?"

"A gift. Do you trust me?"

She looked into his face. "Yes," she whispered. She could not yet believe what he had just said to her, not fully, but there was a desperation to it that spoke of truthfulness and she wanted to believe him, wanted to hope that what he had said was true.

He moved round the hole and began to climb into it, feet on the ladder, slowly moving downwards until his head was at her feet, when he looked up and lifted up his hand to her. "Come."

It was difficult in her dancing slippers and the silk and pearl dress did not help matters, but she made her way down the ladder, hands shaking as she held the rough wood, Laurence's hands pressed gently about her waist, guiding her and stopping her from falling. Finally, her feet touched solid ground and she let go of the ladder, turned to face him.

They were standing in a dirt tunnel. Above them was a domed ceiling containing the hole up to the garden of Belle Vue Cottage. Around them, a wider circular space cut into the earth, the chalk walls the height of a man and a half. Leading away from the space in which they stood were three passageways, each one also full height, the width less than her outstretched arms. All along the walls were little niches, into which were set flickering candles.

Her voice came out as a whisper. "What is this place?"

Laurence stood before her, his face hopeful, excited. "A place for your shells. A place for you and you alone. No-one need know it exists, even, if you do not want them to. You can be alone here with them, if you wish. We will have to be at Ashland Manor for part of the year, but we can be at Northdown whenever you choose and Belle Vue Cottage can be your secret place. It – it is not all finished yet, there was not enough time, but I wanted to show it to you tonight, I could not be patient any longer. Later, when it is all complete, I will have them dig a tunnel from the cellar of the house so that you can come here easily. But for now we had to climb down – shall I show you the rest?"

"The rest?"

He took her hand and began to lead her.

They walked through a tunnel, perhaps thirty feet long, then came to a large empty room, rectangular in shape, at least fifteen by twenty feet, filled with glowing candles, lending the dark chamber an otherworldly air.

"It is like a church," she whispered. "How did you find it? Was it here all along?"

He turned to her, grinning. "I had it dug out."

"All this?"

He nodded.

"For me?"

"For you."

She looked up at him, gazed into his face as though seeking answers.

"I want you to be happy," he said. "I tried before, with your room and the shells but then I realised they were not right."

"I'm sorry," she said, a wave of sadness rising up in her, the familiar sense of failure. "I was rude, and I did not –"

"No," he interrupted. "No. You were right. I did things to please a bride. A human bride. But you are a selkie bride." He gave a laugh and his eyes shone with tears. "You are not like other women, and I gave you the wrong gifts, gifts that would please a different woman. I did not stop to think about what I knew of you, what you showed me of your true self."

"The library –"

He nodded. "The library was better. I learnt from my mistakes."

She looked back at him and then leant her head against his chest, felt his arms come gently about her and then tighten. Once again the tightness was too much, trapping her, squeezing her. But there was another desire inside her, a desire to be held, and she took a deeper breath and let it out, leant into him, the tightness now safety, love, belonging.

They stood there for a long time, in silence. Finally, Laurence loosened his embrace and she looked up into his face.

"Thank you."

He nodded, waiting.

"What you said before…"

"I meant every word. I love you, Frances. Will you – would you be happy to have a true marriage with me? I cannot bear for us to have only a marriage of convenience. You are not a convenience to me. You are – you are everything."

She took a step back and he frowned, but she put out her hand and he took it in his.

"I will."

He let go of her hand, touched her cheek, then cupped her face in both hands and kissed her softly. At once she stiffened under his hands and lips. He looked down at her, disappointed. "Frances, do you not like to be kissed? To be... touched, when we are alone... in bed, even? Tell me."

She frowned up at him. "It is... wonderful," she managed at last. "It is... so much feeling that I think I will... I do not know what, that I might die from so much pleasure."

He stared at her, lost for words. "But..." He tried again. "But you lie so still, you close your eyes, you do not..."

Her frown grew deeper. "My mother said... that a lady must not... must not show..." She swallowed. "She said a lady should lie still and silent, that she should close her eyes and let her husband do as he wishes," she finished, cheeks crimson and voice low. "Is that not right? I tried to do it right, but it was difficult to stay still when I felt... so much."

"Oh, Frances," he whispered. "Oh Frances, my strange selkie. Your mother was... she was so *wrong*, Frances." He grabbed her and crushed her to him, and she startled, but then embraced him as tightly as he held her. "Frances, promise me you will never follow the ways of the *ton*, ever again."

She let out a gasp of laughter. "I have never been adept at following their ways."

"Then leave them entirely behind. I beg you." He held her at arm's length, looking into her face, then gently pulled her back to him and kissed her again and this time she was soft in his arms, her lips moved beneath his, her mouth opened to his touch and they were lost in one another.

"Come," he said after a few moments.

"Come where?" She hoped not back to the ball, although she could bear it better now.

"Down to the sea to find the first shells for your grotto, of course."

"But the ball…"

"You see? You are the perfect guest."

She laughed as he steadied the ladder for her, climbing out and then reaching her hand back for him, his grasp firm on her hand as he reached the top and brushed himself down, sliding the cover back into place.

"We cannot go back like this, anyway," she said. They were both dusty and her train had a little rip in it.

"The other guests will not mind," he said. "They have music, a ballroom and fine food and drink. They do not need us to enjoy themselves."

The horses were munching grass. Laurence helped Frances back into the phaeton, took the reins and they proceeded at a brisk trot down the hill to the beach at Margate. They sat close now, their bodies pressed together, and glanced at one another from time to time as though disbelieving the other was there at all.

"When we walked together that day and were caught by the tides," Laurence said, "I was shocked by you. The way you lifted your skirts and walked through the sea."

She shook her head. "I wanted to show you how wrong you were, about the tides. I was being stubborn. I should probably have let you carry me. It would have been more ladylike. I lifted my skirts higher than I should to scandalise you."

"I saw your stockings and ribbons," he said, his voice grown husky at the memory. "I saw a glimpse of your thighs. I have never desired a woman so much in my life."

She said nothing and he wondered if he had offended her,

but then she reached out and took the reins from his hands, turned the horses' heads to the right.

"What are you doing?"

She did not answer and he, wondering, allowed her to drive them along the cliff path, away from Margate. When she finally reined in the horses, they were at the start of the pathway that cut through the cliffs and down into Botany Bay.

"What are we doing here?"

She held out the reins to him. "Tie up the horses," she said, and climbed down from the carriage, walking away from him down the little path.

He tied them up and hurried after her. "The tide is high," he called after her. "It may not be right for collecting shells."

She only kept walking and he followed her as she made her way to the vast cliff stack and its archway, the space she had once walked through, rendering him breathless. The sea was where it had been that day. The same depth, almost to the knees, and she was not stopping. She knew the tides intimately, must have known they would be the same height as they had been that day. She walked into the sea without stopping, without pulling up her silk dress, and made her way to the centre of the archway, then turned to face him and held her arms out to him.

Laurence stood and stared at her, her white figure ethereal, otherworldly, then he ran across the sand and walked into the sea. The cold water swirled about him but his eyes were only on Frances, her face tilted up to him as he drew closer. He hesitated, but she did not. Her arms slipped about his neck and she pulled him close to her, her mouth on his, eager for him.

He pushed her against the cold hard chalk with one hand, fumbling to undo his breeches with the other. And then she was pulling up her skirt, pearls falling off the netting into the dark water below. He was first shocked at her eagerness, then aroused by it, her panting breath and clenched hands full of silk revealing her stockings and their ribbons and above that, her bare white thighs, which had filled his thoughts since that day a few months ago when she had walked into the sea ahead of him. He reached behind her, pushing past the silk to grasp her buttocks and pull her towards him, her feet in dancing slippers first on tiptoe, but when he pulled her harder upwards her feet left the sand with a gasp, so that she was held between the rock and his body. He gripped himself and watched her face as he entered her, eyes wide, lips parted. And at last this was the Frances he had always desired, who pushed back against him, gripping his shoulders as he thrust inside her, opening her mouth to him, her tongue seeking his with a passion he had never yet found in her, a passion which made him grow still harder as he drove faster within her and yet she matched his rhythm, rode against him, velvet soft and hot inside, as the icy water swirled around his knees. His hands gripped her behind as she cried out, pressed against him so that her breasts strained against the white silk and he felt her pleasure even as his own came, a rush of feeling so great he gasped her name, "Frances," and they panted softly together, mouths still seeking the last moments of delight. All the women Laurence had known until now had been nothing compared to this woman, his wife, his treasure.

Gently he lowered her to the ground, back into the water but she did not flinch at the cold, still pressed against him.

"You are perfect, Frances," he whispered to her. "I love you."

She gave a tiny laugh and half shook her head against his

chest. "I am too rough to be perfect. I ought to be smoother to be a viscountess."

He laughed. "Is that what you think? Do you know what happens to little rough things?"

She shook her head.

"The shell that holds them coats them with layers until they are shining pearls."

"Are you going to coat me with layers?"

"Yes," he said. "I will hold you tight and cover you with love for the rest of our lives."

She nestled into his warm embrace as the cold sea rushed over their feet. "I love you, Laurence," she whispered, so low that he only just heard her.

He was quiet but when she raised her head to look up at him his eyes were shining at her declaration. "My selkie," he said, tightening his arms about her so that she felt the beat of his heart against her breasts. "My pearl."

I hope you have enjoyed *The Viscount's Pearl*. If you have, I would really appreciate it if you would leave a rating or brief review, so that new readers can find it. I read all reviews and am always grateful for your time in writing them and touched by your kind words. There are more Regency Outsiders still to come, so look out for their stories…

Have you read the Forbidden City series? Pick up the first in the series FREE on your local Amazon website.

Lonely. Used as a pawn. One last bid for love.

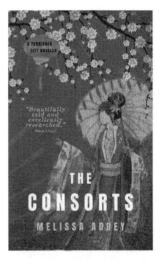

18th century China. Imperial concubine Qing yearns for love and friendship. Neglected by the Emperor, passed over for more ambitious women, Qing lives a lonely existence. But when a new concubine comes to court, friendship blooms, bringing with it a taste of happiness.

For the first time in her life, Qing has a friend and perhaps even a chance at loving and being loved. But when the Empress' throne suddenly becomes available, Qing finds herself being used as a pawn by the highest ranked women of the court. Caught up in their power games, on one devastating night everything she holds dear is put at risk.

As the power players of the Forbidden City make their moves, can Qing find the courage to make one last bid for love? Can an insignificant pawn snatch victory from the jaws of defeat?

Author's Note on History

MARGATE IS A PRETTY SEASIDE TOWN ON THE SOUTH-east coast of Britain, still very popular today with holidaymakers. There's a beautiful book called *Margate in the Georgian Era* by Anthony Lee, which contains a wealth of information as well as amazing images of Margate as it developed from a tiny fishing village to a fashionable holiday destination for the Regency era's high society.

Just outside the main part of the town used to stand Belle Vue Cottage, an unassuming house briefly used as a school for young girls. In its garden, in 1836, was found the most extraordinary shell grotto. Composed of over 4.6 million shells, this subterranean marvel is a mosaic of beautiful patterns, covering every part of a 2.4 metre high, 21-metre-long passageway, including a large room and a rotunda which lets in light from above. The shells are mostly ordinary local shells, but the mystery remains as to who built it – with options ranging from the Phoenicians 3,000 years ago to a Regency folly. It is a beautiful place (look at pictures of it online) and I could not resist giving it to Frances as a gift. My family and I spent some very happy days researching in Margate this past summer.

Two women stand out on either side of this era for their interest in shells and other seaside finds. The Duchess of Portland amassed the largest shell collection of the time, which was sold off after her death in 1785. The story of her life and collection is told in the informative book *The Duchess's Shells* by Beth Fowkes Tobin. The second was Mary Anning, an English fossil collector, dealer, and palaeontologist who lived in Lyme Regis and who made her first serious find of an ichthyosaur fossil in 1811 along the shoreline on which she walked daily, finding every kind of fossil over the years. There are several books, novels, documentaries and films based on her life.

My intention was for Frances to be autistic, as this runs in my family and I wondered what it would be like to be autistic in a time and class of society that required huge social interaction and adherence to social niceties in order to be married. Being able to give enough detail on shells to match her interest was greatly helped by the Marine Biological Association's pages on each type of shell. www.marlin.ac.uk

Northdown House in Northdown Park does exist in Margate. I borrowed it for my fictional world and made some building modifications for the image at the front of this book. If you'd like to read about its real owners and history you can do so here: http://botanyplants.co.uk/northdown-farm-history. It is a beautiful building surrounded by lovely gardens, including ancient mulberry and cherry trees, which I had the joy of wandering through. It is currently being turned into a school for autistic children, one of those odd (or magical!) coincidences that happen when you write. Andreea and Richard: thank you for sending me photos, floor plans and other information to help me build my version. I hope you like your characters!

Lord Barrington's wasting disease is based on limb-girdle

Muscular Dystrophy, which can begin in early adulthood, initially making it hard to do activities like walk upstairs and slowly progressing to a possible need for a wheelchair over 20-30 years. This disease can sometimes also affect the heart or breathing.

The pearl tiara for Frances' wedding is based on the exquisite Mellerio Shell Tiara which belongs to the Spanish royal family.

Current and forthcoming books include:

18th century China: The Forbidden City series

The Consorts. A lonely and forgotten imperial concubine is faced with one last chance for love... if she is brave enough to seize it. Set in China's Forbidden City in the 18th century. (Novella)

The Fragrant Concubine. A new imperial concubine is keeping a dangerous secret. Is the Emperor right to fall in love with her, or is his life at risk? Based on the legends that grew up around a real concubine.

The Garden of Perfect Brightness. Painter Giuseppe Castiglione is tasked with creating a garden fit for an imperial concubine, but as flowers bloom, so do feelings. Based on one man's extraordinary life.

The Cold Palace. Chosen against her will. Elevated to Empress. Accused of madness. Based on a real Empress of China's life, an award-winning novel.

Medieval Morocco: The Moroccan Empire series

The Cup. A gifted healer makes an impossible vow whose consequences ripple unstoppably outwards as an empire rises across North Africa and a future queen reaches for power.

A String of Silver Beads. Seeking freedom, a young Berber woman marries an ambitious Muslim warrior, but finds herself enmeshed in bitter rivalry with his powerful queen.

None Such as She. A false prophecy leads to the rise of a great empire across North Africa and Spain… and a dangerous queen who will stop at nothing to achieve her ambitions..

Do Not Awaken Love. A Spanish nun. A Muslim warlord. The destiny of an empire held between them. A woman must hold true to her faith, which is tested by great dangers… and by love

Ancient Rome: the Colosseum series

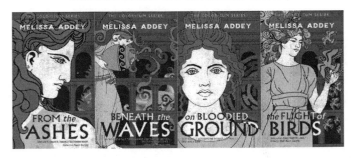

From the Ashes. Follow the quick-witted and fiercely loyal backstage team of the Colosseum as they inaugurate the gladiatorial games through the devastation of Pompeii, plague and fire.

Beneath the Waves. Flooding the Colosseum for epic sea battles brings both hidden dangers and emotions to the surface for the backstage team of the Colosseum.

On Bloodied Ground. Below the Colosseum's arena lies a dark labyrinth and a darker secret. As gladiators die before they even reach the arena, the backstage team grow fearful of what is still to come.

The Flight of Birds. Emperor Domitian has three final tasks for the backstage team to complete and his erratic behaviour is beginning to frighten them. Is he just strange, or is he dangerous?

Regency England: the Regency Outsiders series

Lady for a Season. A young duke declared mad. His nurse masquerading as a lady. One social season in which to marry him off. What could possibly go wrong?

The Viscount's Pearl. He's a carefree rake who wants a marriage of convenience. She's an awkward spinster who doesn't want to marry at all. Fate has other plans in store for them both.

To Win Her Hand. They've been promised since birth, so he sees no reason to woo her. She plans to find true love. Trapped in snowy London, Christmas might just bring them together.

Biography

I GREW UP AND WAS HOME EDUCATED ON AN ITALIAN hill farm. I now live in London with my husband, two children and a black and white cat called Holly who enjoys the editing process as there is so much scrap paper involved.

I mainly write historical fiction, inspired by what I call 'the footnotes of history': forgotten stories or part-legends about interesting people and places. I have a PhD in Creative Writing, for which I wrote The Garden of Perfect Brightness and an academic thesis about balancing fact and fiction in historical fiction.

I like to move from one historical era to another, finding stories to share, like a travelling minstrel. So far I've been to Ancient Rome, medieval Morocco, 18th century China and Regency England. Join me on my travels: browse my books.

If you'd like to know more about me and my books, visit my website www.MelissaAddey.com where there are free novellas, book trailers, interviews, videos of research trips, info for book clubs and more.

Thanks

Thank you to photographer Guru Saini and model Dolly for the front cover image and to Streetlight Graphics, who always have my back and make my life so easy.

Thank you to my beta readers for this book: Helen, Etain, Martin, Bernie, Susanne. Your comments and ideas are always insightful. Thank you to my editor Debi Alper for helping my stories meet their readers in the best possible shape. And to my lovely ARC readers, who are the first to see the book as it sets out into the world, thank you for giving it a warm welcome.

Enormous thanks to the community and teachers at Regency Fiction Writers, who generously share their knowledge and made my research so much easier.

All errors and fictional choices are, of course, mine.

Made in the USA
Columbia, SC
05 March 2025

54709216R00171